THE COTTAGE AT THE EDGE OF TIME

TIME

Bound by Love, Chained by Fate

I0587335

Written By

Simon Mennell

Disclaimer

This book is a work of fiction. Names, characters, businesses, places, events, and incidents are either the products of the author's imagination or used in a fictitious manner. Any resemblance to actual persons, living or dead, or actual events is purely coincidental.

The views and opinions expressed in this book are those of the characters and do not necessarily reflect the views or opinions of the author or the publisher. This book is intended purely for entertainment purposes, and the author and publisher assume no responsibility for any actions taken as a result of reading this fiction.

Dedication

To Graham, my best friend, taken too soon,

never forgotten.

For those who stand alone on the cliff while

the storm rages — do not despair; hope still waits

beyond the horizon.

Table of Contents

Chapter One

The Ordinary Light

York never quite slept, not even in late March in 1987. After the office lights dimmed and the shop shutters rattled down, the city carried on breathing. Taxis prowled the damp streets, headlights sliding across brick façades. Delivery vans clattered over cobbles with crates of bread and milk, drivers yawning into the chill. Bicycles slipped through the traffic like shadows on wheels. From the ring road came the low thrum of lorries heading south, steady as a tide.

There was always someone awake: a couple arguing softly under an umbrella, a drunk laughing too loud as he staggered out of the Minster Arms, a student on the night bus with her textbooks open on her knees. The city kept its own rhythm, as though the walls and streets remembered centuries of watchmen, market cries, and the creak of cartwheels on stone. On summer evenings, open windows spilled music into the dark, Top of the Pops on colour tellies, Spandau Ballet or Ultravox through radio speakers, the muffled cheer of a quiz show audience. The air carried chip-shop vinegar cooling to a tang, the bite of diesel, and the earthy smell of the Ouse, slow and brown beneath the bridges.

Graham Jones walked home with his shoulders hunched against the damp, cutting across Lendal Bridge and following the river, boots slapping the uneven pavement. He paused, as he always did, at the lit bookshop window to eye glossy architecture magazines he never bought; tonight he let the desire pass. The square hulk of the old chocolate factory warehouse pulled him on, the place he and Mara had coaxed into a life.

The building stood solid against the water, red brick weather-beaten and proud. Once it had held sacks of cocoa beans and barrels of sugar; now its cavernous floors were carved into flats with tall windows and opinions about draughts. Inside, the stairwell still smelt faintly of dust and cocoa. Iron pillars rose like blackened trees and footsteps rang up the landings. On the third floor Mr Dyer, carpet slippers, cardigan that had outlived governments, smoked by the fire door with a jam jar for ash.

"Evenin', Jonesy."

"Evening, Mr Dyer. Weather's foul."

"Always is. Best stay in with a pint."

"That's the plan."

By the fifth floor the day had unknotted in his shoulders. Their door, paint scuffed, brass thirty-five hanging a fraction crooked, gave with its familiar catch. Warmth met him: steam ghosting the kitchen window, the soft burble of a DJ talking himself towards a chorus, garlic and onions doing exactly what garlic and onions should.

Mara was at the hob in one of his old jumpers, sleeves shoved up, hair pinned without much conviction. The flat was itself, high ceilings, brick and beam; a jar of screws and coins beside the brass owl

3

she had found in a charity shop; plants crowding the window ledge; the scar in the pine table where he had dropped a chisel and sworn like a man who had met God and been unimpressed. Against the brick wall, the stereo sat like a shrine: silver twin-cassette, black speakers that crackled if you asked too much. The shelves below sagged with records and home-taped compilations. They had named some, Autumn Walks, Rain Evenings, Cooking (Red Sauce), as if a life could be filed and found again.

Without turning she said, "Don't drip on my clean floor," which meant she had heard his keys and smiled before he had crossed the threshold.

"Permission to flood the mat?"

"Denied." The spoon tapped the pan twice. "Towels are on the radiator. Tea is two songs away."

He hung his coat, did the two shakes and sleeve-tug that pretended he was not soaked, and stepped into the kitchen in socks he insisted were not his good pair. He leaned in to kiss the damp curl at her temple; she head-butted him lightly in warning, still stirring.

The DJ faded and the opening piano line arrived, bare and unmistakable.

They both stilled.

Against All Odds slipped into the room. It did what it always did to Mara, a quieting, a softening, the way her gaze seemed to look through steam to somewhere she kept just for herself.

"I love this one," she said, low, as if it might frighten if spoken too loud.

"I know."

"When we split," she went on, eyes on the pan, "I used to put it on and think: stay brave. Sounds daft out loud."

"It doesn't."

He stepped behind her and slid his arms round her waist. The jumper was a little rough against his forearm; her hair smelt of rain and that citrus shampoo she had smuggled onto his side of the bath.

"You came back," she said.

5

"You told me to."

She let the spoon rest and leaned back into him for the chorus. "Then it's not just mine anymore," she murmured. "It's ours."

They stood like that until the final held note fell away and the DJ returned, sheepish about the weather. The room woke up. She nudged him off with her hip, mock-stern. "Set the table, builder. This sauce needs witnesses."

He laid two places without looking, brass-riveted knives; the salt turned so its good side faced out, because it mattered. As they sat down to eat, he told her about the apprentice who had finally found plumb. Shouted out, and stood like he had discovered a new planet; the lad would dine out on that bubble for a week. She told him about Mrs Albright and the cousin who came to translate the law until offered a biscuit and the ultimatum: let's agree the biscuits are real and start from there. The story earned its laugh and the day eased in their bones.

The lights blinked, once, twice, and the radio fizzled and died. The flat exhaled.

"Oh, good," Mara said into the hush. "Power cut."

"Romantic," Graham said. "If you ignore the onions."

He struck a match and lit the candles around the room. He also had an old camp gas lamp that provided a lovely glow across the living room. Pantea: grim and perfect. They sat at the candlelit table with steam ghosting their faces and listened to the building rearrange itself by sound, feet on stairs, a door slamming two floors down, Mr Dyer's cough doing its rounds like a sermon.

A knock, three brisk raps. Mara raised an eyebrow.

"I'll go," replied Graham.

Mrs. Penhaligon stood in the doorway in a defiant dressing gown, wielding a torch like a truncheon and a watering can shaped like a goose. "Is it everybody, or just my fuse?"

"Everybody."

"Good. I thought it was just me at first. Tell Mara I've a scarf for her if she wants it. And you" — she poked Graham with the goose's beak — "when's the next charity quiz? The last raised thirty-seven pounds and a jar of pickled onions."

"We can't top pickled onions."

"You can always top pickled onions."

Her beam flicked over his face, clocking the grin he had failed to tidy away. Her voice softened. "You two all right?"

"We're... good."

"Keep it that way," she said, and swept off to terrify the fifth floor.

Mara had pulled on her coat. "Come on, let's go out for a walk."

"In this?"

"Power cut. You and your Cub Scout stove can't fix everything. I want chips, grab that torch."

They took the stairs; lifts in old buildings strike at the first whiff of adventure. Mr Dyer saluted with

8

his jam jar. "Evenin'. Weather's foul," he repeated, pleased to be right twice in an hour.

Outside, rain had been waiting just for them. Stonegate shone like a postcard; the Minster loomed and vanished in cloud. Shopfronts were dark except for the tea rooms doing their last pots and a jeweller who refused to accept closing time. By the time they reached the chip shop, all the lights around were back on and business was in full swing. The chip shop steamed like a locomotive. Vinegar lifted and made their eyes water.

They ate under the awning like burglars casing a safe, burning their tongues and not caring. A gust off the river brought a raw salt tang that made Graham think, inexplicably, of open water, edges where land had to try.

"So," she said around a chip, "beer."

"Thought you'd never ask," he said, appalled.

"Deal." She grabbed his arm as they headed off towards the Woolpack.

A ghost tour drifted past, lanterns bobbing, guide in a cape telling excellent lies. A lad in a bomber jacket declared love was tragic and asked the bus shelter if anyone could lend him fifty pence. York kept doing York.

By the time they arrived at the Woolpack the electricity was back on and the pub was warm and cosy.

"What will you have?" the landlord asked.

"The usual," replied Graham.

"We are only having the one mind, it's a school day tomorrow," Mara said, laughing.

True to her word, after one they headed back home. Back in the stairwell they heard shouting, high and frantic, and the sound of water where water should not be. Graham was up the steps two at a time before Mara could say his name. On the third floor a young couple were ankle-deep in a kitchen that had decided to become a pond. A joint had failed where new met old; the building was making its opinion known.

"I'm a builder," he said, which in the circumstances was exactly the right thing they wanted to hear. He found the stopcock half under a cupboard that should not be a cupboard; water sulked and slowed. He wedged a bucket that would not hold and said soothing nonsense that meant you are not on your own.

"Jonesy," Mr Dyer said from the landing, approving as if Graham had fixed gravity. "You're a good lad."

By the time they climbed back to the fifth they were soaked and laughing, the kind of laughing you do when you have stopped disaster and everything in the day is pitching towards a larger thing that makes sense of even the daft bits.

The power blinked on as they stepped inside. The radio cleared its throat and, cheeky as anything, gave them the last few bars of Gold by Spandau Ballet.

"You forgot to turn the radio off before we went out," Mara said.

"Well, with no power, who could know it was on."

Graham put candles out one by one. The building settled. In the quiet that followed, with the rain easing to a tired whisper, Mara took her hands from the mug she had let go cold and laid them flat on the table.

"Ok, I'm off to bed, busy day tomorrow," said Mara.

"Me too," replied Graham. They both fell asleep quickly, and soon it was back off to work for the usual routine. By the time Graham came home that night, Mara was sat at the table with a mug of tea, staring into space.

"You ok, darling?" Graham asked tenderly.

"I think I'm late," she said.

It landed between them with the weight of a mislaid stone.

He sat down next to her. "Late?"

"A week. Maybe more." She tried a smile that didn't quite hold. "I wanted to say it last night, but with the power cut and everything, it didn't feel the right time."

He took her hands, warm and damp from the mug. The freckle by her lip that he'd kissed a thousand times seemed newly important, as if facts needed noticing properly now.

"Bloody hell," he said, chest splitting tidy down the middle in the best possible way. "Bloody hell, Mara."

"Scared?" she asked.

"Terrified," he admitted, grinning anyway. "In the best way, I'm going to be a Dad."

Relief lit her face.

"Well, I'll make an appointment to see the doctor tomorrow, then we can get scared. But I know my body and I'm always regular, so I really think I am."

They sat there grinning like fools while the river kept its brown counsel and the building clicked back into itself.

"What if they have your nose?" she said.

"Poor sod. Better your eyes."

"And your chin. You always pretend it's too square, but it's exactly right."

"What about the dancing?"

"Tragic," she said promptly, and he laughed until his sides ached.

They talked like people who didn't want to wake the future by shouting at it: she'd ring the surgery; he'd clear the hall cupboard and find the pram-bits cousin Claire swore were somewhere in her loft; Sunday at his parents if they could bear the fuss; a note to Blue Rhino for a blank tape because Cooking (Red Sauce) might need a sequel after all. They promised to be kind when they were tired and to take turns being brave.

Later, when the saxophonist four doors down conceded defeat, they switched the room lights off. In the bedroom, the charity-shop boat curtains gave the river back its small story. Mara found his chest by memory; he covered her hand.

"You'll be wonderful," she whispered.

"So will you."

"We're going to be somebody's parents, Graham."

He watched the city's leftover light paint the ceiling. Somewhere a bus sighed; the Ouse went on as if none of it were new. "We're going to be all right," he said, and for once the room didn't argue.

Chapter Two

The City that Waits

By morning the shock of discovery had softened into a secret; by spring it had grown into a rhythm of its own.

Spring thickened into summer, and York glowed with the kind of light that made even its oldest stones seem young. The city had always carried its centuries like a second skin—walls that had outlasted wars, crooked lanes where traders once hawked their wares, the river Ouse slipping silently through it all. In 1987 the streets were as busy as ever, thronged with tourists clutching guidebooks, coaches idling by the station, day-trippers spilling into shops, shopping bags rustling like a tide.

For Graham and Mara, York had never looked brighter. Their lives had tilted into a new shape, a gentler rhythm marked by clinic appointments and quiet excitement, but they still walked hand in hand through the city as they always had.

On Saturdays, they wound their way down The Shambles, where butcher's hooks still jutted above the windows and the timbered houses leaned in close enough to whisper. Tourists craned their necks to take photographs, children pressed sticky faces against sweet-shop glass, and the air smelt of sugar, leather, and old stone. Mara loved it all. She threaded through the crowds with amused grace, pointing out things Graham would have walked past: a gargoyle peering down, a crooked doorframe, a cat curled like a monarch in a bookshop window.

Sometimes they wandered to the Minster, its towers rising pale and defiant above the rooftops. To Graham it was labour made miraculous—thousands of hands across hundreds of years fitting stone upon stone, lifting the vaults like sails into heaven. To Mara, it was something quieter, an anchor. She liked to sit on a bench in the shadow of the south transept, watching the tourists funnel through the doors.

"Imagine," she said once, her palm resting absently over her still-flat stomach, "bringing a child here. Letting them climb those steps, teaching them to spot saints in the glass."

Graham only nodded, because he couldn't find words for how that picture struck him.

York in summer was noisy with possibility. Street musicians and jugglers claimed corners the way stallholders claim market pitch: fiddlers by the square, guitarists under archways where the stone lent them grandeur. Ghost tours, still a novelty then, gathered outside old taverns as dusk approached, guides in black cloaks holding lanterns, weaving tales of Roman soldiers and grey ladies. Mara dragged Graham along one night, laughing as the guide pointed to darkened windows and told of footsteps echoing where no one walked.

"You don't believe any of this, do you?" Graham whispered, his arm around her.

"Not the details," she admitted, eyes gleaming in the torchlight, "but the feeling of it. The way history presses against you in this city. Don't you ever feel that?"

He thought of the centuries of hands that had built the Minster, of cobbles worn smooth by hooves and boots, of walls still standing when everyone who had laid them was dust. "Aye," he said softly. "Sometimes I do."

They lingered after the tour, strolling along the city walls while the sky bruised into evening. The tourists had thinned by then, leaving only the sound of their own steps on the worn stone. The rooftops fell away on either side, and the Minster glowed behind them, lit from within like a lantern. Mara leaned on the parapet, looking out across the roofs, her profile pale against the fading sky.

"Do you ever think," she said, "that we're just passing through? Like all of this will still be here long after us."

"Morbid thought for a Thursday night," Graham replied, though he slipped his arm around her shoulders all the same.

"Not morbid," she corrected gently. "Comforting. It means our little one will be part of something that lasts."

He kissed her temple, but a small chill crept through him nonetheless.

In the days that followed, York wrapped them in its ordinary splendour. They shopped in the open-air market by Parliament Street, haggling over carrots and cauliflowers while buskers competed with each other for tourist coins. Mara bought a knitted baby cardigan from an old woman whose hands shook as she wrapped it in brown paper.

"Too soon," Graham murmured, but Mara only smiled and tucked the package into her bag as if she were tucking away hope itself.

Afternoons often ended in a café off Stonegate, where the tables wobbled and the tea tasted faintly metallic. Students crowded the corners, arguing about politics in voices meant to carry. Graham would stir his tea slowly, half-listening, while Mara scribbled notes in a pad she carried everywhere, legal arguments mingling with lists of baby names she never let him see.

Evenings returned them to their flat, their little refuge above the city. The radio spilled music into the kitchen—Paul Young's Everytime You Go Away, Simple Minds' Don't You (Forget About Me)—songs that stitched themselves into the rhythm of their days. Mara's favourite remained Against All Odds, and every time it played, she stopped what she was doing and let it wash through her. Graham teased her for being sentimental, but secretly he loved how the song lit her face from within, as if she were remembering something that hadn't happened yet.

One night, as they cleared plates and the rain tapped steadily on the panes, Mara caught Graham sketching again at the table. She leaned over his shoulder, curious. On the page was a rough outline of a small house on a cliff, its roof pitched against the weather, the sea sketched in heavy strokes behind it.

"Not exactly York," she teased.

"Just a thought," he said, embarrassed. "Sometimes I think about leaving the city. Somewhere quieter."

She tilted her head, considering. "I can't imagine you without the noise. Without the scaffolding and the radio blaring on site."

"Noise is fine," he said, shading the roof, "until it's not."

Mara smiled, brushing the back of his neck with her hand. "Well, if you ever do drag me away to some windswept cottage, make sure it's got a fire that doesn't go out."

He caught her hand and kissed it, but he didn't say how vivid the picture was in his mind.

That night, as they lay in bed with the faint sound of the saxophonist from down the hall, Mara shifted closer and placed his hand gently on her stomach. "Do you think they can hear us yet?" she whispered.

Graham laughed softly. "Bit early, love. But maybe."

She fell asleep quickly after, breath warm against his collarbone. Graham lay awake a while longer, listening to the rain at the window, the city murmuring beyond the walls, and the echo of ghost stories still drifting through his head.

Sunday mornings belonged to football. Graham had played since schooldays, and even now, with his knees stiff from years on scaffolding and the occasional twinge in his back, he still turned out for the Woolpack pub team.

The pitch on the Knavesmire was one of many used on weekends, worn bald at the goalmouths, with dog walkers weaving around the edges. The referee was usually a retired postman with a whistle that didn't always work, and the changing rooms smelt permanently of mud and liniment. But for Graham and his mates it was everything: ninety minutes to forget the week, to kick and shout and feel twenty again.

That particular Sunday in June, the sun broke through early, burning the dew off the grass and sending steam curling from the pitch. Graham laced his boots, pulling them tight, and jogged a short circle before the kick-off. His best mate from the site, Davey, clapped him on the back.

"Got your shooting boots on, Jonesy?"

"They're welded to me," Graham grinned, though the truth was he hadn't scored in months.

The whistle blew, and the game began in the usual blur: shouts of "Man on!", the thud of the ball, the satisfying crack of a clearance. Graham played centre-half, steady and stubborn. He wasn't fast, but he read the game well, knew when to step up, when to hold. By half-time his shirt clung with sweat, and the Woolpack lads were one goal down, but spirits were high. A couple of pints after would soften the blow either way.

On the touchline, a small crowd had gathered: girlfriends, wives, children kicking their own smaller balls in the long grass. Graham hadn't expected Mara—she often used Sunday mornings to catch up on sleep or casework—but just before the second half began, he spotted her at the edge of the pitch. She stood in the shade of a sycamore, sunglasses hiding her eyes, her hand resting absently against her stomach.

"Bloody hell, Jonesy," Davey muttered, following his gaze. "She's a good one, coming out to watch this lot."

"She's the best one," Graham replied, and jogged back onto the pitch with his chest a little fuller.

The second half passed in a haze of sweat and shouted encouragements. Graham made one last-ditch tackle that left him sliding through mud and nearly taking a lump out of his shin, but the Woolpack salvaged a draw in the final minutes. The whistle went, the lads cheered as if they'd won the league, and they trudged off laughing, muddy, aching, alive.

Mara waited with his favourite, a can of Dandelion and Burdock, and that look she always gave him after football—amusement and affection stitched together.

"You're limping," she said, handing him the can.

"Part of the act," he said, taking a long swig.

"You'll be hobbling by Tuesday."

"Worth it." He glanced around, lowering his voice. "Did you see that tackle near the end?"

"I saw you nearly break your neck."

He laughed and slung an arm around her shoulders, unbothered by the mud streaking his sleeve onto her blouse. Together they walked towards town, the bells of the Minster tolling noon above the rooftops.

That afternoon, they joined his team-mates at the Woolpack, a low-ceilinged pub with beams blackened by centuries of smoke. The carpet was threadbare, the dartboard missing two numbers, and the fruit machine sulked unless you slapped it. The landlord, built like a barrel and grinning like a man who had outlived three refurbishments, pulled pints into dimpled glasses and rang the till like a dinner bell.

The air smelt of old hops, spilt lager, and the ghost of cigarettes.

Graham claimed the corner snug. Mara perched beside him with a half lager shandy while the men retold the match in increasingly heroic tones.

"Jonesy timed that tackle like a Swiss clock," Davey announced.

"Swiss clocks don't slide ten yards on their backsides," someone said, and the table roared.

Talk turned, as it always did, to life outside the lines. Davey leaned in, elbow on the table.

"So, Dad-to-be," he grinned, "that's you done for Sundays then. No more centre-half when you're pushing a pram, eh?"

"Rubbish," Graham said, though he was smiling. "I'll strap the baby to me like a rucksack. Put them in goal."

"Name the kid after whoever scores you a winner first," another lad chimed. "Alan if it's a boy. Alana if it's a girl."

Mara rolled her eyes, fondly. "No child of mine is being called Alan because a postman in shorts shinned one in from six yards."

More laughter. Graham felt a swell of pride that almost knocked him over, with Mara there beside him, their secret no longer secret, his mates treating him like he was carrying gold in his pockets.

"Get your last pints in while you can," Davey went on. "Sleep'll be rationed. Football too."

"Let him have this one," Mara said, squeezing Graham's knee under the table. "He's earned it."

They stayed for one more round. Someone fed coins into the jukebox and chose a run of soft rock that made the whole pub hum along without knowing the words. Beer left their ears warm and the day soft around the edges; they let the city carry them.

By the time they stepped back into the afternoon, the sun had leaned west and the city had shaken off its Sunday sleep.

Walking home along Stonegate, the streets were heaving with tourists spilling from coaches, snapping photos of crooked shopfronts and queuing outside tea rooms. A fiddler played outside a jeweller's, his bow flashing, and children danced clumsily in circles while parents clapped along. The air smelled of roasting nuts and diesel, of the river not far away.

Mara slowed near the Minster, her gaze drawn upward. Sunlight caught in the stained glass, throwing colour across the pavement like spilt paint.

"It never feels real, does it?" she murmured.

"What doesn't?"

"All of this. That it's ours, in our time. That people centuries ago built it knowing we'd still be walking under it." She glanced at him, smiling faintly. "Sometimes I think York itself is watching us."

He didn't answer; he tightened his hand around hers and let the bells answer for him.

That evening, the weather turned. Clouds gathered heavy over the rooftops, and rain began to pelt the windows of their flat. Graham lit the old gas fire, its hiss and click filling the room before the flames caught. Mara curled on the sofa under a blanket, her legs tucked beneath her, reading a brief by lamplight.

When the storm reached its peak, thunder rolling like a drum above the city, the Minster bells tolled again, strange and out of rhythm, carried on the wind. Mara shivered, though the fire was warm.

"Only a storm," Graham said, setting a mug of tea on the table.

She closed the file and leaned against him, letting the thunder roll on. "Promise me," she whispered, "no matter what happens, you'll keep going."

He looked at her, startled.

"Where's this coming from?"

She shook her head quickly. "Nowhere. Just... promise."

He kissed her hair. "Alright. I promise."

The bells tolled again, and for a moment it felt as though the whole city was listening.

By late summer, the pregnancy was no longer a secret whispered among family and friends but a truth visible to the world. Mara's body began to change, her once-tailored skirts giving way to looser dresses, her movements slower but no less graceful. Graham became a hawk at her side, snatching shopping bags before she could lift them, insisting she take the last seat on the bus, fussing if she looked pale.

"Graham, I'm not made of glass," she would tease, but she allowed his arm around her when they crossed the cobbles, her hand resting on his forearm as if to thank him for worrying.

The clinic visits became milestones. The waiting rooms smelt of disinfectant and warm paper, posters of smiling infants pinned to the walls. They sat together, knees touching, leafing through outdated magazines until Mara's name was called. Graham never missed an appointment, no matter what was happening on site. He wanted to be there, wanted to hear every heartbeat, wanted proof that their child was real and not just a dream spoken in the dark.

The first time they heard it, the quick and insistent thrum like a sparrow trapped in a box, Mara squeezed his hand so tightly he thought his fingers might break. Cold gel clung to her skin; paper crackled beneath her; the monitor's green light flickered across her face. He looked at her and saw tears in her eyes, the same as his own.

"That's ours," she whispered. "That's us."

From then on, everything bent towards the future. Saturdays at the market turned into treasure hunts: tiny cardigans knitted by pensioners, booties soft as clouds, picture books with dog-eared corners. Graham carried each purchase home as if it might blow away.

Their flat began to change too. The spare corner of the bedroom sprouted a cot borrowed from a cousin, its paint chipped but sturdy. Graham gave it a fresh coat of paint.

"Look at that, like new," Graham said as Mara entered the room with a cup of coffee for him.

Mara had also found curtains with a pattern of boats at a charity shop and hung them proudly, declaring the space a "nursery" even though it was barely the width of a wardrobe.

At night, Graham stretched on the sofa with his sketchbook. Mara, feet tucked beneath a cushion, leaned over to watch his pencil move. He still drew cottages more often than not, small houses with sturdy walls and wide hearths, always facing the sea.

"One day," he said, shading a roof. "When there are three of us, we'll find a place like this. Out of the city. Just us and the gulls."

Mara smiled, her hand resting on the curve of her stomach. "Promise me it'll have a library. Even if it's just one wall."

"And a football pitch in the garden, and a Scalextric set," Graham countered.

"And a proper kitchen," she said firmly. "None of this two-ring cooker nonsense."

"Deal." He kissed her temple and let the pencil roll to the floor.

As autumn arrived, York dressed itself for the season. Leaves skittered along the cobbles, tourists wrapped in scarves pressed into the Minster for shelter, and the smell of roasted chestnuts hung over the marketplace. Ghost tours grew busier as the nights lengthened, lanterns bobbing through the streets like will-o'-the-wisps. Graham and Mara watched one pass from the window of a café, laughing as a group of schoolchildren squealed at the guide's tales.

"Maybe we should go again," Mara suggested, stirring her tea.

"You'll give yourself nightmares," Graham teased.

"Not me," she said with mock solemnity. "This little one." She patted her stomach. "They need to know York's stories."

Their world narrowed around those stories, those hopes. Every song on the radio seemed meant for them; every future felt within reach. Even when

Mara came home tired from the law courts, eyes shadowed, she brushed it off with a smile.

"Just work," she said, slipping off her shoes. "Our real life is here."

Graham believed her. He wanted to believe her.

One evening, as November rain lashed the windows, they sat together by the fire. Mara curled in the armchair, a blanket draped over her, her book resting on the rise of her stomach. Graham sat on the floor at her feet, sorting through the screws and nails he had spilled from his pockets, a habit she never quite broke him of. The radio played softly, static tugging at the edges of the songs.

Then, as if on cue, Against All Odds began again.

Mara closed her eyes, smiling faintly. "There it is," she whispered. "Our song."

Graham looked up at her, silhouetted by lamplight, the shape of her more beautiful than anything he could build with his hands.

"Do you ever think," she said, "that life can be too good? Like we're holding something we can't possibly keep?"

"Don't say that," he said quickly, but she only reached down and brushed her fingers through his hair.

"I don't mean it in a bad way. I just mean… if it ended tomorrow, I'd still be glad it was ours."

He caught her hand, kissed her palm, and shook his head. "It's not ending. We're only just starting."

Outside, the storm kept its drum; somewhere the Minster tolled off-beat again. They held each other and didn't try to count.

Chapter Three

The Snow and the Silence

Autumn came down hard on York. Frost filmed the pavements in the mornings, turning the cobbles treacherous and bright. The Minster wore the cold like armour; even its bells sounded sharper, as if the air itself had become glass. Chimneys pushed smoke into the white sky, leaving the air tinged with coal and wood ash. By mid-December their flat felt like a ship in harbour, small, snug, holding steady while weather rattled the windows and drove people quickly from street to street.

They were ready. That was the strange, giddy truth of it. The hospital bag sat by the door with a list tucked into its pocket, Mara's handwriting neat and insistent: toothbrush, cardigan, baby blanket (blue), snacks, camera (film?). The borrowed cot stood in the corner with the boat curtain drawn across the window, a bit of seaside in a city of stone. On the chair lay the cardigan from the market, tiny pearl buttons winking as if in on a joke.

Graham found tasks to give his nerves somewhere to go. He sanded the edge of the old pine toy box they had rescued, varnished it until it shone, and stencilled a small gull in one corner for luck. He fixed a loose cupboard hinge, sorted the cutlery drawer, and rewired a lamp that did not strictly need it. When he ran out of work, he sharpened pencils and made a stack of blank pages ready for lists he never wrote. Even the smell of varnish clung to the flat, sharp and hopeful, as if he could coat the future against harm.

Mara slowed without complaint. Her work had tapered to paper and phone calls, the firm capable but suddenly solicitous. She spent afternoons in the armchair with a book, feet up, one hand parked on the curve of her belly as if guarding a door. She liked the sound of the city in winter, the hiss of buses, the occasional squeal of children let loose on icy patches, the distant calling of a stallholder too stubborn to close. Sometimes she dozed and woke to find the light different, the room rearranged by shadow, and Graham watching her as if afraid to blink in case time moved without him.

They had a last supper out at the Woolpack on a Tuesday when the snow threatened but did not arrive. The pub was a fog of smoke and chatter, its low ceiling trapping the warmth of beer and bodies. The air smelled of gravy and fried onions, mixing with the tang of spilt ale. The landlord, cheeks red as the hearth fire, brought them a shepherd's pie on the house and embarrassed them with a toast. "To the Joneses, soon to be three." The darts team banged their flights on the table like a drumroll. Mara blushed and raised her glass of water as if it were champagne. Graham felt the room tilt towards them, friendly eyes and laughter pressing in.

They lingered afterwards, listening to the landlord's booming voice mixing with the soft thuds of darts and the clink of pint glasses. When they finally buttoned coats and stepped out, the cold clutched them with both hands. Their breath puffed white as they cut across the square. They pressed their hands to the leaded glass of a toy shop, looking in at a wooden train set looping eternally around a paper mountain. The window smelled faintly of dust and varnished wood when Graham leaned close.

"Soon," Mara said, not quite to him, her eyes fixed on the tiny train as though she could will it into their lives. He nodded, though his throat had tightened around the word.

They did not say the frightening things out loud. They did not name the silent hours each had kept pretending sleep, the sudden thought that rose like a fish and vanished before it could be identified. They took comfort in preparation, in the ordinary, in the way the kettle still boiled and the radio still chattered and the Minster still marked time in great, careful strokes.

The first pains came on a night when snow finally fell, neat as confetti, flakes fat and unconcerned. They were halfway through a game of rummy and nonsense when Mara paused, when she blinked rapidly, her eyes unfocusing for a moment, her hand slipping to her side.

"Is that...?" Graham began, and she nodded, the smallest smile touching her mouth.

"I think so," she said, and then, after the breath had passed, "Don't fuss."

He fussed anyway. He checked the bag by the door twice, then a third time, then laughed at himself and zipped it shut. He changed his shirt because it felt important to be clean, then changed back because the first one had the right collar. He rang the number taped by the phone and listened hard as the midwife asked sensible questions in a voice that sounded like someone mending a bicycle, competent, unflustered, practical. Not yet, she said. Time them. Breathe. Ring again if anything changes.

They walked the flat as if rehearsing for a performance, two figures tracing paths between chair and window, sofa and kitchen door. The contractions braided the hours, bright strands of pain threaded through the ordinary. Between them they watched the snow deepen on the sill, and Mara teased him for counting aloud like a football commentator. When the intervals shrank and the air felt thin with it, Graham rang again, voice too loud, and the midwife said come in now, love, and he helped Mara into her coat though the effort of sleeves felt ridiculous and immense.

The streets were swallowed, their edges smudged into softness. Boots crunched on fresh snow, the sound swallowed by the muffled city. Chimneys wrote their smoke into the night, and a fox darted across the road, its paws vanishing without trace. The taxi slid once and corrected itself, the driver talking like a man soothing a skittish horse. "We'll get you there, don't you worry." In the back seat, Mara worked through each pain like a wave, knuckles white around his hand, then loosening, then white again. Graham tried jokes. He tried silence. He tried being a wall for her to lean against; he tried being air. The smell of petrol and damp upholstery clung to the car, the heater clicking on and off, blowing too hot then too cold.

The hospital was a long, lit brightness at the rim of the dark, heat hitting their faces as they pushed through the doors. Time changed its shape there. It always did in places built for beginnings and endings. Corridors bright as noon led to rooms where lamps burned low. The air was thick with bleach and overheated radiators, and the hum of fluorescent lights was constant. Nurses walked with the smooth efficiency of people whose bodies had learned to save steps. Papers were taken, questions asked, machines wheeled, and all the while Mara's breath kept up its steady labour, the body flexible and fierce, the mind riding inside it like a rider on a wild horse.

They put her in a room with a window that showed nothing but a flat white square of snow. Paper was pulled tight beneath her and crackled whenever she shifted. Graham sat, stood, sat again, coat rack, water bearer, the idiot making the wrong jokes, and the hand to be gripped until it sang.

At first there were smiles. He fetched ice. He walked the corridor and returned with news that the vending machine dispensed hot chocolate if you gave it a firm tap. She sent him for it, sipped, grimaced, laughed, then rode another contraction while he counted, whispered, and clenched his jaw in useless sympathy.

Then something shifted. He could not say when. The light felt different. The voices grew complicated.

"Just a minute," the midwife said, in a tone that meant now. Another voice arrived. Older. Certain. Words split the air: "Heart rate... distress... we are going to..."

Graham stood as if the order had been given to him. He tried to read faces the way he read walls, signs of movement, stress in the line, inevitabilities, and found only the blur of people moving fast towards a point he could not see. Someone told him to wait outside. The words landed on him with the weight of a beam. He kissed Mara's forehead and found it damp and shockingly hot. She looked at him from far away and said his name in a voice he had never heard before, both request and apology, and he stepped backwards into the corridor because that was the sum of what he could do.

The corridor was a world of waiting. No bells, no seasons, no snow. Just the stink of bleach, the hum of strip lights, the thunder of footsteps hammering past. Graham could not sit. He tried once, his knees bouncing, hands shaking, but the chair bucked him off. He stood. He walked the tiles until he lost count. He dropped to the floor, palms on the cold, his forehead pressed to it like prayer. He whispered her name, over and over, as though repetition might hold her to the earth.

The screams tore out of the room and down the corridor. Mara's voice, hoarse, animal, nothing

45

like the woman he knew. It gutted him. He tried to rush the door, but a nurse shoved him back, her eyes hard with the kind of pity that meant no. So he stayed outside, listening, fists thudding against his knees.

Inside, chaos ruled. He could hear it all, clattering metal, shouted orders, boots skidding on linoleum. "Pressure is dropping!" "Clamp, now!" "She is bleeding out…" A crash, a tray hitting the floor. Another scream. Then silence. Then Mara again, weaker, raw, until it broke off into something worse, nothing.

He knew before the handle turned.

The corridor filled with running bodies: green scrubs and pale faces, hands red to the wrists. A nurse flew past carrying a basin streaked scarlet. Another dragged a machine, its alarm shrieking like an animal in pain. Graham staggered against the wall, breath gone, his heart beating so loud he thought it might split his ribs.

He knelt again, because standing was a lie. He rocked forward, forehead to the tiles, and muttered,

"Please. Please. Please." He had never begged God in his life, but now the word tore from him like breath.

And then the silence came. The silence that was worse than any scream.

The door opened. A doctor stepped out, pale beneath her mask. Behind her, a nurse followed, her eyes like winter, clear, merciless, nothing soft left in them. Graham did not need the words. He saw it in their faces first. Still he waited for them to speak, because until they said it, it might not be true.

They asked if he was alone. He said yes. He said no. He did not know which was true. They told him the baby had gone first, a boy. They told him they had tried. They told him Mara had lost too much blood, that sometimes no hands, no skill, no begging could stop the body obeying its own brutal laws. They said she had been brave.

Brave. He clung to the word like it was rope in a storm. Something to hold when everything else had been ripped away.

They asked if he wanted to see her. He did not want to. He did not want that final picture to stamp itself over every other one. But he followed anyway, because following was all that was left.

The room was small, unbearably quiet. Machines dark. Metal tools abandoned on trays. Shadows sharp against white walls. The clock ticked without moving. The strip light clicked and never changed. Mara lay still, her skin pale but not yet cold. She looked more herself than he expected. And less herself than he could bear.

He sat, because standing was impossible, and took her hand. It was warm. He gripped it as though he could anchor her back to him, as though the world had made a mistake that he could correct by refusing to let go.

He had the absurd thought that he should be polite, tidy, not cry too much, not disturb the sheets. As if grief were a guest in the room, something to be hosted with restraint. But the sobs came anyway, tearing out of him, breaking his chest wide open.

They left him there as long as he wanted. Kind. Impossible. Time had no edges anymore. The only thing he remembered later was the window: a square of snow against black sky, luminous as a blank page. A page he knew he would never be able to write on again.

He went home just before dawn because a nurse said gently that he should, that there was nothing he could do here now and everything at home would need him to come back to it, to stand in its rooms, and be alive. He stepped into a city reshaped by night. The snow had stopped; the streets were clean and brutal in their quiet. The taxi turned in front of the Minster, and he looked up because habit said look up, and the building answered with its immensity as if to say what Mara had said once: We will still be here after you have gone.

The flat was too warm. Or perhaps he was too cold. He kept his coat on and stood in the kitchen where the lists were and the kettle was, and the postcard wall kept on requesting attention for harbour towns and Roman roads. The bag by the door waited, its zip already obediently closed. He carried it to the table because his hands did not know what else to carry, and he sat opposite it like a man across from an enemy with whom a negotiation had stalled.

The cot stood in the corner. He crossed to it without deciding to and put his hands on its bars as if it were a railing and he were on a ferry trying not to be sick. The boat curtain was half open and let in a light that made everything ridiculous and exact. He read the spines of their paperbacks as if they might contain instructions: Repair, Mend, Restore.

He sat in Mara's armchair and positioned himself so that if he turned his head he would see the cot, and if he turned it the other way he would see the door, and if he closed his eyes he would see both.

Snow began again, thin flakes now, undecided in the early light. On the windowsill, the brass owl watched. Graham set both hands on the chair arms, found that he could breathe, and hated that knowledge like a betrayal. The Minster, miles and centuries away, tolled for a service that would start without them. He did not cry then. That came later, like weather. He sat in the quiet his life had become and learned the size of it by listening.

The phone waited on the small table beside him. Its silence was heavier than the tolling bells, heavier than the hush of snow. He had been turning from it for hours, knowing that every moment of delay was a cruelty of its own. At last, with fingers that no longer felt like his, he lifted the receiver.

The dial tone filled the room, steady, unfeeling. He pressed the numbers one by one, each click an act of treachery against the world he wanted back. The line rang.

When the voice came, warm, expectant, innocent of what was about to be placed upon it, Graham closed his eyes. He drew a breath, and in that breath he felt the whole weight of what he was about to do: to tell them that their daughter was gone, and with her the grandchild they had been waiting to hold.

His mouth shaped the words. His heart broke
as he gave them away.

Chapter Four

Carry Her With You

The days that followed blurred into one another, as if time had slipped its gears. Morning arrived, but Graham barely noticed it. The curtains stayed drawn, the air thick with the smell of stale tea and the faint tang of plaster dust that clung to his skin no matter how many times he scrubbed.

His parents came to try to help and support him. Even though they were kind and loving, it could not break through the grief. His heart was broken, and nothing they said could fix it. Eventually they had to go back to their home, though they called every day, offering support and love.

Most days he sat in Mara's armchair, not reading, not watching, simply existing in the hollow of the cushions she had shaped. Sometimes hours passed with him staring at the cot in the corner. Other times he found himself in the kitchen, the kettle boiling without his remembering how it got there. Meals came and went untouched. The bread went hard on the counter, and fruit in the bowl shrank in on itself, skins puckering like old faces.

When the day of the funeral came, York seemed hushed beneath a pale winter sky. The Minster's bells tolled, each strike like a hammer against his chest. The crematorium chapel was packed—rows of faces: family, friends, neighbours, football lads—all gathered, all in black, all carrying their own measure of sorrow. The air was heavy with lilies, their sweetness thick enough to choke; radiators clanked, and the curtain motor purred, indifferent.

He sat rigid in the front pew, the paper shaking in his hands. Mara's photograph on the order of service blurred and cleared and blurred again as his tears kept coming, a tide he could not turn. Beside the pulpit, a small white coffin rested next to hers—two boxes no husband, no parent should ever be asked to look at. The chapel was too warm, too bright; lilies soured the air; the hymn faltered into silence. When the curtains drew and the coffins began to slide from view, the rollers gave a soft, ordinary clatter, and something tore clean through him. He lurched to his feet with a sound he did not recognise as his own, but Davey's arm came round his shoulders, and his father's hand found his sleeve and held him down. His knees buckled. His chest worked like a bellows with no air to find. In that dizzy, breaking instant, another room rushed up: their kitchen on a Tuesday, Mara leaning into him, mug warm between her palms, her cheek against his shoulder, her hands resting on the round of her belly.

"Listen," she had whispered, laughing at nothing and everything, "he's doing cartwheels." The memory landed with such force he could taste the steam of her tea, hear the click of the old clock, feel the tiny thud beneath his palm. Then the curtains met, and the sound in the chapel changed—no rollers now, just the hush people make when there is nothing left to say—and he understood that time would go on without them. He bent forward until his forehead touched his knuckles and let the grief take him, great heaving sobs that shook his ribs, while Davey and his father held him as if their hands alone could keep him from falling straight through the world.

Afterwards, the mourners drifted towards the Marcia for the reception. The snug and the bar filled quickly, coats steaming from the cold, voices hushed but insistent. Plates of curled ham sandwiches and sausage rolls appeared on tables, bowls of crisps, cups of tea balanced awkwardly beside pints. The place smelt of beer, damp wool, and the faint tang of floor polish, but over it all was grief, its own smell, raw and metallic.

People tried to help in the only ways they knew. Aunty Jean pressed a sandwich into his hand and said, "Eat, love, it'll keep you standing," though he only set it down, untouched. Old lads from the Woolpack clapped his back, muttering, "She was a good 'un, Jonesy," before turning away, their eyes too wet to linger. Neighbours told him stories he half-knew already—Mara carrying their shopping when knees gave out, Mara organising the church raffle, Mara laughing loudest at the pub quiz when she had got the answer wrong.

For a moment, the pub almost seemed warm with her presence, her life stitched into every memory. But the sound of it was unbearable. Their stories kept her alive for them; for him, it only deepened the hole she had left.

He slipped outside to the garden. The benches were slick with frost, the air sharp in his lungs. He sat with his pint untouched, watching his breath fog in the pale air. From inside came bursts of laughter, sudden and sharp, as people remembered her dancing at weddings, singing off-key, teasing Graham in ways that made his ears burn red. It was not cruel laughter—it was love, memory keeping her close. But he could not join them. He could not laugh.

He sat until his hands were numb on the pint glass, until the world inside the Marcia blurred into a dull hum, the warmth of it just out of reach.

Anna found him there. She wore a dark blue coat, her hair longer than Mara's, streaked with Californian sun. She looked exhausted from the flight, but her eyes—Mara's eyes—were steady.

"Graham," she said softly, sitting beside him on the frozen bench.

He looked up, blinking. "Anna."

Mara's sister took his hand, her grip firm, her voice steady despite the crack in it. "She loved you more than anything. You know that?"

His throat tightened. "I know."

"York feels so heavy. Everything grey and small. You should come to California when you can. Stay with us. See something different. There's light there, Graham. Proper light. The kind that fills you whether you want it or not. The mornings start with sun spilling over the mountains. The ocean smells of salt and eucalyptus, not cold stone. And in the evenings… the sky turns every colour at once. Orange, violet, pink. Sometimes you just stand there and forget to breathe."

He tried to imagine it, the warmth of a place where you did not need two jumpers indoors, where the sky itself tried to heal you. But the thought of it also hurt. "I can't think past today," he whispered.

"I know," Anna said, her voice breaking. "But I needed to say it. You're family, Graham. Always. When you're ready, we'll be waiting. She'd want you to live again."

She kissed his cheek and went back inside, leaving him alone in the frost, her words echoing like a promise too big to hold.

Days followed, heavy and shapeless. His parents brought casseroles, his mother smoothing curtains as though grief could be pressed flat. His father clapped his shoulder, urging him home for "fresh air." Friends tried too. Davey, still in his muddy kit, said, "The lads miss you." The Woolpack boys stamped snow from their boots, coaxing him out for "just the one pint." But Graham only shook his head each time.

Neighbours left pies, cakes, soups. The counters filled with kindness, slowly turning to waste. The only sound was the clock ticking, like water dripping into a sink that never filled.

There was a knock at the door—three quick raps, a pause, then two more, the Woolpack rhythm. Graham didn't move at first. The knocking came again, and Davey's voice came through the letterbox, winter air riding in with it.

"Jonesy? It's us."

He opened the door to Davey and two of the lads, Gaz and Mick, stamping snow from their boots onto the stair mat like schoolboys caught out. They smelt of cold air and the Woolpack's lunchtime hop; scarves looped high, faces raw with the weather.

"All right," Davey said, meaning not all right at all. He lifted a paper bag. "Brought you a pasty. Proper one. And the landlord says your stool's sulking."

Gaz peered past Graham into the flat. "Thought we'd kidnap you for just the one. Half, even. The snug's quiet. Landlord asked after you."

"We'll sit in the corner where you can't hear the blasted jukebox," Mick added, trying for lightness and missing. "We won't talk about… y'know. We'll talk nonsense. Ten minutes. We'll walk you back."

Graham stood with one hand on the door edge, the other on the frame, as if bracing against a wind that had got inside the building. The flat behind him smelt faintly of varnish and lilies gone to sweetness. The pasty bag crackled in Davey's grip.

"Not tonight," he said, the words feeling like pebbles in his mouth.

Davey nodded, took it on the chin. "Tomorrow then. Or Saturday. Or after that. We'll keep trying."

Gaz lifted the bag, awkward now. "We'll leave this, yeah? Eat it or throw it at a gull. Your choice."

Mick fished in his pocket and set a folded fixture list on the hall table beside the brass owl.

"If you fancy standing in the rain shouting at men who can't trap a ball, we'll be at the Knavesmire on Sunday. Your boots'll be waiting."

They didn't step inside. No one asked to. Davey squeezed his shoulder once—hard, a builder's clumsy blessing—and they backed away down the stair, voices low, boots creaking. Cold air lingered in the doorway after he shut it, then thinned, leaving the flat unchanged.

He took the pasty to the kitchen and set it beside an untouched casserole, then pinned the fixture list under the magnet shaped like a gull. He stood there until the clock ticked him out of the moment and back into the quiet.

Down at the Woolpack a little later, Davey fed coins into the payphone and spoke to Graham's dad.

"He won't come out for us," he said, palm cupped over the mouthpiece. "But he might pick up for his gran. Would you… could you ask her to give him a ring?" The landlord hovered nearby with a tea towel and a nod, as if granting permission for the intervention.

That was how the phone call that finally broke the stillness came to be.

It was the phone itself that announced it—an old bell, shrill, cutting through the flat like an alarm. Graham lifted the receiver, half-dreading who it might be.

"Hello?"

"Graham, love." The voice was soft, worn at the edges, but carried the unmistakable strength of his gran. Too old to travel now from St Andrews, but as present as ever.

"Gran," he breathed.

"Och, my boy. I've been thinking of you every hour."

"I don't know what to do," he admitted, his voice cracking. "It's all... gone, Gran."

"Aye," she said simply. "You've suffered the loss of two people at once—a moment of true joy turned into the worst thing imaginable for anyone to carry. Nothing I can say will stitch that hole closed. But listen, my darling. Grief's a tide. It'll drown you if you sit still and let it. You've got to move, even a little, or it'll take you under."

"I can't stay here."

"No. York's full of her. Every street, every stone. You'll spend your life walking through ghosts. You need somewhere new. A place to set your hands to work again. Do you remember, when you were a wee boy, telling me you wanted a cottage by the sea? Go and find it, Graham. Live again. And carry her with you," she added, gentle but firm. "Not as a weight—as the part of you she made."

He rubbed his eyes, knuckles rough. "She made me promise, Gran. She said if anything happened, I had to carry on. As if she knew."

Gran's voice softened. "Then keep that promise, my darling boy. You honour her by living, not by wasting away in your flat. Build something again. That's who you are."

The line went quiet but warm, as if she were still holding his hand across the miles of wire.

When they hung up, Graham sat with the receiver in his lap. Outside, snow felt steady, softening the rooftops of York. For the first time since Mara's death, he felt something shift—not relief, not hope, but the faintest suggestion of direction.

It didn't happen all at once. The idea of leaving gnawed at him. He walked through York as if testing Gran's words. Everywhere he turned, Mara was there: in the Minster bell, in the market stalls, in the Woolpack snug. He lived among ghosts.

So he began to look south. Property pages became his nightly reading. Most houses were too neat, too polished. He wanted something that needed him—something broken enough to match the wreckage inside.

It was a small advertisement, half-hidden at the bottom of a column, that caught him:

For sale: former cottage, late 17th century. Cliffside location near Looe, Cornwall. Requires full renovation. No services connected. Price: offers invited.

The words require full renovation might have chased off most buyers. To Graham, they felt like an invitation. An invitation to carry her with him into whatever came next.

Within a fortnight, he was on the train, a rucksack at his feet, his toolbox lashed with string beside him. The journey pulled him through changing landscapes—flat fields, wooded hills, and at last the wild edge of Cornwall, where the air smelt different, full of salt and promise.

He hired a battered van at Liskeard and followed twisting lanes toward the coast. At last the road climbed, narrowed, and opened onto a headland where the sea smashed itself endlessly against the cliffs. There, perched at the edge of it all, was the cottage.

It sat like a forgotten sentinel, hunkered low against the wind. The slate roof sagged; one chimney leaned like a drunk. Ivy clawed across the walls, almost swallowing a window.

He cut the engine and sat for a moment, staring. The air rushed around him, clean and fierce. Below, the sea roared. It was raw, unpolished, utterly apart from the world he had left.

Inside, the air was heavy with dust and salt. The floorboards creaked; the fireplace was half-choked with fallen stone. A gull shrieked outside, its cry echoing through the empty rooms like a warning—or a welcome.

The place was ruinous. It was also perfect.

That first night, he lay on a camp bed in the sitting room, listening to the storm drag itself across the sea. Wrapped in his coat, staring at the low beams, with a camping lamp offering a small, stubborn glow, Graham felt the ache of absence pressing into him. But he also felt something else: the first fragile stirrings of purpose.

Here, at the cliff's edge, there was no one to tell him what to do. No casseroles, no polite invitations, no corridors full of loss. Just work. Work he could sink his hands into until exhaustion dulled the pain.

The cottage didn't care who he had been. It only demanded what he could give.

And Graham, broken as he was, was ready to give it everything. And he would carry her with him.

Chapter Five

Where the Silence Cracks

The days fell into a rhythm of work. Graham woke early, not because he slept well, but because the wind through the rafters made sleep a fragile thing. Each morning he boiled water on a camping stove balanced in the old fireplace, drank tea strong enough to sting, and set about trying to bring the cottage back to life.

The place had been empty for thirty years, and it showed. Floorboards sagged, plaster crumbled at a touch, and the chimney spat soot whenever the wind shifted. The windows rattled in their frames, and one upstairs pane had given up entirely, leaving only a hole through which the gulls jeered at him.

Still, he worked. He stripped rotten timbers, patched the roof with salvaged slate, and scrubbed walls until his knuckles split. The labour filled his days

69

and wore him down in a way that kept the grief at bay—at least until night returned.

By the end of his first week, he admitted he needed supplies. His hammer had cracked, his saw was blunted, and the nails rattling around in his pocket would hardly last a day. So he set off down the cliff road into the town, the van bumping along lanes that seemed built for carts rather than engines.

Looe revealed itself slowly, a jumble of narrow streets pressed between hills and sea. Fishing boats rocked in the harbour, their masts clinking like cutlery in a drawer. The air was thick with the smell of salt, diesel, and fried batter from the chip shops. Shops spilled onto the pavements: a butcher with hooks in the window, a greengrocer stacking cabbages like cannonballs, and—what he was after—a hardware shop with a peeling sign that simply read FERRIS & SON, IRONMONGERS — EST 1760.

A bell jangled as he pushed the door open. Inside, the shop smelt of oil and wood shavings, the kind of place where everything had a place, even if you couldn't see the logic. Shelves bowed under the weight of nails, screws, brushes, hammers, locks, ropes, chains. Behind the counter stood a man in his sixties, sleeves rolled, glasses perched at the end of his nose.

"Morning," the man said, eyeing him with polite curiosity. "Don't reckon I've seen you in here before."

"Just moved in," Graham replied. "Up on the cliff road. Old cottage."

The man gave a low whistle. "That place? Nobody's lived there since… oh, must be the fifties. Damp as a haddock's pocket. You've work cut out, lad."

"That's the idea," Graham said simply. "I'm Graham."

"Ferris," the man added, tapping his badge. "You'll be needing nails, timber seal, new locks if you're wise. Roof slate too, I shouldn't wonder."

By the time Graham left, his arms were heavy with bags and his wallet considerably lighter. He paused outside, blinking in the sudden sunlight. People passed by carrying shopping bags, children tugged dogs on leads, fishermen shouted to one another across the quay. It was life, ordinary and undisturbed, and he felt at once far from it and desperate to be part of it again.

On his way back to the van, he stopped at the bakery for a pasty and a loaf. The woman behind the counter asked where he was staying, and when he told her, her eyebrows shot up.

"That old place? Folk say it was a smuggler's den, once upon a time. Tunnels in the cliffs, so they reckon." She handed him his change with a smile that was half-teasing, half-wary. "You be careful up there."

"I will," he said, though he wasn't sure of what.

Back at the cottage, he ate standing by the window, looking out at the sea as it heaved itself against the rocks. The pasty was hot and flaky, the bread still warm in its paper bag. For the first time in weeks, food tasted like something more than duty.

That afternoon he returned to the work. He replaced hinges on the doors, fitted new panes of glass, swept centuries of grit from the flagstones. The cottage resisted, every task harder than it should have been, but that was all right. Resistance kept his mind quiet.

It was while he was pulling up a loose board in the bedroom that he found it. His crowbar slipped under the plank, levering it up with a crack. Beneath, in the dust, lay a coin dulled with age. He picked it up, rubbed the grime with his thumb, and squinted at the faint outline of a crowned head.

"Huh," he muttered aloud. "Old penny."

He turned it over, the coin heavy and oddly warm in his hand. Who had dropped it? A smuggler, a fisherman, a child hiding treasure? He held it longer than he meant to, the weight strangely comforting. He slipped it into his pocket and carried on, never guessing that it was gold—a George III guinea—and worth far more than he imagined.

That night, he sat by the fire with the coin glinting faintly in the lamplight. Outside, the sea roared, the gulls screamed, and the wind pressed at the shutters as if trying to get in. Graham leaned back in his chair, staring at the "penny," and for the first time wondered if this place had chosen him as much as he had chosen it.

Work filled his days, but the nights refused to be tamed. When the sun dropped behind the sea, the cottage seemed to swell with silence—each creak of timber amplified, each gust of wind like a hand rattling the shutters. He began to buy bottles in town along with his nails and sandpaper—beer at first, then whisky, the burn of it quicker to quiet the ache.

At first it was just a glass to help him sleep. Then another to push back the memories. Soon the bottles emptied faster than he could remember drinking them. By nightfall, he'd sit in the armchair staring at the fire, Mara's absence blooming in the room like smoke. The coin lay on the bedside table, but he often carried it in his pocket, rolling it between

74

his fingers like a worry stone. Its weight anchored him and taunted him all at once.

The townsfolk noticed, though they said little. Mr Ferris at the ironmongers would frown when Graham came in smelling faintly of drink, but he still set aside the nails he knew the man would need. The baker slipped him an extra loaf more than once. At the Jolly Sailor in Looe, where he sometimes stopped for a drink, the landlord tried to draw him into conversation, but Graham gave short answers and hurried back to the cottage.

One night in January, the weather turned. The wind rose from the sea with a howl that shook the windows. Rain lashed the roof, finding its way through gaps he hadn't yet patched. He sat in the dark, whisky bottle at his feet, the radio crackling on the table beside him. Stations came and went in bursts of static—snatches of voices, half-songs, weather reports warning of gales along the coast.

Then, through the static, the unmistakable piano chords began. Against All Odds.

He froze. For a moment, he thought he'd imagined it. But then the voice came, raw and pleading, filling the room with Mara's memory. He saw her in the York kitchen, eyes closed, hand resting on her belly as she whispered, Our song.

The bottle slipped from his hand, thudding against the floorboards. His breath hitched, the sound tearing from him before he could stop it.

He stumbled to his feet, the radio still pouring the song into the room, and lurched to the door. The wind hit him like a wall, rain driving sideways, soaking him instantly. He walked out anyway, down the narrow path toward the edge of the cliff.

The sea raged below, waves smashing white against the rocks. The rain blurred everything, the world reduced to water and wind. Graham stood at the edge, his boots sliding on the mud, the abyss yawning below.

He wanted to step forward. Wanted the roar to take him, to end the ache. His body shook with it, the whisky in his veins urging him on.

76

But when he leaned forward, the sea surging beneath, something inside him broke. His knees gave way. He fell to the ground, fists pounding the wet earth, his voice hoarse and torn.

"I'm sorry, Mara!" he shouted into the gale, each word ripped from his throat and swallowed by the storm. He struck the ground again, mud smearing up his arms. "I'm sorry! I can't do it!" he sobbed uncontrollably.

The sky flared with lightning, the cliffs shaking with thunder. He crouched there, broken, a man shouting apologies into a void that never answered.

At last, shuddering and hollow, he forced himself upright. He turned from the abyss, stumbling back along the path toward the cottage. His legs felt carved from stone. The wind clawed at him, rain needling his eyes.

Then it happened.

With a shriek like tearing canvas, something ripped free from the roof—a slate, loosened weeks ago, finally claimed by the gale. It spun through the air and struck him hard across the temple.

The world cracked white.

He reeled, blood warm against the cold rain, staggering like a drunk. Somehow, blind with pain, he lurched toward the cottage door. His hand fumbled at the latch, missed, tried again.

He half-fell into the room, dragging himself across the floorboards. The fire was cold, the walls closing in. He crawled toward the bedroom, the coin slipping from his pocket, clinking once against the boards before his hand closed over it instinctively.

He clutched it tight, every ounce of strength pouring into his fingers. His body gave way, collapsing onto the boards.

Darkness rose like the tide.

And when Graham opened his eyes again, the year was no longer 1987.

Chapter Six

The Stranger in the Window

When Graham slowly opened his eyes, the room didn't feel right—something was wrong. At first, he blamed the whisky, the storm still humming in his skull like a struck wire. But no—this was different. The ceiling above him didn't sag with damp, brown blooms. Heavy oak joists ran across it, blackened by decades of smoke, polished smooth where hands had worried them absentmindedly while rising from chairs. Between the beams, an uneven coat of limewash—chalk-white, pocked with hairline ripples—caught the lamplight like frost on milk. The air smelt of tallow and salt, with something sour beneath, the old-rancid edge of fat that clings at the back of the throat.

He pushed himself upright, head ringing though he couldn't remember the blow that had felled him. The nylon camp bed was gone. No squeak of elastic, no zip, no crumpled sleeping bag. Instead, he sank into a heavy oak frame—a four-poster stripped of finery, its carved posts nicked and notched with small histories. A quilt lay over him, thick and hand-stitched in rough diamonds, smelling of lavender gone bitter with age and, behind it, lanolin—the ghost of the sheep still clinging to the wool.

Yesterday—he was certain of it—he'd been in frayed jeans, trainers kicked under the bed, a cotton tee sticking to his chest, his bomber jacket draped on a chair he meant to fix. That was yesterday.

But now—

His hands met cloth he had never owned. A coarse linen shirt, undyed and faintly scratchy, clung to his skin; the collar lay wide and raw at his throat, closed by bone buttons that sat imperfectly down his chest. Over it, a woollen waistcoat had been pulled tight; the seams were stiff with smoke, sweat, and years. His thighs felt bound in; breeches of heavy fustian hugged to the knee where rough stockings grazed his calves. On his feet, stout square-toed shoes creaked with every shift, their brass buckles dulled to the green of old pennies.

He tugged at a seam—expecting costume stitching, some theatre trick. The cloth held with the stubbornness of garments mended more than replaced. Frayed edge, darned knee, shiny seat. Lived in. Worked in.

On the table where his radio had sat, a lamp burned with a thin, lapping flame: whale oil—sharp and fish-thick, sea turned to fire. Its brass collar was blackened with use; smoke had smudged the chimney. Shadows crawled over the walls, over the beams, turning the low room into a cave that breathed.

Beside the lamp lay coins. He reached for one. Weight hit his palm with a warm, human gravity. Not copper's dullness but the deep, patient glow of tired gold: a spade-shield crisp though softened by fingers, GEORGIVS III DEI GRATIA ghosting round the rim. A guinea—no replica, no souvenir, but a thing that had moved from hand to hand while men bargained and bragged and died.

His breath snagged. He turned to the window. The old casement's small panes—wobbly glass, seeded with bubbles—rippled the world beyond. The cliff and the long heave of sea were the same, but the track no longer choked with bramble and ruin. Beaten earth, rimmed with gorse. And on the headland where only broken walls had crouched yesterday, smoke lifted from two squat chimneys as if the cottage had drawn breath.

His reflection swam in the clouded glass. His eyes were his. The rest... not quite. Not the neat, short side-parting he had combed each morning since school but long black hair, loose and salt-tangled, falling to his shoulders. A stranger wore his bones.

Cold washed through him. He pressed both hands to the sill, feeling the oak bite crescents into his skin. Too sharp for a dream. He looked down at the guinea again, edge biting his palm until it hurt.

Nothing dissolved. The room stayed. He walked out along the passage—narrower than it had ever been in his lifetime, because furniture compressed it, pegs held coats and shawls, and the air was full of smoke and steeped herbs. In the scullery he found no enamel sink. A granite trough sat there instead, a wooden ladle on its rim, brown water tracking down the stone from an iron spout. A pail. A scrubbed board. Onion skins clung to a knife. On the hearth, a trivet held a black pot; fat and onion rode the air, peppery mutton stewing down into something blunt and generous.

This wasn't renovation. It was the cottage as it had been—whole, worked-in, alive.

Panic sent him to the door. He dragged the bar, lifted the latch. Wind slapped him bright with salt, and the sight beyond stopped him mid-breath.

The headland wasn't empty. A low-roofed byre hunched against the weather; a grey pony stamped outside it, breath smoking in steady puffs. Two women in shawls trudged past with baskets on their hips, skirts tucked high out of the mud; their hands were red from the cold. Farther down the lane, a cart rattled over ruts, iron rims ringing on granite. The barrels it carried tapped and thudded with baritone hollowness.

"Morning, Michael."

The voice came easy, a fisherman's burr that carried humour without effort. An old man in a patched frock coat, tar glistening on the cuffs, lifted two fingers to his cap without breaking stride. He smelt of rope and herring and cold sleep. He said Michael as if the word belonged to the weather.

Graham opened his mouth. No sound.

Another pair of neighbours followed, shawls tight over hair. "Mornin', Michael," the older called, sure he would be where he always was. The younger slid him a quick, appraising look. "You'll be at the cove afore tide, then," she asked.

He nodded, because not nodding would mean explaining, and there was no explanation anyone could swallow.

He followed the track downhill. The world narrowed to the feel of it under his shoes—the way many feet and hooves had furrowed it, the way water obsessed over the same two edges and gnawed them back each winter. Below, the harbour jabbered with rope and gulls and men's voices. Where ruin had hunched yesterday, boats now shouldered one another, their tarred sides dull as seals. Nets hung black and wet. Women bent to their work with their backs like question marks—guts to gut, scales to scrape, children to scold. Kelp. Fish-gut. Coal smoke. Damp wool. Hot tallow from a chandlery door. A broken crate leaking rum's sweet, dangerous perfume. The air was a broth, scalding and thick and, in a way he didn't want, comforting.

A barefoot boy shot past, hair like weed drying on pebbles, grin wide as bottom tide. "Michael!" he yelped, and was gone with a slap of feet. The way the name leapt from other people's mouths—fitted, like a well-cut plug—made Graham's scalp prickle.

He touched his shirt as if to steady himself—coarse homespun. Not his. A rough blue coat cut square sat on his shoulders, the collar rubbing his neck raw in a way that said: you've always had me. He looked at his hands and saw the paint and pencil he knew were gone. Instead, ground-in black. The half-moons of old rope burn. A nick on the thumb where a knife had slipped weeks ago. A healing scrape. He rubbed until the skin stung. The history didn't shift.

"You're late."

He turned. A broad man of thirty stood planting the lane with his boots as if it were a deck. Square jaw shadowed by a day's growth. A pale old scar ran from ear to collar like a careless stitch. Hat angled against the wind, short coat hem tar-darkened. His eyes were that flinty, patient grey of men who've learned to expect other people's mistakes and factor them into the plan.

"Late?" Graham said, fighting to keep his face the way the man expected.

"Aye." The man glanced at the tide without needing a clock. "Work tonight. Tide nor revenue wait on your yawns. You've not turned soft, have you?"

Somewhere in Graham, the old labourer's instinct—carried from scaffolds and sites and men who don't forgive dithering—straightened his spine. "No."

The grey eyes weighed him, scraped for rot in the grain. Something shifted. A decision landed with no sound. The man's palm, heavy as a mallet, smacked his shoulder. "Cove," he said. "Two hours afore high water. No lanterns till the last. And keep your head down—cutter sniffin' off Rame yesternight."

He turned and was gone, dragging the air with him.

Graham stood and let the harbour move around him. He could not say: my name is Graham Jones, I came here from—From what? From radio static and neon? From York, where the Minster shouldered the sky and a woman called Mara pressed a hand to a neat curve of belly and said the word ours like a spell?

He pushed his thumb into the guinea until the edge bit. Pain sharpened him into usefulness.

He was a little confused as he made his way back to the cottage, though not afraid. A strange calmness had settled over him, quiet but sure, as if the air itself recognised him. The path curved like a memory under his feet. He couldn't say why, but he felt he belonged here—as though some small part of him had always belonged. The sea's voice in the distance, the smoke rising from chimney stacks, the measured rhythm of the place—all of it folded around him, steadying. Michael, he thought, hearing the name as if someone else had spoken it. Yes. Michael.

He climbed back to the cottage. Passing faces nodded and called to him in a cordial rhythm that left no room for argument. A boy ran with a hoop, a dog skittered stone to stone after it and decided against the chase halfway. A woman at the well hauled rope hand over hand; the bucket rose with the groan of swollen hemp.

"Have 'ee still got that cough, then?" she called over her shoulder to a neighbour, laughter rising and falling in the easy way of people who have seen too many winters to be surprised by one more.

Inside, the fire had banked itself into a red grin; the stew had skinned over and looked unapologetic about it. On the table, someone had forgotten a pewter tankard half-full of ale. He lifted it and tasted bitter malt with a lick of iron. He stared into the hearth until the flames doubled, almost placing him into a trance.

He drew the guinea from his pocket. Warm— like it had been living against skin all morning. Things with no right to a pulse sometimes felt like they had one.

"Michael."

He stared. A girl of about thirteen—shawl pulled tight, cheeks chapped to a berry-red—stood in the doorway, squinting as though she might bring him into focus by sheer effort. She carried the brisk wariness of someone who knows a day will spill work onto her the moment she stops moving.

"Mam says if you're about, there's milk to fetch," she said. "And she told me to pass a word from Eliza: hands ready for the tide."

"Eliza," he said, and the name came like a rope thrown across a gap.

"Aye." The girl tipped her head, giving him the sort of sharp, side-on look a woman uses when judging a horse's temper rather than its teeth. "You look queerer'n a threepenny bit today." She sniffed, then bobbed a quick curtsey—neighbourly, not servile—and slipped away, leaving the door breathing in her wake.

Eliza. The name hung in the warm air like tobacco smoke. He turned it over as he turned the coin. Eliza. Eliza. Who could she be—and what business had she with him?

As dusk crept in, he wrapped himself in the blue coat and took the cliff path. Gorse snagged at him; crushed blossoms breathed out their warm, almond-sweet scent against a winter sky. The sea shifted from pewter to iron. Down in the fold of the cliff, the cove opened—an indrawn breath you could hide inside. In daylight it would be raw rock and shingle; at night, with the wind corked and the stones oiled dark by tide, it was a pocket built by God for secrets.

Figures moved low and quick. Voices spoke in whistles and single nouns. Rope thumped. A keel hissed over wet stones, then shoulders took the weight with a grunt that sounded like prayer. Rum. Tobacco. Tea, perhaps. The names themselves felt like offences in his mouth—curious, how language could be evidence.

The scarred man materialised at his elbow, eyes already past Michael to the water. "About time." A barrel was levered against Graham's shins. "Roll. No clatter."

Michael crouched—back remembering scaffolds; thighs remembering ladders; hands remembering that weight gives you its centre if you ask properly—and tipped the barrel into a quiet sideways roll. Brined, sloshing, heavier than his guess. Work found its lanes in his muscles and ran.

"Quiet," someone hissed. "Lantern east— beyond the snag."

They froze in the same heartbeat. Out beyond the shoulder of rock, a light bobbed, dipped, returned—the slow pulse of a ship's lantern. The air went singe-thin. Small sounds sharpened: water licking at stones; a checked breath; the faint, furious crackle of a wick cupped under a coat.

"Faster," the scarred man—Jory, as Michael suddenly recalled—said, his voice like a blade being honed.

They moved as a single creature—barrels shouldered, ropes coiled, cart wheels coaxed into their first grudging turn. The pony tossed its head and listened with its whole skull, ears flicking like shutters in a gust. Lanterns swung low; men slipped through the half-light like bone beneath skin.

Then the shout:

"Stand there!"

Lanterns flared, throwing stretched monsters up the cliff. Two horses clattered over the shingle, iron shoes striking sparks that ran like minnows. The revenue men wore their hats cocked square; one carried a pistol low, the other held a musket not quite aimed, its steel making quiet promises.

The whole cove froze—breath, muscle, thought—as if the night itself had stopped.

A lantern wobbled where a foot shifted too fast; oil slopped and flared, but only for a heartbeat before someone stamped it out. A barrel, nudged by nerves alone, rolled a few yards downhill before a man caught it with a murmured curse. The pony tossed, whites showing, but a handler soothed it with a steady hand.

"Easy there," Jory called, tone friendly as wet rope. "Didn't expect company."

The nearest revenue horse edged forward. "Routine patrol," the man said. His lantern swung, its light cutting across faces that tried to look bored and hands that tried to look idle. "Quiet night."

"Aye," Jory replied. "Quiet as we can hope for. Just seeing the pony sure-footed before morning. Tide's rougher today than it has a right to be."

A pause. The revenue men's lanterns hovered, searching, weighing. They saw carts, a pony, a few shapes that could be fishermen—or could be smugglers—and nothing they could point to with confidence. Suspicion thickened the air, but nothing broke it.

"Mind the headland path," one of them said finally. "Wind'll knock a man clean over."

Jory touched his cap. "Kind of you."

The lanterns lingered a moment longer—two bright doubts in a dark place—then turned inland. Hooves scraped. Harness rang once, twice. Slowly, the revenue men slipped away, light thinning to a thread and then to nothing.

Only when the last echo had been swallowed by the cliffs did the cove breathe again.

Jory let out a breath that might have been laughter if relief hadn't strangled it. "Close as skin," he muttered. "Another step and they'd have been asking questions no one wants to answer."

Barrels were shouldered again; ropes coiled; the cart's wheels gave their first quiet, grudging turn. The pony flicked its ears, listening with its whole skull. Lanterns swung low. Men slipped through the half-light like bones beneath skin.

Up on the headland, the wind had teeth again. Jory clapped Michael's back hard enough to rattle coins in heaven. "Never seen you keep so still. Thought the sea had taken the iron out of you. Keep it up and you'll live long enough to regret it."

Laughter followed—thin, messy, the kind men use to push danger away an arm's length.

They moved inland. Lamps shuttered. Hooves muffled with sacking. They kept to lanes neither parsons nor excise liked to think about. Where the town gathered itself round yards and wells, gilt letters briefly caught the moon:

FERRIS & CO., IRONMONGERS — ESTABLISHED 1760.

The window showed neat drawers of nails, polite coils of rope, lanterns fit for respectable porches. But at the back gate, Jory rapped three times in a rhythm that belonged to people rather than doors. A latch slipped. Stone steps drank them downward.

The air cooled. The cellar stretched, brick-vaulted and deep, the smell of oak and spirit thick enough to touch. Barrels. Bales. Crates. Brandy. Tobacco. Lace enough to dress a dozen weddings the law would prefer naked. A network of hands made it quick. Barrel kissed floor here; bales stacked in the north wall's dry pocket; chalk slashed on each cask to mark its soul.

A boy, ink at his cuticles, kept tally, whispering his totals as though sharing them with the walls. Ferris himself—broad, smooth-faced from years of bargaining—moved like three men: one who sold hinges, one who smuggled, one who counted debts of kindness and paid them back with interest.

"Eliza keeps it straighter than the law ever could," Jory murmured, catching Graham's glance. "Safe as houses—so long as you don't bring the King's nose to the door."

Eliza oversaw without waste. Where a man might have barked orders, she let competence speak. A gesture placed a crate; a palm sealed a barrel; the smallest twist corrected a knot. She seldom raised her voice; men turned anyway, as though the tide itself demanded they face her.

When the last rope was coiled and the last wheel chocked, she looked at Graham. Not thanks. Not approval. Acknowledgment—the weight of being counted on. One nod: you are in this now.

There'd be no stepping back without tearing something.

By the time he reached the cottage, the fire was a red smile. He stirred it, set the kettle near the coals. Nicks stippled his hands; his sleeve was torn; his cheek still rough with grit. Hollow and overfull—danger ringing him like a bell stuffed with rags.

On the table lay the guinea. Bright, remembering daylight he hadn't seen. He touched it. Weight. Warmth. A truth that didn't care whether he understood.

A knock came. Soft. Deliberate. Not neighbourly.

"Michael?" A woman's voice—low, edged with command and a hint of salt wind.

He opened the door. Eliza stood easy in the lamplight, hood forward, a damp curl pasted to her cheek. Weather clung to her.

"You kept your head," she said. Not praise—a ledger entry. "Most don't, first time the King's men pass close."

"They didn't see anything."

"Aye. Because no one gave them reason to." Her gaze lingered on the fine scatter of grit on his cheek, reading the night as if it were written on him.

"Careful with different. Different draws notice. Notice draws King's men. King's men bring Tyburn."

She stepped inside, warming her scarred hands at his hearth like one who'd known it all her life. "We'll move the rest at dawn. Black Spring track. Ferris'll hold what's left. You'll come."

He nodded. It wasn't agreement. It was alignment.

At the door, she paused. Her mouth almost shaped a smile. "Drink less," she said. "You smell more of rain tonight than tavern. Keep to it."

Then she was gone, the night folding around the space she left.

Michael stood in the quiet while the kettle chattered. He poured something bitter into a beaker and cupped it like it might teach his fingers what century they belonged to.

He didn't mean to speak. The name slipped out anyway, soft and guilty:

"Oh, Mara."

The room held its silence. Only the guinea caught the firelight—bright, unyielding. A tether across time, or a lure. He could not tell which.

He set it on the mantel like a last letter, and watched the flame bow once, acknowledging a guest that had no intention of leaving.

Chapter Seven

The Tin Beneath the Boards

Morning crept into the cottage in thin stripes, pale light slipping through the small panes and laying bars across the floor. Graham woke as if he'd been dropped from a height. His head felt thick, his shoulders and arms heavy, every muscle complaining after the night on the cliff and the barrels in the dark.

For a moment he lay still, keeping his eyes closed and listening.

The sea below, restless and constant. Gulls arguing above. From the track came the sounds that passed for rush hour in 1789: a door being unbarred, a latch clacking, a woman calling a child, a cart's harness jingling as someone coaxed a pony into work.

No rumble of buses. No central heating ticking. No radio muttering the weather. Only this world. He opened his eyes.

The ceiling above him was low and smoky, beams dark with age. The quilt, still rough but warm, had slid from his shoulder. His right hand ached as if he'd been clenching it all night. When he uncurled his fingers, the guinea lay there, pressed into his palm like it belonged.

In his time, it would have been behind glass with a small white card: Guinea, George III, c. 1785–1790. Gold. Do not touch.

Here, it was pocket change. He sat up, joints protesting, and set the coin on the table beside the oil lamp. In the cold daylight its gold looked tired but stubborn, catching the light and throwing a slight shimmer across the room.

He swung his legs out of bed. The boards complained under his weight. One plank dipped a fraction more than the others, his heel sinking into a slight hollow. He rocked his foot, testing. There. A different sound. Not the solid knock of oak on joist, but something thinner—a hollow note.

He froze, feeling suddenly as if he'd stepped on a landmine. Old habits from health-and-safety lectures mixed with movie scenes; somewhere in his brain a voice said, don't move. Ridiculous. There were no bombs yet. Not here.

Slowly, he crouched, fingertips running along the seam of the boards. The nails were little more than stains, iron long since eaten away by salt and damp. He worked his fingers under the edge and levered up. The board lifted with a soft, reluctant creak, like an old man rising from a chair.

Beneath, something metal glinted in the half-dark. He slid his hand into the hollow. His fingers closed around cold tin. The box was small and plain, the sort of thing an elderly aunt might use for buttons. Here, hidden under the floor of a smuggler's cottage, it weighed more than it should. His hands shook slightly as he drew it out and laid it on the bed. Dust smeared his fingers. The lid stuck, then gave with a sharp click that sounded too loud in the quiet room.

Coins.

Neatly stacked, side by side as if someone had measured them into place: guineas, shillings, half-crowns. Their faces were dulled, but the shapes were unmistakable. Beneath them were heavier pieces, thicker discs of silver and gold stamped with unfamiliar designs: Spanish pieces of eight, hacked at the edges; French louis d'or, faint fleur-de-lis glimmering; and deeper still, the warm, dense glow of Spanish doubloons.

More money than he'd seen in years. More than any builder's wages. Here, in this century, enough to change a life; perhaps enough to end one. He lifted one of the heavier coins. It bit into his skin, solid and cold. Not a replica. No museum glass, no polite sign. Just history sitting in his hand.

In York, this would have lived on a plinth under soft light in the museum with a quiet alarm. Here, it lived under a floorboard.

His breath caught. The room seemed to tilt, as if the weight of the gold were dragging the world off true. What had Michael been, exactly? Smuggler, certainly. The night on the cliffs had proved that. But this tin was more than wages tucked aside. This looked like a hedge against disaster. A hoard to run on. Money to buy a new name in a new town, if you were lucky enough not to be caught with it.

If the revenue men ever found this, the best you could hope for was a short drop and a quick stop. His heart thumped. He snapped the lid shut. The crack of tin rang like a shot.

Instinct dragged his eyes toward the door, then the tiny window, as if someone might burst in and shout got you. No one came.

He slid the box back into its hiding-place, lowered the board, and pressed until the plank sat flush with its neighbours. Only when the seams looked ordinary again did his breathing ease.

In the kitchen, he splashed cold water into a bowl and washed, the chill biting his skin in a way that felt almost welcome. The scullery's stone trough finished the job; he dunked his face and came up sputtering, hair dripping, eyes stinging. He chewed on a heel of bread that had gone tough overnight, more to put something in his stomach than from appetite.

Outside, the day was opening itself in small layers. A latch clicked. A child shrieked, then laughed. Somewhere a pony snorted and stamped. Smoke rose from squat chimneys, blue at first, then thickening as damp peat and kindling caught.

If he was going to live here—properly live, not just survive the odd night—he needed to walk among them as if he belonged. Listen. Copy. Learn which words were Michael's and which were Graham's. Every wrong phrase, every too-modern reflex, was a loose nail in the disguise.

He pulled on Michael's coat, the wool heavy and smelling faintly of smoke and salt, and stepped outside. The air tasted of brine and woodsmoke. Gorse on the bank let out its peculiar faint coconut smell when the breeze brushed it; it made him think of supermarket shampoo and summer holidays, which felt obscene in a world where people still measured heat in hearths.

Down the track, the village stirred itself. Low cottages huddled against the slope, their whitewash already stained by weather. Women wrapped shawls tighter around their shoulders and shouldered baskets towards the harbour. A boy coaxed a reluctant dog along; the animal dug its paws in, determined to debate the day. Along a lichen-covered wall, a row of men sat mending nets, fingers blunt and nimble, twine rasping under calloused skin.

They looked up as he passed.

"Morning, Michael," one called, eyes dropping back to the torn net.

"Busy night, was it?" another added with a sideways grin.

Michael gave what he hoped was the right nod. Not too cheerful, not guilty. Just a man sore from a long night. He felt his tongue wanting to say yeah and swallowed it, letting the silence stand. No one seemed to find it strange. Their gazes slid off him. To them he was what he appeared: Michael Parry, part of this place.

The harbour drew him down. The air there was thicker: tar, fish-gut, coal smoke, the sour-sweet reek of a bucket of offal left too long in the weak sun. Rope and wet wood, too. Always rope. Boats bumped gently at their moorings, hulls knocking. Gulls wheeled and screamed, dropping in a frenzy whenever anyone flung scraps onto the water. Men rolled barrels over cobbles slick with salt, guiding them with a practised rhythm.

Across the little square, a tidy frontage drew his eye—FERRIS & CO., IRONMONGERS – ESTABLISHED 1760. The gilt letters looked steadier and more patient in the daylight, marching across paint that had weathered without fuss. Behind the glass, the place seemed almost to greet him: rows of neat drawers, each carefully labelled—Nails 1", Nails 2", Boat Spikes, Hinges. Coils of rope and loops of chain hung with a quiet pride. Two polished lanterns waited as though they expected decent company, not the shadowed den he had slipped through the previous night with the smugglers.

He felt the tug of familiarity—unexpected, almost comforting. It was like spotting an old friend on a foreign street. He couldn't help grinning. Daylight had softened everything, made it honest again, and he'd spent enough years in places just like it. In York, tucked behind the glass of a narrow ironmongers off Micklegate, he'd once passed whole afternoons choosing plugs and screws while Mara laughed at him for reading every label twice. Here, for a moment, that world didn't feel quite so far away.

Now he watched a woman go in, skirts wet from the quay. Through the window, he saw Ferris weigh a kettle-hook on a scale with the seriousness of a man measuring something precious. The whole scene might have been a painting in a museum in his old world. Here, it was just Wednesday.

Ferris glanced up and spotted him. Recognition was quick and discreet: a small, decisive nod towards the alley that led to the back door. Later, that meant.

The bell over the shop clinked as the woman left with her purchase. A farmer went in and came out with a twist of paper and an opinion on the price of salt. Ferris smiled for both men, but his eyes did other work.

"Michael!"

The shout bounced off stone. Jory, scarred and broad, strode along the quay, coat flapping, boots loud on the wet cobbles. The scar that dragged his eye was lighter in daylight; the eye itself was sharp.

"Dreaming on your feet, are you?" Jory said. "We've business. Come on."

He didn't wait for agreement. His hand tightened on Michael's arm and steered him towards a low storehouse near the waterline. Michael let himself be guided. Protest would have been wrong, and wrongness drew attention.

Inside, the air smelled of pitch, damp, and stale rope. A few lamps threw dull light over a scarred table where half a dozen men stood close, voices low. On a board laid across two barrels, someone had chalked tide times, moon phases, and a short list of signs whose meaning he did not yet know. Barrels and crates lined the walls. Some bore foreign chalk marks; others carried harmless English names, for anyone who asked the wrong questions.

And there she was. Eliza stood at the end of the table. Yesterday's bonnet was gone; her dark hair was braided tight and pinned up, neat without fuss. Her gown was plain; her sleeves were rolled, showing strong forearms. The men's attention pointed toward her like iron to a magnet. Every time anyone spoke, their eyes flicked to her, seeking approval or instruction without seeming to.

"Michael," she said. "About time."

Jory grinned. "Told you he'd drag his boots."

The men laughed, shoulders loosening. The sound died as quickly as it came when Eliza lifted her gaze. She didn't need to raise her voice. The room knew to listen.

"We've a rum due from Roscoff next week," she said. "Brandy and lace, good stuff, not ditch-water. High value, high risk. The cutter's sniffing along the coast. We'll need heads clear and eyes sharper."

Her tone was even, but the words tightened the group. Michael felt it. In his old life it was how men spoke on site when a wall was about to be lifted or a dangerous pour was coming: no fuss, no drama, but everyone caught the seriousness.

She picked up a stub of chalk and wrote on the plank: NEW MOON – TALLAND WEST COVE – THREE KNOCKS.

"Where're we landing, mistress?" Kit asked. Fair-haired, cap askew, younger than the rest. His voice was steady, but his hands worried the edge of the table.

"Not here," Eliza said. "Too many eyes in this harbour now. And too many ears in the Jolly." Her glance slid once, briefly, towards the tavern up the slope. "We'll take the cove west of Talland. We'll give the lantern as we do. Michael"

His breath caught.

"you'll take first watch on the headland. If the revenue so much as breathes our air, I want to know it before they see the sand. No lantern until the last. Owl call twice. If your throat fails you, use the reed."

She slid a slim bone whistle down the plank. It spun once and stopped by his hand.

Michael picked it up. It was small and cool, easy to hide. He had no idea what a real owl sounded like outside films and late-night television, but he wasn't about to say that here.

Jory scratched new marks on the plank. "Signals," he said, half to Eliza, half to the room. "Three knocks on the capstan post is go. Two and a whistle is scatter and every man takes care of his own skin. Anyone starts singing—"

"—and Mary brains him with a ladle," Eliza finished, dry.

That earned a proper laugh. Everyone believed Mary would.

They broke the plan apart and passed it round between them: how many hands at the cove, where the ponies would wait, which farm tracks were quiet, which lamp in which cottage window meant danger. Michael listened like a man cramming before an exam, catching names, routes, habits, trying to lay them over the map in his head.

Kit was sent to fetch sackcloth from the loft above the capstan. Jory would walk the lanes, checking whose cart was where, reading the mud for hooves and wheels.

"Ferris, lamp oil?" Eliza asked without looking.

"In the ledger as farm wicks," Ferris said from the doorway, half in shadow, apron already on. "If the King's pup asks, I'll say I'm pious about early milking."

The men drifted away in twos, boots creaking on damp boards, talk thinning. Soon only Eliza and Michael remained.

When the last footstep faded, she came to stand beside him. Up close he could smell salt on her hair, and clean soap over old smoke.

"You're quiet," she said.

It was observation, not accusation, but it still landed like a hand on his chest. For a moment he was in another kitchen entirely: Mara at the stove in York, radio playing Phil Collins, steam on the window, her asking *are you alright?* with that look that meant *tell me the truth.*

"I'm tired," he said. A lie of sorts, but the least dangerous one.

She watched him. Her brows drew together slightly, like someone reading a plan that nearly made sense. "Rest," she said at last. "Next week, no one will sleep."

She walked towards the door. The light picked out the silver in the pins holding her braid. He almost said her name then—Mara, not Eliza—but bit it back so hard his teeth hurt.

Outside, the village had grown louder. Women scrubbed steps, brushes rasping stone. The cooper hammered hoops onto a cask; each blow rang down the wynd. Ferris's bell clinked twice in quick succession. A boy chased a hoop that bounced off a rut and nearly took out a passing fisherman. A dog slept in a doorway with one eye open, as if afraid of missing anything important.

From the Jolly came Mary's voice, big as the sea and twice as relentless.

"No, Tom Treglown, you'll not have ale before noon unless you bring me the eggs you owe from Whitsun," she declared, half inside, half out. "And if you say what eggs I'll nail your ears to my lintel and hang a sign from your nose."

Tom laughed in the bright, careless way of a man who'd never yet believed a threat. "Later, Mary. I'm good for it."

"You're good for the square root of nawth," she said, and smacked him with a cloth for punctuation.

She spotted Michael at the door and jerked her chin.

"You," she said. "Sit. Eat. Men who fall off cliffs do it either for love or for lack of stew, and I can't mend the first."

A bowl appeared as if she'd conjured it: barley, carrot, scraps of yesterday's mutton, thick enough to stand a spoon in, and a heel of bread still warm from the oven.

"And keep your ears open," she added. "Ears make money. Mouths make widows."

"Does preaching pay?" he asked. The words came instinctively, sounding oddly like himself.

"Not in coin," she said. "In necks."

For a moment her gaze softened, flicking over his face the way someone checks a roof for leaks.

"You've a different air about you these days," she said quietly. "Keep your head. There's shadow on the lanes."

"What shadow?"

"The kind that walks on two legs and writes your name wrong on a paper," she said. "Excise pup was in here this morning, sniffing for coffee and sin. I told him I only serve Christians. He said he was one. I suggested he prove it by paying his slate." She snorted. "He laughed. I didn't."

She thumped the ladle once on the bar. That was the end of that topic.

Michael ate. The stew was hot and honest. It grounded him in a way he hadn't realised he needed, anchoring his thoughts in taste and heat instead of fear and memory.

Tom wandered past, humming something too close to one of their signals, and earned a sharp rap of the ladle on his knuckles.

"Whistling's for birds and thieves," Mary said. "Be a man and shut your gob."

Later, crossing the square, Michael caught Ferris's look and followed it to the back of the ironmongers. The front room stank cheerfully of oil and metal. Ferris measured out nails with a scale that looked like it might measure souls if you asked it nicely.

When the door knock rattled into emptiness and no one else was near, Ferris slid the bolt.

"Back," he said, and the shopkeeper's smile fell away like a mask put carefully aside.

The storeroom behind was another world. Rails stacked against one wall. Sacks of charcoal and crates that pretended to be flour and weren't. The floor gave a slight echo in one place where it shouldn't. Ferris moved aside a pile of scrap and lifted a hatch. Cool air breathed up from below.

"In the cellar we hide the tuns," he said. "We shift rails over the top, then lay an iron bar across each bung. If some pup of Harker's taps it, he'll hear the ring and think it a crate of bolts."

"Sound as a disguise," Michael said before he could stop himself. "Clever."

Ferris's eye sharpened. "You always did have a head for sense," he said slowly. "A man taught me that trick. Didn't live long enough to boast of it."

He handed over two books. One was a tidy ledger for any official eye: nails and hinges and lamp oil, all straightforward. The other was narrow, older, its pages thick with handling, its ink blotched.

The names in it weren't names at all. Birds. Winds. Bits of weather.

"If I say two owls and a south-wester," Ferris said, "you'll know what's meant?"

"I'll learn," Michael said. And he meant it. Not just for his own neck, but because to refuse would draw the wrong kind of attention.

Ferris's hand landed heavy on his shoulder. "You were always steady," he said. "Don't go brittle. Brittle men break, and they break others with them."

The afternoon stretched itself into small tasks threaded with danger. Michael mended nets under the eye of an old man who looked like he'd been tying knots since the beginning of time itself. He carried a sack of meal up a steep lane for a widow whose doorway faced straight into the weather. He walked past the harbour twice in a way that looked casual and wasn't, counting faces he recognised and ones he didn't.

Michael was adjusting to his new surroundings and the people in it. Work, talk, small favours. That was how belonging was built, in any age.

Near dusk, Jory came down from the headland, coat wet, scar whiter than usual.

"Cutter off Rame," he said to Eliza at the storehouse door, pitching his voice so only she and Michael could hear. "Sitting like a crow on a sheep's back. Wind's changed twice. She hasn't."

"Waiting, then," Eliza said. "They've learnt something."

"Or someone's told them," Jory said. For a heartbeat his gaze drifted towards the tavern, where Tom's laughter rose too loud, too often.

Eliza's eyes cooled, but she didn't follow the look. Not yet.

"We tighten the circle," she said. "No word in the Jolly after dark. Signals only."

121

She turned to Michael. "You'll walk the western path after moonrise. No light. If you hear three knocks on wood and no owl after, you leave the ridge and go to ground. Understood?"

He touched the bone whistle in his pocket. "Jory showed me how to use the reed."

"Good." She hesitated. "And keep Thomas Treglown out of your shadow tonight. He thinks cheer is a kind of safety. It isn't."

Evening wrapped itself around the village. Cooking smells, onion, cabbage, a trace of fish, mixed with the ever-present tang of smoke. Children's shrieks turned to yawns. Doors thudded as latches dropped. The fiddler tried a tune outside the Jolly; Mary shooed him in with a flap of her cloth so the notes wouldn't carry where they shouldn't.

Clouds slid in from the sea, dark and low. A fine, irritating rain began to fall, pricking skin rather than soaking it.

Michael walked the cliff path in a loop Jory had shown him: ash tree to gully, gully to the old lime kiln,

kiln to a black spring that left the rock wet even in dry weather. He memorised the feel of the ground under his boots, where it tilted, where it narrowed, where a slip would mean more than bruises.

Below, the sea went about its work, hurling itself against stone. The sound was constant, big enough to swallow smaller noises. Twice he crouched and pressed his fingers into the mud where hooves had passed. The older prints were crumbling at the edges; the newer ones still sharp. Once he thought he saw a lantern far out among the waves, but the rain blurred it into nothing.

By the time he came down again, the square was mostly dark. The Jolly's shutters were closed; light leaked around their edges. Mary had barred the door and was scrubbing a table as if she could scour worry out of the wood.

"Late," she said, not looking up. "You'll take broth or you'll take my temper."

"Broth," he said. He was learning.

"You're already wiser than half the village," she replied. She slid a bowl to him through the half-open door, rich and steaming. "Tom went off with a grin and a lie. I told him his wife has a better claim on his legs than any barrel. He said women were born to worry. I told him some men exist just to prove us right."

She scowled into the rain. "If the rope comes to Boscawn this winter, it'll come laughing."

He ate standing under the eaves, the broth warming him from throat to stomach. Across the square, Ferris lifted his shop latch once, then again, as if testing something only he could hear. The little metallic sound carried clearly. A signal, if you knew how to listen.

Eliza crossed from the storehouse, cloak pulled tight. The lamplight caught on the pins in her hair, turning them briefly to sparks. For a moment her head turned in his direction, as if she'd felt his gaze, then she moved on.

Back at the cottage, the fire sulked in the grate until he coaxed it into life. He shut the door on the wind and the sea and the smell of the village and walked the narrow corridor. The board with the faint give waited under his foot like a question.

He knelt, levered it up, and brought the tin into the lamplight again. The lid opened more easily this time. Gold and silver gleamed back at him, patient, unchanged.

Guineas, louis d'or, doubloons. Pieces of eight nicked at the edge. Crowns and half-crowns. A small fortune in any age.

With this, a man could vanish. Buy passage, pick a new name, go somewhere the King's men didn't know his face. With this, a man could do a great deal of good or a great deal of harm.

With this, a man could hang.

He shut the lid and slid the tin back into its hole. The board went down over it with a soft sigh. He pressed his palm flat to the floor as if he could hold the secret still.

Smoke from the fire clung to his hair. Salt still tingled in the back of his throat.

Memory rose hard and fast, like waves over rock: the cliff in his own time; his hands full of mud; the storm pulling at his clothes. Mara's voice in the wind, whether real or imagined, he still couldn't say. His own raw shout, I'm sorry, Mara, I can't do it. The burn of whisky. The radio struggling through static to reach the chorus of Against All Odds. The taste of salt in his mouth, grief, sea, or both.

Now, here: a bed older than most of the buildings he'd ever worked on. A tin of smuggled coin under the floor. A woman with Mara's face, more or less, organising men by the quay.

"What am I supposed to do?" he whispered to the beams.

The fire cracked once. The sea answered with its constant grind. That was all.

He slept eventually, the way bodies do when they have been pushed far enough. His mind didn't agree, but it didn't get a vote.

126

He woke before light to wind shouldering at the shutters and gulls screaming their hunger above the roof. The day that followed was grey and unsettled, the sort of weather that made everything look like it was thinking twice.

He washed his face in water that bit, drank a mouthful that felt like knives going down, and did his best not to think about the tin.

By mid-morning, someone knocked.

Not a neighbour's tentative tap or Tom's careless thump. Three firm, measured knocks. Enough to say I know you're there, but not enough to say I own the door.

He opened it. Eliza stood on the step. Cloak fastened at the throat with a plain pewter pin. Mist on her lashes and in her hair. The weather had reddened her cheeks but softened nothing else about her.

"Michael," she said. "Walk with me."

He glanced once towards the hearth, where the loose board sat harmless and innocent in the floor.

Then he took his coat from the peg, pulled the door to behind him, and followed her.

The cliff path was slick with last night's rain. Grass bent under their boots. Below, the sea battered the rocks without rhythm or mercy. Eliza walked with purpose, skirts brushing gorse, eyes on the horizon. A boy waved from a cottage doorway; she lifted a hand in reply without breaking stride.

"The men look to you," she said after a while.

"Me?" The word came out before he could tidy it.

"Aye." She did not slow. "You have always been steady. Last night you were different, quiet, but when Kit went down you had him up before he drowned in his own fear. That counts."

He swallowed. He did not remember doing it in the way she did, as part of long years of shared nights, but his muscles remembered enough.

"You know who I am," she went on. "And what I stand to lose."

He nodded. It was easier than speaking.

"I cannot afford men who shake," she said. "Not after Newgate. Not with Harker's cutter sitting off Rame like a carrion bird." She turned her head and looked straight at him. "So I'll ask it plain. Are you with us, Michael, or do you doubt?"

I'm not Michael at all rose in his throat like sickness. He saw himself trying to explain: 1980s, York, electricity, a storm, a slipped slate. He saw her face if he said it. At best she would think he was cracked. At worst she would think he was lying.

"I'm with you," he said. His voice did not break.

She studied him. Her gaze was sharp, as if she were weighing timber and mortar and deciding if they would hold. Then she nodded once.

"Good," she said. "Then prove it."

They reached a bend in the path. Below, a steep, mean track dropped to a narrow inlet. The cave at its foot was a dark mouth; weed slicked the rocks. The sea leapt and slammed at the entrance like something trying to get in.

"There's a keg cached in that cave," she said. "Three nights ago. I want to know if it's still there. Fetch it. Alone."

His stomach knotted at the sight of the path. It was not far, but it was nasty, wet stone, bad footing, and no rail. Once, in his own world, he had had a physiotherapist and a steel-framed walking aid; now he had an eighteenth-century cliff and a woman watching.

"If it's gone?" he asked.

"Then I'll know," she said simply. "If it's there, bring it up. Either way, I'll see whether you can be trusted when the ground shifts."

No anger. No coaxing. Just a measure being taken.

He went. The first steps were the worst. The ground sloped and slid under his boots. Twice he caught himself on rock, skin scraping. Spray blew up from below, hitting his face, cold and salty. The air in the cave was rank—old weed, trapped water.

He found the keg half-buried in shingle behind a rock lip, wedged there like someone had known what they were doing. It was no bigger than a beer barrel, but dense with liquid weight. He dug it loose, muscles straining, and heaved it onto his shoulder.

The climb back hurt. His legs burned, his breath rasped. The keg shifted against him with every step, trying to pull him off balance. He stopped twice to brace and go again, forehead pressed briefly to wet rock, forcing himself not to look down.

At the top he staggered onto level ground and let the keg drop at Eliza's boots. He bent double, hands on his knees, lungs dragging at the air.

Eliza crouched, worked the bung loose with a knife from somewhere in her skirts, sniffed the spirit, and nodded. She drove the bung back in with the heel of her hand.

"Well done," she said.

For a heartbeat approval lit her face, bright and surprising.

"You've not lost your edge," she added. "I needed to know."

"And now?" he managed.

"Now I know you'll stand when I call."

They turned back towards the village. At a stile above a tangle of furze she paused and looked down at the tracks that threaded through Boscawen—lanes, footpaths, the narrow ways between cottage and field.

"You'll hear talk that Harker's sent for more men," she said. "Farmer near Morvah swears a sergeant paid him a sovereign to keep a lamp in his window whenever the air smells of rum. Lamps lie. Men lie better."

Her breath smoked in the cold. "We'll change the signs. Three knocks and an owl is go. Two knocks and no owl is scatter and let the barrels drown." She looked at him. "Tell Jory. Tell Ferris. Tell no one else."

"I will."

Near the cottage she slowed. A loose strand of hair had escaped her braid and whipped across her cheek.

"Well done," she said. "But loyalty is everything. Fail me once and there'll be no one between you and the rope. Do you understand?"

"I do," he said. And found, to his own surprise, that he meant it.

For a moment something eased in her face—the barest hint of warmth.

"If you're to follow me into storms and shadows," she said, offering her hand, "you'd best be sure I trust you to keep up."

He took it before he thought. Her grip was warm, firm, the grip of someone who'd hauled nets and weathered more than the sea. He already knew her name—Eliza—but standing this close he found himself staring, caught by the way the light touched her face. For the briefest moment, in the shape of her jaw and the quiet defiance in her eyes, he saw Mara.

Not Mara—never Mara—but some echo of her that struck like a misstep on a familiar stair.

"Eliza," he said anyway, as if saying it might steady him.

A flicker crossed her expression—curiosity, maybe, or caution—but she withdrew her hand and turned toward the village.

"Rest while you can," she said. "The tide waits for no man. Nor do I."

She walked away, boots sure on the path, cloak snapping in the wind. He watched her go, the ache of memory tugging at him. Eliza trusted him—at least enough to let him follow—but she was her own person entirely. And he would do well to remember that.

Back at the cottage a skin of frost was forming in the hollows. The grass crunched faintly under his boots. The gorse clicked as it cooled, the sound like small pieces of metal settling.

Under the floor the tin lay where he'd left it, heavy and silent. Out beyond Rame a cutter hung off the coast like a dark bird on a fence-post, waiting for something it thought it understood.

In the village below, Mary banged her ladle on her bar and dared the world to send trouble through her door; Ferris weighed truth and lies on his scales; Jory read the road like a psalm; and Thomas Treglown laughed too loudly at a joke that wasn't funny.

Michael—Graham underneath—stood in the centre of his small room and put his hand on the loose board, feeling the slight give, the hidden weight.

For the first time he knew without flinching that the life behind him and this life in front of him were not going to let go. Not of him. Not of each other. He was caught between them.

The tin. The tide. Eliza.

Three anchors. Three ropes.

Sooner or later he would have to choose which one he would let drag him under.

Chapter Eight

Smoke and Silver

Morning came lean and grey, the sort of light that makes a village hold its breath. Wind combed the gorse, the tide chewed at the shingle, and the cottage floors creaked the way old timbers do when they are deciding whether to forgive another day of footsteps.

Michael woke to the ache left by cliffs and barrels and a night that had asked too much of his muscles. The tin under the board lay where he'd pressed it; he could feel its fact through the floor as keenly as if it had been tucked under his ribs. When he opened the door the lane already wore its first prints. Mary crossed it with a heel of bread wrapped in cloth and the kind of look that counts a man's sleep.

"Eat," she said, pushing the bundle into his hands without ceremony. "And mind: London folk sharpen their knives on strangers' smiles."

He blinked. "London?"

"Ask her," Mary said, tilting her chin toward the square.

Eliza was there, hood back, ledger under one arm, speaking with Ferris in a low voice that stayed low even when the wind tried to lift it. Jory loitered at a respectful distance, whittling nothing into less than nothing. Thomas Treglown leaned on the capstan post and made his grin do a job his hands rarely did sober.

Eliza saw Michael and ended two conversations with one nod. "Coach at the turnpike inside the hour," she said. "We take the road east."

Ferris coughed into a glove already blackened with soot. "Harker's boys slunk along the quay at dawn, kicking at crates like they were cats. You'll find the city no kinder."

"We don't go to be loved," Eliza said. "We go to be paid."

Jory flicked his whittle-scrap into the wind. "Keep your head down and your purse down deeper."

Thomas pushed off the post, swaggering two steps closer than sense allowed. "If the coach tips in a ditch, don't you fret," he declared to Michael with the airy largesse of a man who had not yet been asked to be brave. "We'll drink the roads dry until you return."

"Drink the roads and you'll talk them too," Mary said, arriving like weather. She placed a small sack in Eliza's hand—hard cheese, two apples, a twist of salt. "My advice is worth three times the price I ask," she added. "Don't let London put you in a pocket and sit on you."

Eliza's mouth tugged, almost a smile. "I don't fit in most pockets."

"You'd be surprised what men will try to stuff away," Mary said, and kissed the air near Eliza's cheek, as if blessing and warning used the same gesture.

They took their leave with the economy of people who had done so too often: few words, a squeeze of a wrist, a look held a fraction too long. Eliza set a pace that made the coachman—an affronted man with a red scarf and a sense of his own importance—blink and adjust. They climbed in; the door thumped; the square slid away.

The journey took two days of jolting decisions. Hedgerows went past in a scroll of thorn and sparrow; sheep lifted their heads and misjudged the importance of coaches; turnpikes collected coins with the solemnity of priests collecting souls. They changed horses at posting inns that smelt of singed hair, sour ale, and the hope of hot food: pewter tankards sweating by hearths that had known better jokes, spit-boys turning joints with the automatic misery of boys given jobs that burn.

Eliza travelled like a ledger travels—kept open, kept neat. She wrote while the wheels hammered ruts into a rhythm, pausing to wet the nib and to measure, by ear alone, if the road ahead promised a bend or a broken spring. In the lamplight of the coach her features gentled, but the bone of resolve stayed beneath the skin like the keel under a hull.

Michael watched the world with the hungry, frightened curiosity of a man stepping into a story already half told. When the inn doors opened he breathed London early—coal smoke drifting ahead of the city like rumour, a sharpened noise that made the very air feel crowded. He tried not to look when Eliza, thinking herself unwatched, pressed two fingers to the inside of her wrist and breathed out, as if steadying herself before harbour.

On the second morning a pedlar fell in with the coach for an hour, keeping pace on a lean mare with opinions of her own. He traded weather and politics through the leather—"French give speeches while we give rope; makes a change, that"—then hawked combs of bone and small books of bawdy verse no one admitted to wanting. Eliza bought needles and two skeins of thread. "Nothing draws notice like a tear left torn," she said, tucking them away. The pedlar looked at Graham and decided, sensibly, not to ask questions that weren't for sale.

The city rose as a smudge and became a judgement. Its smoke sat heavy on the tongue. The Thames moved like a beast too old to rush; its smell climbed into the coach and settled opposite Michael like a fourth passenger. Streets narrowed until the hubs kissed walls; streets widened into brick avenues where lamps would later coax honest shadows into pretending they were safe. People occupied the air: apprentices with flour like early snow in their hair; ladies carrying tiny dogs like accusations; boys darting with oysters held aloft and shouting; men who had no business to show and so showed their knives.

"Speak when spoken to," Eliza murmured as they entered Wapping's pulse. "Listen as if there's coin hidden in every word."

Warehouses shouldered the river; cranes creaked; the very ropes looked prosperous. Their coach rolled into a lane where the Thames pressed close enough to scold. Eliza stepped down first, the river's breath flattening the edge of her hood, and led Graham into a building that had learnt how to keep secrets under the rasp of ledgers.

Inside, pipe smoke stroked the rafters and sat there fat and pleased. A long table, scarred and shining where palms had polished it, held dominion. Behind it, three buyers: hawk-nose and watch chain; a florid fellow with rings that would remember the warmth of his vanity; and a sallow man whose eyes counted faster than his mouth could lie.

"Mrs Trevelyan."

Hawk-nose stood, voice smooth as a blade sheath.

"Eliza," she corrected, sitting without being offered. She laid her ledger flat, her hand steady upon it. "I trust you've discovered a thirst."

"London is a city of thirsts." Hawk-nose's smile was meant to be seen and not believed. "Some more... pressing than others. Rum, for instance, is scarce this winter."

"Then imagine the joy when it isn't," Eliza said.

The bargaining came on in waves. Numbers were launched and recovered; excuses were fished up and thrown back. The florid man tried a compliment shaped like an insult; Eliza ignored it the way a woman ignores weather—noticed, measured, not obeyed. When the sallow man floated a figure that would have left Cornwall chewing on its own knuckles, she looked at him until even his rings seemed to doubt their worth.

"Fair," she said, and the word sounded like a law. "Or the barrels sit and the cutters rest and I take my trade to Dorset."

"Gulliver?" Hawk-nose's eyebrows took interest.

"Who I choose is my conversation," she replied. "Your conversation is price."

Michael kept quiet and counted breaths, but he saw it: how she let silence do sums the men didn't want to show; how she tipped the table by reminding them that their bravado was fed by the backs of coastal villages; how she smiled exactly once, at a figure that looked like a concession and was, in fact, the one she had come for. When the quills scratched, the sound had relief in it.

Florid Rings flicked his gaze to Graham. "And Cornwall sends a new face. Michael, is it? You keep her books or her doors?"

"I keep what I'm told," Michael said, letting the coast roughen the words. A ripple—approval from some, irritation from others—ran like a rat along the table's underside.

They left with coin promised and dates named. Eliza's step did not quicken—victory, for her, was a balance kept upright. Outside, the river made its opinion known by smelling worse. "Two more buyers to remind," she said, "then food."

"Do you enjoy it?" he asked before he could stop himself. "This… bargain work?"

"I enjoy men paying what they should," she said. "And I enjoy taking bread from the King's mouth and giving it to those who buttered it in the first place."

The tavern near Wapping had earned its heat by swallowing too many stories to count. Smoke lay along the beams like old cats. The fiddler's bow scraped a tune that had seen better fiddlers. Sailors and clerks and men who pretended to be neither formed a stew of laughter and watchfulness.

"Keep your eyes on your own cup," Eliza said, and then her gaze snagged on a man who did not need to be announced.

He sat as if the chair were a throne he had decided would do for now. Broad shoulders, hair tied clean, a pale scar like a punctuation mark at the temple. His ease told its own story. Around him men leaned in with the posture of those who discover that gravity has a voice. He raised a tankard and did not hurry.

"Isaac Gulliver," Eliza said under her breath. "Dorset's king."

Michael stole a look and found the man's eyes already on him—brief, weighing, uninterested in being caught at either. The glance left a mark as light as chalk and as stubborn.

"Do we speak to him?" Michael asked.

"Not unless we want to owe him for the privilege," Eliza said. "Gulliver sells safety by the yard and has a way of measuring wrong on purpose. Remember his face. Spend no other coin on him."

They ate bread that had not seen a good oven and meat that had seen too many; they drank ale that made Michael miss even bad whisky. At one point a sailor tried to teach him a song that required a better memory for lies. Eliza's hand on his sleeve was warning enough; he let the chorus die in his mouth. Later, when the tavern's warmth grew mean with fatigue, they took rooms at an inn that smelt of river mud and wishes.

The room had a narrow bed, a candle that pretended to be brave, and a window that did not fit the hole it had been given. Eliza stood at it, looking out at the lamps stroking the Thames into a false gentleness. He watched the set of her shoulders and recognised something—Mara used to stand at their York window and look at the Minster as if the stone could answer back.

"You're wondering about the name," she said at last, as if the window had spoken.

He didn't deny it.

"Trevelyan sits wrong in some mouths here," she went on. "Too neat for the cliff folk, too cliff for the neat."

She told him then, not like a confession but like the straightening of a page: Devon father, law for breakfast, ledgers for play; a life drawn on good paper with a careful hand. Then Jacques—laughter, fight, salt—and the way love can be a tide that ignores the lines men draw with ink. She said Newgate like a place in a prayer you don't want to say and said widow like a duty, not a wound.

"I kept his name," she finished, "and I kept the work. It keeps bread in mouths that would otherwise chew the inside of their cheeks. If I'm to hang, I prefer to hang for something worth a loaf."

He thought of Mara and of the tin and of how wanting two truths at once can split a man along a seam he didn't know he had. "I understand," he said, and found that he did and didn't. She studied him and filed the answer somewhere inside a ledger he would never read.

"Sleep," she said, and blew out the candle with the finality of a page turned.

They left at dawn when London pretends to be repentant. Frost skinned the gutters. A woman threw dirty water that tried to be clean into the street with the indifference of habit. The coach rattled away from the river; London unspooled into hedgerow again.

Fields lay brittle and bright. Crows stitched black across them, busy with their own accounts. Eliza's face closed like a shutter against the cold; Graham kept his hands tucked and tried not to remember the pistol beneath her cloak, because the remembering made the world tilt.

Near noon the road narrowed to a throat between two stands of oak. The coachman clicked to the team; their breath smoked like tired engines.

Michael felt the stillness first—the way birds edit themselves out of a scene that's about to change.

A figure stepped into the road with the confidence of a man who has rehearsed the moment in his head a hundred times. Tricorn low, mask higher than his courage, pistol in a steady line. A horse behind him tossed an opinion.

"Stand in the King's name!" he barked, borrowing majesty for a job that rarely ends with it.

The coach lurched to obedience. The driver raised his hands the way men who know their lives are worth less than their cargo raise their hands.

"Out."

Michael's body remembered fights badly won and worse avoided. He lifted the latch. Eliza's "Wait" cut through the air like a string pulled hard.

She stepped down first, boots biting frost. The highwayman started his patter, a little too pleased with the rhyme of purse and curse. He did not finish it.

Eliza's pistol came out of her cloak like an answer to a question no one had asked her, but everyone should have expected. French make, clean lines, a promise in steel. The crack of it split the cold. Powder bit the air. The man yelled, dropped his own weapon, clutched a bleeding arm, discovered that horses do not respect human emergencies, and banged off up the lane with more speed than dignity.

Silence fell with one last shudder of the coach springs.

Eliza swabbed the barrel with a cloth she conjured from nowhere, seating the habit with the same care she gave to figures in a column. She spoke without looking at Michael. "Hesitation's a grave," she said. "I don't dig."

He found his voice in the ruts. "You didn't blink."

"I've blinked before," she said. "It always costs more than a shot."

They rolled on. For a long while no one—not even the coachman—tried a joke to lighten the load. The hills grew friendlier, the air less crowded. Somewhere a thrush bullied the morning into being.

At the next posting house the ostler—a boy with red hands and a curiosity he couldn't afford—stared at the scorch on Eliza's glove and wisely decided to be interested in hoof pickings instead. Eliza wrote a line in her ledger with the same pen that had signed a buyer into honour and a thief into pain.

By the time the coast lifted its familiar shoulder, Michael had a new noise in his head that wasn't the coach or the wheels or the river's stink. It was a thin, cold thread that said: you asked for work, and the work answered. The square received them with the kind of welcome villages give to risk that has gone out and returned with coin: nods that meant both satisfaction and new lists of tasks.

Ferris was in his doorway pretending to admire the straightness of a nail while actually counting the number of men across the street. He lifted a hand. "Bring us news and not trouble?"

"Both," Eliza said. "Men who pay and men who try not to. London breeds them like lice."

Mary leaned on her broom as if it were a staff of office. "You didn't let the city chew your boots, then."

"It took a bite," Eliza allowed. "We bit back."

Jory stepped from shadow with the air of someone who has been waiting long enough to deserve an answer. "The cutter's been sniffing. Harker himself asked after our nails." He said nails as if it were the punchline to a dirty joke the sea had told him.

Eliza's eyes sharpened. "Then we keep the pattern and pretend to break it. Tonight: three kegs into Ferris under rails and iron, four to Boscawen. Signals as set. And Thomas—"

"Thomas is already telling the fire what he'll do to any man tries to stop him," Mary said, expression flat.

"Then he can tell the yard the same thing until midnight," Eliza replied. "Sober."

Her gaze found Michael and held. "You saw how London counts. You saw what the road demands. Cornwall will ask more. You still with me?"

He felt the tin under the board as a physical pull, felt Mara's name like a bruise, felt the crack of the pistol still living in the air between his lungs. "Aye," he said, and in his mouth the word tasted like salt and iron and something darker.

"Good," she said. "Then eat, and sleep with one ear open. Men who mean us harm sleep with both."

That evening the Jolly filled and emptied and filled again. Thomas laughed too loud and too long, then sulked when Mary gave him soup and no ale; he pressed his hand to his heart and declared himself invincible to three different men who had already seen ropes in their dreams. A stranger's face flickered at the door and was gone before anyone could decide whether to notice it. Isaac Gulliver did not appear, but the idea of him sat in the corner like an extra chair.

Michael walked home when the village's lights went from friendly to thin. The cottage accepted him with the complaint of familiar wood. He set the ledger Mary had smuggled into his hands—loaves, lamp oil, and a note that read simply: "Don't be a fool"—on the table, then lifted the board by the bed and touched the tin. It was still cold. It was still heavy. It was still a decision waiting to make him into someone he might not like.

He slept badly, and when he woke before dawn to the sound of gulls telling lies to each other, he found that the road and the pistol and Eliza's ledger had woven themselves into one thought: the sea does not care, but people do, and that's the trouble.

They would ride the next tide of work into consequence. London had given them prices. The highway had given them a rule. Cornwall would give them both a test.

And when the sun finally split the cloud thinly enough to be called morning, he was already on the path to the storehouse, the taste of powder still a grit on his tongue, Eliza's voice in his head like a line drawn true: Hesitation is a grave.

Chapter Nine

Across the Narrow Sea

The tavern smelt of tar, wet wool, and sour ale. Smoke from the hearth clung to the beams, mixing with the reek of men who had lived too long at sea. Dice clicked. Tankards knocked. A fiddler scraped something that sounded like a fight trying to be a tune. The door blew open and a sailor stumbled in with salt still bright on his coat and a look that turned talk to hush before he reached the bar.

"François is dead."

Tankards paused halfway to mouths. Dice froze mid-cast and rolled no further than knuckles.

Eliza did not stand. She leaned forward over her untouched mug, voice cool and sharp enough to cut cloth. "How?"

The sailor stared at his rope-burnt hands. "Saint-Malo. Tavern by the quay. Dice and drink. Steel in the ribs afore the night was out. Buried him in the sand with no marker." His eyes lifted, hollow. "No François, no cargo. He were the bridge."

Someone swore into the rushes. Another man made the sign he saved for storms.

Michael felt the words weigh his chest. François—Jacques's old contact, the man who smoothed the passage from French cellar to Cornish cove. Gone, and with him a whole thin chain that fed half the village.

Eliza rose, the bench scraping stone. She didn't look at the sailor; she took the room the way a helmsman takes a sea, steady. "Then François is gone. The trade is not. France is wide," she said. "Coin finds ears. We go to Paris. We find another."

The name shivered through the room like a bell struck once—Paris—far as China to most of them. And even among hardened sailors the word carried a new weight. Whispers of revolution had crossed the

157

Channel on the same ships as brandy and lace. In France, Paris was no longer just a city but a tinderbox, sparking in the dark.

Her gaze found Michael. "You'll come with me, Michael."

It wasn't a request, and it left no place to put refusal.

They spilled out into a wind that made the quay's ropes sing. Word reached the square faster than feet. Ferris shut his ledger and came at a trot; Jory slid from shadow like someone the night forgot to keep. Thomas Treglown arrived last with a grin that had too much ale in it and not enough sense.

"You'll be needing a man for your bags," Thomas announced.

"We'll be needing silence," Eliza said. "Which leaves you behind the bar with Mary."

Mary folded her arms; ladle tucked in the crook. "He'll be polishing pewter with his tongue if he argues," she said, and Thomas's grin mislaid itself.

Ferris pressed a folded paper to Eliza's palm. "A name in Wapping who owes me two favours and reckons at three," he murmured. "If you have to double back through London."

Eliza slid it away without looking. "If I'm in London on the return, we're already losing," she said, but her eyes softened a fraction. "Thank you."

Jory took Michael's sleeve and tugged him a pace aside. "If you're stopped, you're farm folk buying cloth," he said. "Speak slow. Let her speak fast. If you must speak, speak truth's outline and none of the colour."

"And if that fails?"

Jory's smile lived in one corner of his mouth. "Then run sooner than your pride says. Pride is bones in a ditch."

Mary reached up and fastened a narrow ribbon round Michael's wrist, no wider than a shoelace, faded blue. "From my Jim," she said. "He didn't need it where he went. You keep it and don't make me sorry."

He nodded, throat tight. Eliza watched, said nothing, and turned for the harbour.

As they walked, Eliza lowered her voice. "Paris is no longer safe ground. The people rise against their King, and every stranger is an ear to suspect. English faces draw eyes we don't want. You must let me speak for you, Michael—always. If they think you're a spy…" She didn't finish, but the cut of her glance across the harbour was enough.

Two mornings later the Channel lay pewter under a pewter sky. A stout brigantine waited in the harbour, patched canvas tugging at its lashings like an old dog straining at a lead. The deck was a racket of orders and rope-slap, the smell of tar and fish and human effort thick enough to chew. A boy in bare feet ran with a coil on his shoulder like glory, and an old man with a face pickled in salt spat, nodded at Eliza, and said to no one: "Weather's got teeth." The crew took this as a prayer and an insult both.

Eliza walked the gangplank with her cloak drawn close. Michael followed, boots uncertain on wet wood, feeling the first insistent lift and drop as the tide tested the hull.

Canvas boomed. The quay slid sideways. London diminished to a smudge and then a line and then the kind of memory the sea eats. Michael held the rail and tried to teach his stomach what his hands already knew—hold fast—but the horizon rocked and his belly rocked with it.

By noon a man with a bosun's voice and a cathedral of scars across his knuckles shoved a mop into Michael's hands. "Holystone the deck or feed it," he said. "Sea takes men who stare at it too long."

Michael scrubbed. The grit rasped, the salt stung skin split by work, and the plain labour steadied him in a way the view could not. A gull skated the wind like a small god. The old man who'd spoken of weather came and leaned on the rail and watched Michael with interest.

"Michael, is it?" he said, tasting the name.

Michael nodded.

"You've the look of a landsman who forgot how to be one." The old man nudged the mop with a toe. "There's many ways to drown. One is counting waves."

"What's your way?" Michael asked, sweat running chill under his shirt.

"Keep your mouth shut and your hands busy." He grinned, revealing a good tooth among ruins. "And don't whistle. Calls wind, that. Men laugh till the wind answers."

The crew laughed later—not cruelly but like men who had seen this play a hundred times and knew all the lines—when Michael first went green. "Michael's sea legs live in his boots," one called, thumping a cask. "Not under him."

Eliza said nothing. She stood near the quarterdeck, hair braided tight, cloak tugged by the wind, her profile carved against the bruise-coloured sky. If she pitied him, she didn't show it. If she approved that he'd come anyway, she didn't show that either.

Below deck was worse. The air was a stew of bilge, damp oak, tallow smoke, and men. Hammocks swung like slow pendulums. Rats ticked unseen. Michael lay in canvas and clutched its edge, gut wrenching with every lurch. He shut his eyes against the sway and tried to remember York—solid steps, the gas fire's hiss, Mara's hand heavy on his chest—but the memory mocked him, as if the sea had even taken that.

He remembered another crossing, another life: Dover to Calais, diesel smoke drawing a grey ribbon in a clean sky, a paper cup of coffee warm in his hands. I've been to London, I've been to France, he muttered to the dark, to the stink. But it wasn't like this.

Here the Channel was not a delay between pastry and petrol. It was the old moat of an island, the hand that drowned fleets, the jaw that chewed men to splinters.

The storm came on their second night.

Wind tore canvas. Rain hammered. The brigantine pitched like a toy a child had grown bored of and shaken. Men went aloft into blackness, their lanterns brief coins of light that swung and vanished. The sea roared black and white, foam exploding over the gunwales to soak the deck, then being dragged back down by its own weight.

The bosun bellowed and was wind-swallowed; still the men moved like they'd been born to it. A pump thudded somewhere below and kept thudding. A saint's medal flashed at a throat. A man kissed his fingers and pressed them to the mast as if comfort and superstition shared a roof.

Michael flung himself from the hammock and into a passage where water sluiced to his calves. The ship threw him into ribs of timber and back again. He swallowed salt and fear and the certain thought that he would be swallowed by a century that hadn't even a name for him.

A hand clamped his arm. Eliza, face cut from lantern flame and rain, eyes steady in the chaos. "Hold fast!" she shouted—not counsel but command. She jammed a line into his hands and braced his shoulders against a beam. "Always hold fast."

She was gone again, boots hammering up to the screaming deck.

He wrapped the line twice around his forearms until it burned and held until the storm lost its appetite and lay back down to a sullen heave. Only then did he crawl, shaking, to the stink and the swing and the scratch of rats. Hold fast thudded in his skull like a drum.

Dawn came like a mercy you didn't trust. The brigantine creaked, water dripped from everywhere, and gulls wrote thin white lines against a thinning sky. The crew moved like men who had spent more of their lives with one leg longer than the other. Some looked at Eliza with curiosity, some with hunger, some with the old, sour calculus men spend on women who step where they're not meant to. Two watched too long.

Michael saw them watching: the broad-shouldered pair—boys really, with hair salted and eyes mean with boredom. At first it was only glances that didn't bother to hide. Then it became lingerings at the scuttlebutt, shoulders turning when she passed, grins that looked like knives you keep in boots.

That evening the sea lay easy, lanterns swung lazy, and the ship's breath slowed to a tired dog's sigh. Eliza left the deck alone, coil of rope in one hand, knife sheathed in the seam of her cloak because Eliza left no room that did not have an exit. The boys glanced at one another and slipped after her into the dark throat of the companionway.

Michael followed, lantern held low, his stomach flipping from habit now as much as motion. The passage stank of tar and bilge and damp wool. Voices hushed ahead—a laugh he didn't like, soft as grease.

Steel hissed. He turned the corner in time to see one boy pinned to timber, eyes wide, throat under a blade's kiss. Eliza held the knife like an argument

166

she had already won. The other had his hand arrested midway to her sleeve, mouth open on a word he'd not be proud of.

"Try it again," she said, voice low as the storm's growl, the metal bright where it touched skin. "And you'll feed the gulls afore dawn."

The boy under the edge made a sound too small for his size. His mate bolted. Eliza shoved and the first fled too, boots clattering, shame and fear snapping at his heels.

She wiped the blade on her cloak with clean, unhurried movements, slid it home, and turned into the lantern light where Michael stood braced against the wall as if the ship had moved again. Her eyes weighed him and then shrugged off the weight.

"Men mistake silence for weakness," she said. "Better they learn otherwise."

She brushed past him—lavender, salt, a ghost of whale oil clinging to the cloth—and climbed into night as if nothing unusual had occurred.

On deck later, an old sailor squinted at Michael and jerked his chin after Eliza. "She's the kind that stands where she plants," he said. "Men don't like to be reminded their mothers did the same."

"You'll cross with her again?" Michael asked.

"If she pays on the nail," the man said. "And if she keeps boys like that from growing bones they can't use. There's worse captains stand on two legs."

"Worse?"

"Wind that lies," the sailor said, and went to coil rope.

"Land ho!"

The cry snagged on the morning and pulled it open. Michael lurched to the rail with a head still floating and saw France haul itself out of the sea: pale chalk cliffs streaked with green, a harbour alive with gulls and masts like a forest pressed into water. The smell ran out to meet them—fish, mud, old smoke, the sour press of too many bodies in too little space.

Dock lines sang. Timbers groaned and accepted stone. On the quay a carriage waited, black lacquer dulled by salt, wheels spattered with last week's road. Its horses stamped clouds into the cold. The driver wore a tricorn empty of interest and a face emptied of the habit of asking questions.

A harbour clerk appeared with a quill behind his ear and a ledger big enough to damn a town. "Nom?" he demanded, looking at Eliza and then beyond her at the world that might pay him to look elsewhere.

Eliza smiled with only her mouth. "Deveraux," she said in polite French. "Linen and lace. Samples to purchase." She offered a folded paper with a wax that looked more important than it was and, beneath it, a look that suggested his day would be shorter if he didn't read too closely. A coin changed hands without the need to announce itself. The ledger developed a gap where questions might have gone.

Eliza stepped down as if she had never been at sea. Michael followed and the ground moved under him like a joke that had gone on too long. He put a hand to the carriage and felt it hold still. The driver touched his cap to no one in particular and cracked the reins.

The road north and east was a ribbon of frost-edged mud. Smoke rose from cottages in tight ropes; geese exploded affronted onto verges; bare trees clicked their bones together. The smells were a stranger's grammar—garlic and dung and hot chestnuts from a brazier where a boy warmed his hands and shouted for coin. Michael watched, hollow with the phantom sway, and thought how different the word Paris felt in his mouth now—less a place and more an answer they had to drag out of a world that owed them nothing.

They stopped at a roadside tavern with a roof that looked as though it had lowered itself by slow degrees to warm the heads beneath it. Inside, the air was a wrestle—smoke that stung, wine turned to vinegar where it had dried, roasting meat, damp wool, bodies. Dice rattled. Cards slapped. Laughter hit hard corners and came back sharp. Women prowled the room in painted cheeks and bodices laced like traps, their perfumes fighting the sweat.

One woman took one look and made straight for Michael. She had the assured sway of someone who had never gone hungry if she could help it, and a bodice so low it did half her work. Before he could shift, she swung a leg over the bench and dropped into his lap. Her weight pinned him to the wall. She leaned in until her breath—wine-sour and sweet with some poor flower—washed his face, and her breasts, high and heavy, pushed against his chest then up under his chin until his nose drowned in them.

"Un monsieur anglais," she purred, grinding her hips, fingers already searching the line of his coat for purse and appetite. "Tu paies, je te fais oublier la mer."

Michael scrambled for French he barely had. Heat rushed his face. He tried to turn his head, but she caught his chin and pressed him back into the swell of flesh, the world reduced to perfume and sweat and the roar of men who always cheer someone else's disgrace.

"Eliza—" he managed, muffled and mortified.

A laugh cut across the room. Eliza, cloak loose over one shoulder, had seen it all. She leaned back on the bench with her mug in hand and laughed—not cruelly, but with bright delight, teeth flashing in the firelight, eyes dancing as if the storm had left a joke behind and she had just found it.

The woman in his lap, mistaking the laugh for encouragement, ground closer and tossed her hair at Eliza as if to say watch me work. Michael found his hands and shoved; bench scraping, he sent her spilling to her feet with a squawk and a string of French he didn't need translated. She flounced away, skirts swishing, already measuring the next man's knee.

Michael dragged in air, cheeks burning hot enough to sear off the stink. Across the hearth Eliza's laughter softened to a crooked smile. She lifted her mug in a small, mocking salute, then took a sip as if to bless his survival.

172

"Careful," she said later, in English shaded with French so it could hide in the room. "Some things are cheap twice, and costly the third time."

"I'll try to remember that," he said, eyes watering from smoke and humiliation both.

The boy who brought their trencher of stew had ink on his fingers and the posture of someone who had read a dangerous sentence and liked the taste. He nodded toward a back table where a packet of pamphlets changed hands like illicit bread. "Les droits de l'homme," he whispered, proud to know the title. "Says the King's head sits lighter these days."

"Does it?" Eliza said, as if discussing the weather. She leaned close to Michael when the boy left. "This is what I meant. France eats itself. Words can be as sharp as steel here. A careless question in the wrong ear and we'll be called spies before we find another bridge."

They pushed on. Frost rimed the hedges; horses changed under them like arguments resolved by money. Near Rouen the road widened, and the world admitted a river that moved with the slow confidence of age. Barges hunched under loads, men hauled lines along towpaths, and the cathedral's lace of stone rose over it all like a hand held up to swear a difficult truth. Michael craned for it and felt briefly, foolishly, as if he'd brought York to look at a cousin.

At a barrier outside a town the carriage halted. A gendarme with a mouth like a knuckle rapped the step with a baton. "Papiers."

Eliza had them already—neat, folded, faintly scented with lavender because everything she touched learned to carry something of her. The gendarme read and did not understand half, which helped. Eliza let a coin stand in for any nouns that gave him trouble. He handed the papers back and tried to boast about Paris while he did it.

"Citizens, everywhere," he said, as if citizen were a word he personally had invented. "Cockades. Songs. People standing on barrels to shout."

"Paris will teach you to listen," Eliza said.

He blinked. "Pardon?"

174

"Nothing," she said, and the whip flicked and the wheels rolled and the gendarme admired his baton to see if it looked more important in the cold.

That night they lodged at a larger hostelry, the sort of place that existed because the road insisted on resting there. The yard was a theatre of steam, manure, curses, and hooves; the common room a tide of talk and smoke. Laughter had teeth; the stew too much onion because onion was cheap; the wine was young and resentful. Men spoke in pockets about pain, impôt, guerre—bread, tax, war—and about pamphlets flying faster than pigeons. Several voices muttered about "les Anglais" with a suspicion that prickled Michael's neck. Eliza caught it too. "We must be careful," she murmured, hand shielding her lips from view. "To them, every Englishman is a spy now. Even whispers can tie ropes."

When they climbed the crooked stair, the treads counted every foot that had ever used them; the corridor smelt of damp and secrets. Eliza's chamber was two doors down from his. He pictured her setting her back against the wood for a breath, head tipped to listen, then crossing to the window and cracking it, letting the cold strip the inn's smells from her skin. He did not know if she prayed; he suspected she counted—routes, coins, loyalties, variables. The small scrape that reached him after—metal on leather—might have been the pistol slipping from her cloak and onto the table. Or his imagination sliding steel into her hand because the picture would not hold without it.

He slept and woke to the carriage. The driver's shape was a cut-out against a paler sky, shoulders hunched against cold and habit. Hooves beat the road to the same old argument. Paris grew from rumour to direction to certainty in the way of things you do not so much approach as are approached by.

They changed horses at a hamlet where the well bucket wore a rind of ice and the hens muttered their disapproval at a world that refused to warm. A toothless woman sold them chestnuts from a brazier that smoked like a confession; their skins burned his fingers and their heat reached places stew had not. A man with a scar from ear to jaw whispered "Paris" like a dare and laughed, but not with joy.

By afternoon the road broadened and the air thickened. Smoke did not rise so much as loiter. Traffic swelled: carts that leaned under sacks, wagons that shouted their merchandise in paint, riders who kept their hats low and their eyes lower. The smell changed—less earth, more city—tanneries, coal, horse, cabbage boiled to surrender, and somewhere a bakery turning out loaves at a pace that admitted hunger.

A final gate—octroi men taking their due for bringing anything decent into a city that pretended to make its own. Eliza paid with an expression that suggested she was filing names for later. Cockades flashed in hats. A boy sold tricolour ribbons with the air of a priest selling relics. A pamphlet blew against the wheel and clung there like a leaf; the driver cursed it off with his whip.

Eliza drew the curtain with two fingers to look, then let it fall again. "We'll not reach the centre before dark," she said.

"Why?"

"Because Paris in daylight asks who you are. Paris in dark doesn't care, so long as your coin is good."

"Comforting."

"True," she said, which was, he had learned, her preferred comfort.

Inside the walls, the city's sound arrived as a weather of its own—wheels and shouts and the clatter of trade, a lower, stubborn murmur of people talking to themselves about how things should be. Men with trays of hot chestnuts shouldered through with cries that cut the cold. A woman argued with a clerk from a doorway barred by a bolt and an office. Someone sang "Ça ira" as if the words might nail themselves to the air and make a scaffold of chorus.

They stopped at a house built when kings travelled with their own beds and now served anyone who could pay. Eliza took the same seat she always took—back to the wall, view of the door, angle on the stairs—and the room rearranged itself around the fact. Their food arrived and tasted, as always, of onion and the meat promised by smell but delivered mostly in memory. The wine was less young, which did not make it wise.

Nosing the rim of his cup, Michael caught again, like a current under louder noises, the talk that ran this road: a baker struck for mixing sawdust into flour and his wife struck for complaining; a crowd that had found its voice and was deciding what to shout next; a head somewhere with hair still pinned that had been lowered into a basket last week and people had cheered, which told you more about the crowd than the head. Eliza's gaze measured and moved on.

Later, when the room's pitch dropped from shout to hum and then to the soft, dangerous quiet of men too tired to fight and too angry to sleep, Eliza leaned across the table. "Horses at first light," she said. "Maps are no use in cities like this. Keep your pockets close and your eyes closer. Speak only when I tell you."

He gave her a look. "Only when?"

A corner of her mouth acknowledged the joke. "When it matters. Men in fine coats do not trust silence unless they think they own it."

"And if they think they do?"

"We teach," she said again, and whatever ghost of laughter the tavern girl had left sat far behind her eyes now.

They went up. Michael set his palm flat on the bedside table and felt, under splinters and stains, the old truth of wood. It steadied him. He set the guinea down and watched it catch the rushlight. He thought of the tin under the floor in the cliff cottage—the doubloons and pieces-of-eight, the fortune hidden because fortunes in daylight bring rope. He thought of the knife at a sailor's throat and Eliza's laughter that had surprised him more than the steel. He thought of Mara, of a kitchen radio, of Phil Collins telling them to do the impossible—look at me now. He thought of hold fast and the way the words had made a wall inside him he could lean on.

Sleep came and held.

Dawn scraped frost from the world. The road rose to a low ridge and Paris announced herself not with trumpets but with roofs—an iron sea of them—and chimneys, and a brown snake of river with too many bridges, and spires and domes shouldering one another for the right to stab the sky. Smoke hung like a second weather. The sound of it reached them before the gate.

Eliza looked out and did not look away. "We'll start with the Quai," she said. "Then the Rue aux Ours. If coin has ears, it listens there."

"And if it doesn't?"

"Then we give it some," she said, and the carriage rolled on towards the roar.

Chapter Ten

The French Connection

Paris after midnight was a creature with too many eyes and not enough mercy.

Fog crept low along the Seine, thick with the smell of wet stone, horse sweat, stale wine, and the sharp tang of riverweed. Lanterns struggled against the dark, casting halos of weak gold that dissolved before touching the ground. Voices drifted across the bridges—argument, laughter, the scrape of boots, the iron bark of a patrol sergeant calling someone a fool.

Michael kept close to Eliza as she cut through the maze of alleys behind the Quai des Orfèvres. Her pace was steady, deliberate, the stride of someone who moved through danger the same way other people moved through their own kitchens. He followed, the hem of her cloak brushing his knee now and then, and every time it did, some taut line inside him tightened further.

He had been in cities before—York, London, Bristol—but nothing like Paris, especially in 1789. This place crawled under the skin, humming with a feverish energy as if it were thinking. Plotting.

Ahead, a drunk sang half a verse of À la Bastille!, trying and failing to remember the rest. Somewhere deeper in the night, a dog barked, then whimpered, as if reconsidering the wisdom of making noise.

"This way," Eliza said softly. Her breath ghosted the chill air.

She turned into a narrow passage between two leaning houses, their upper floors nearly touching above. Rain had slicked the cobbles into dark mirrors. Michael's boots slipped once; her hand shot out, steadying him without looking back.

That touch lasted only a heartbeat, but it grounded him more than any rope or railing ever had. At the end of the passage stood the tavern with its sagging roof, crooked beams, and windows fogged opaque from decades of breath and smoke. The same tavern from earlier—where deals whispered in shadow and fists did the talking when words failed. But now the night had deepened, and so had the mood.

Inside, the roar had thickened to something more dangerous. A fiddler scraped frantically in the corner, trying to outrun a roomful of men who had decided the day hadn't given them enough to fear. Tankards slammed. Dice clattered. Shouts cracked the air like broken glass.

Michael had barely stepped through the door when a hand clamped onto his shoulder.

"Citizen!" A man with a tricolour cockade and breath like rotting apples leered at him. "Where's your ribbon, eh? All patriots wear a ribbon!"

Before Michael could answer, Eliza moved.

"Here," she said smoothly, plucking a scrap of blue-white-red from the table behind her. She tied it around Michael's arm herself, fingers sure, her expression unreadable. "Satisfied, monsieur?"

The man grunted and lurched away. Eliza inhaled once, the faintest release of tension, then led him through the smoke-thick din to the back wall— toward the secret door hidden behind hanging nets and storage barrels.

The barman caught her eye, muttered something about "pas longtemps, la Garde est nerveuse ce soir"—not long, the Guard is jumpy tonight—then pressed the hidden latch. The door eased open and cold air spilled out. Michael followed Eliza down the narrow stair into the smuggling cellar.

The lamps were lower tonight. Faces more guarded. Maps and ledgers lay across the tables, ink glistening like fresh blood. Men spoke in quick bursts of French, Breton, Dorset English, and the universal tongue of people who lived by the moon and died by the dawn.

Gulliver waited at the far end, arms crossed, his pale eyes hard as flint.

"You're late."

"The streets are thick with militia," Eliza replied. "Someone stirred the pot."

"Aye," Gulliver said. "Durand's men."

Michael felt the name land between them like a warning bell. Durand—the cheat. The liar. The man who'd led them into that empty warehouse with promises that rotted as quickly as the mould on his barrels. And the man who now lay dead at Gulliver's hand.

"Word's spreading," Gulliver continued, lowering his voice. "Durand's kin are stirring. Turning stones. Asking who last met him breathing."

Michael felt the muscles in his neck tighten.

"They'll try to find us," Gulliver said. "Tonight. Tomorrow. The week after, if God's cruel enough."

Eliza's face did not change. "Let them come. We've other business."

"More dangerous business," Gulliver said grimly. "The Paris links won't hold long—not with Durand gone and half the city baring its teeth. We

186

have one night to secure replacements. One night to set the chain

He turned to Michael.

"You proved yourself once," Gulliver said. "Tonight will ask more."

Michael wasn't sure what to say, so he simply nodded. The truth vibrated in his bones: he was out of his depth, out of his century, and yet utterly unwilling to leave Eliza facing this city alone.

Gulliver gestured them closer over the map-littered table.

"There's a merchant in the Rue des Lombards who deals in grain by day and contraband by night. Name's Fournier. Dangerous, slippery, but he hates the tax officers more than he hates competition. He'll talk if the price is right."

"And if it's wrong?" Michael asked.

"Then he'll hand us to the Garde Nationale," Gulliver said. "A man like that never misses a chance to sell a secret."

Eliza tied her cloak tighter. "Then we give him no secrets. Only choices."

Gulliver gave a single nod. "After Fournier, there's a man in the Faubourg who calls himself 'Le Passeur'. He moves people in and out of Paris when the bridges close. Vigilantes guard his street. Not soldiers—worse."

"Vigilantes?" Michael echoed.

"Aye," Gulliver said. "Men who answer to hunger, not law."

Eliza's gaze sharpened. "If the Faubourg is that hot, we go armed."

Gulliver tapped the cane-pistol at his side. "Armed, aye, but quiet. The wrong shot tonight will bring half Paris down on us."

He folded the map closed.

"You two go to Fournier. I'll deal with Le Passeur alone."

That startled Michael. "Why alone?"

"Because if anyone in this city can smell an Englishman," Gulliver said dryly, "it's a man who spends his life ferrying them."

Eliza stepped forward. "Isaac—"

"No arguments," he said. "You do your part. I do mine."

A beat. Then Eliza nodded. "Midnight at the Pont St-Michel."

"Midnight," Gulliver agreed.

He held Michael's gaze one last time. "Keep your head low and your tongue lower."

Then he was gone, cloak melting into the cellar shadows.

Eliza breathed in once and lifted her hood.

"Come," she said. "Fournier waits for no one."

Michael followed her up the stair, heart pounding, the hidden door closing behind them like the mouth of a grave.

Paris lay different when they re-emerged into its night—tenser, tighter, as if the buildings themselves were listening. Somewhere a bell tolled the hour, muffled by fog thick enough to feel on the tongue. The wind carried the stink of the tanneries, warm horse dung, yeast from a distant bakery, and something metallic beneath it all, like blood drying on iron.

Eliza walked with purpose through the arteries of the Île de la Cité, choosing streets Michael wouldn't have braved alone. Shutters snapped shut as they passed. A woman dragging a sack paused to stare at them with wide, hollow eyes, then hurried inside before a patrol rounded the corner.

A group of militia marched past—tricolour cockades pinned to their hats, muskets slung with sloppy confidence. The officer in front barked orders in a bored rhythm:

"Cherchez les étrangers. Trouvez les contrebandiers. Pas de pitié."

Find the foreigners. Find the smugglers. No mercy.

Michael angled his face down, letting the ribbon Eliza had tied around his arm show. The officer's eyes flicked toward them, lingered, then moved on.

Only when the patrol's boots faded did Eliza speak.

"Paris is closing its doors."

"Against who?"

"Everyone," she said. "That's what fear does."

They pushed further into the medieval knot of streets. Stalls sat shuttered, half-frozen oranges covered by stiff cloths. A butcher slapped a carcass on a hook with more force than needed—either anger or nerves. A pair of boys darted past carrying stolen onions, laughing the brittle laugh of children who knew adults were too occupied to chase them.

Michael quickened his step to match Eliza's. "This Fournier—what's his game?"

"All of them," she said. "But he plays best for himself."

They passed under an archway into the Rue des Lombards, once the street of wealthy bankers, now choked with taverns, warehouses, and shadow markets. Lanterns swung in the damp breeze. A knife-grinder's wheel shrieked sparks into the night. Prostitutes in threadbare shawls tapped knuckles against shutters, calling out prices like vendors at market.

"Over there," Eliza murmured.

The shopfront looked ordinary: wooden sign, shuttered windows, a stack of grain sacks near the door. But the double knock she gave—three quick, one slow—was not the knock of a customer.

A bolt slid.

The door cracked.

A narrow face peeked out, eyes sharp and suspicious. "Qui?"

"Eliza Trevelyan," she said.

The eye widened. Then the door opened.

Inside smelled of millet, ink, and lamp oil. Shelves reached the ceiling, stacked with crates and sacks, but Michael sensed immediately that the grain was the least valuable thing the shop traded in. Fournier emerged from behind the counter—a wiry man in a velvet coat whose best days were decades behind him. His smile was too thin, too polished.

"Madame Trevelyan," he said, in French smoother than his boots. "You are either bold… or desperate… to walk Paris tonight."

"A little of both," she replied.

His gaze slid to Michael. "And this one? Not Parisian."

"Does he need to be?" Eliza asked.

Fournier chuckled. "Names, Madame, not nationality. Names matter to a man in my business."

"No names," Eliza said. "Only trade."

"Then you've brought coin."

"We've brought opportunity."

Michael noted how Fournier's eyes sharpened. Men like him always listened harder when the bait became intangible.

Eliza leaned one elbow on the counter, casual but coiled. "Durand is gone."

Fournier froze.

Michael saw it: fear, quickly smothered. "Gone?" Fournier asked, voice thin.

"Missing," Eliza corrected. "Likely fled. His… warehouse was empty."

Fournier pursed his lips. But his eyes did not match. "Durand fled Paris? That rat? Impossible."

Michael felt a cold twist inside. Fournier knew far more than he let on.

Eliza lifted her gaze. "We need a new point of contact."

"And you thought of me," Fournier said, smiling without warmth. "How flattering. Though you come on a dangerous night."

"You're always dangerous," she said. "That's why we're here."

The merchant preened, but his hands drummed. Too fast. Too nervous.

"Eliza," Michael murmured, leaning close, "he's expecting someone."

She didn't answer aloud, but the flicker in her eyes told him he was right.

Fournier gestured them toward a narrow staircase leading to the cellar. "We should talk below. Less… scrutiny."

Eliza stepped once toward the stair, then stopped. Michael watched her read the room in a heartbeat. The hanging curtain in the back swayed— not from draft, but from movement. A faint scrape of boot leather on stone. A single shadow too dark for the lantern light.

She whispered, almost inaudible, "We're not alone."

Fournier saw her hesitate and his smile vanished.

"Madame," he said softly, "I advise you step down the stairs. Now."

"No," Eliza said. "We talk here."

Fournier sighed. "Then I apologise."

And he clapped his hands.

Two men stepped from behind the curtain— thick-shouldered, faces half-covered with cloth. One carried a cudgel. The other, a knife.

Michael tensed.

Eliza did not.

"Really?" she said. "You think this will end well for you?"

Fournier shrugged. "The Garde Nationale pays more for smugglers than smugglers pay for grain."

Michael's stomach tightened.

"It's not personal," Fournier continued. "It's arithmetic."

Eliza moved first.

A sack of grain split open in her hand as easily as ripping cloth. Flour exploded into the air—blinding, billowing, choking.

Michael lunged, grabbing the cudgel arm, twisting hard. The man crashed into the shelves, sending crates thundering down. The second attacker swung blindly, slashing wild. Eliza ducked, swept a crate into his kneecap, and the man howled as he collapsed.

Fournier stumbled back, coughing, eyes streaming. "You fools!" he shouted. "The Garde are near—"

"Good," Eliza said coldly. "They can collect what's left of you."

She yanked him against the counter, twisting his wrist until the ledger dropped from his hand.

"Who are you working with?" she demanded. "Durand's kin?"

"I—I—" Fournier sputtered.

Michael grabbed a fistful of the man's coat. "Tell her."

Fournier broke instantly.

"Durand owed money," he gasped. "He borrowed from men in the Faubourg. Bad men. He promised them a cut from his next shipment. He never paid."

"And when he died?" Eliza said.

"They looked for his partners."

"You mean us."

Fournier closed his eyes. "They know your names. They know your faces."

Michael felt the floor drop away.

Eliza did not blink. "Then we're already dead unless we keep moving."

Voices erupted outside—the bark of officers, the clang of musket butts striking cobbles.

"Eliza," Michael warned, "we have to go."

She released Fournier with a shove. "If you shout after us," she said quietly, "they won't find enough of you to bury."

Then she grabbed Michael's sleeve.

"Back exit."

They ran and burst through the curtain. Down a cramped corridor that smelled of mildew and fear. A door stuck; she kicked it open. Cold air slapped them. They exploded into a narrow side street just as militia boots thundered into the shop's front entrance.

Eliza pulled Michael down behind a stack of barrels. "Wait."

Shouts inside and then a crash. Fournier screaming and the militia roaring over him.

Eliza exhaled once, a thin thread of relief.

"He's busy," she whispered. "Move."

They sprinted into the dark, the city rising around them like a predator. Their shadows stretched long across the cobbles as Paris swallowed them again.

They didn't stop running until the Rue des Lombards was a memory behind them and the streets widened into the sprawling market district near Les Halles. Lanterns flickered overhead, caught in the winter wind like dying insects. The fog had thickened, swallowing edges, making the world seem half-formed.

Women haggled over sad vegetables. A fishmonger dumped buckets of melted ice into the gutter, the water streaked with blood. A drunk slept upright against a doorway, hat pulled low. Everything looked normal at a glance.

But Michael felt the city watching. Eliza slowed only when they reached the cover of a cart piled with crates. Her breath wasn't ragged; her eyes were bright with calculation, not panic.

"We don't have long," she said, voice low. "Fournier's arrest will only buy us minutes. His attackers saw enough to name us."

"They'll tell the Guard?"

"No," she said. "They'll tell someone worse. The men Durand owed."

Michael swallowed. "Who are they?"

"Not a gang," she said. "Not thieves. Vigilants."

He frowned. "Vigilantes?"

"Not English ones. Not masked heroes." She shook her head. "These are men of the Faubourg: citizens who believe the law isn't harsh enough. They police their streets the way storms police cliffs."

"And they're looking for us."

"Looking for anyone connected to Durand. But yes, us most of all."

Michael's pulse hammered.

"Eliza… what do they do when they find someone?"

She didn't soften it. "They don't use ropes. Too quick. They prefer knives."

Michael looked away, bile rising.

"We keep moving," she said. "There's one more contact we need tonight."

"Gulliver's man? The ferryman?"

"No. Someone else. Someone who can tell us exactly how much danger we're in."

They slipped back into the moving river of people: fishwives, porters, children stealing apples, men in threadbare coats with knives hidden where the militia never bothered to search.

The sky above Paris was the colour of soot. As they approached the eastern alleys, the buildings shifted: taller, meaner, leaning over the streets like eavesdroppers. Windows were barred. Doors reinforced. Lanterns fewer. Voices hushed.

Michael realised suddenly, physically, that they were no longer in the merchant quarter. This was the Faubourg. Eliza knew it too.

"We walk," she murmured. "No fear. No hesitation. Hood low. And don't look at anyone longer than you must."

Michael tucked his chin. He tried to push his shoulders into a shape that belonged here. He tried to look like a man who had business in a neighbourhood where business got you killed.

They passed men warming hands over a brazier made of scrap metal. The flames lit their faces in jolts—hard eyes, a few scars, one missing ear. They watched Michael and Eliza pass but said nothing.

A woman stood on a doorstep with her arms crossed. She had no cloak, no shawl, only a hardened stare that could've carved stone.

"You're not from here," she said in rough French.

"No one is," Eliza replied smoothly. "Everyone borrowed this city from someone."

The woman barked a short laugh and let them go.

Only when the street bent sharply did Michael ask quietly, "Where are we going?"

"To speak to someone who knows the vigilants. Someone who knows what they'll do next."

"And who is that?"

"The Undertaker."

Michael blinked. "You're joking."

"No," she said.

They turned down another alley. This one was lined with shuttered shops: barber, cobbler, and one with black crepe hanging in the doorway. The sign above read:

POMPES FUNÈBRES — FAVREAU

A funeral house. Eliza stepped inside. The air chilled. It smelled of lavender, tallow, and something faintly metallic. Shelves held candles, urns, and folded cloth. A coffin stood propped in one corner, lid open, waiting.

A man appeared from behind a curtain: tall, thin, with a face like carved ivory and fingers stained with ink and wine. His black coat was immaculate.

"Mademoiselle Trevelyan," he said gently. "I did not expect you tonight."

"Favreau," Eliza said. "We need your ear."

He looked at Michael. "Your friend looks pale."

Michael cleared his throat. "It's… been a long evening."

Favreau smiled, but it did nothing to ease the room. "Most long evenings end here."

"Durand," Eliza said. "His death has stirred something."

Favreau exhaled slowly. "Yes. The Faubourg talks of nothing else. Someone claims to have seen you leaving his warehouse."

Michael stiffened.

Favreau raised a hand. "Calm, monsieur. It is rumour. Yet rumour is a hungry thing. The vigilants are sharpening their knives. They believe Durand betrayed them, stole from them, and that someone helped him do it."

"And they think it's us," Eliza said.

"They think many things," Favreau said. "But your names have crossed several lips. And lips become blades."

Michael's blood ran cold. "So what do we do?"

Favreau stepped closer, lowering his voice. "You have until tomorrow night. Maybe less. After that, they will hunt—not through whispers but with torches. If they catch you…"

His eyes met Michael's.

"You will not see dawn."

Silence thickened.

Eliza did not flinch. "We need to get across the river. No bridges. They'll be watched."

"Then you need Jeanne," Favreau said. "She ferries the unwanted. Her boat sleeps under the Pont au Change. But she will not take you unless she believes you can pay and keep quiet."

"We can."

Favreau studied them. "There is something else. You must leave tonight. Now. A patrol passed here half an hour ago asking questions. Men with red sashes."

Eliza's head snapped up. "Vigilants?"

"Yes."

Michael felt his throat close.

Favreau reached behind the counter and lifted two dark cloaks. Heavy. Plain. Anonymous.

"Wear these," he said. "Walk like people used to being ignored."

Eliza took the cloaks. "Favreau… thank you."

He tilted his head. "I bury many. I would prefer not to bury you."

They stepped outside.

The sky above had no stars left. And the street behind them echoed with approaching boots. Eliza didn't hesitate.

"Left," she whispered, and the two of them slipped deeper into the alley just as the boots turned the corner behind them.

Michael risked a glance. Four men—thick coats, red sashes tied at their arms, cudgels in hand. Vigilants. Their faces were cold as cut stone, eyes searching for someone to blame. Someone like them.

Michael swallowed. "They're sweeping the street."

"And they'll sweep harder once they smell the trail," Eliza murmured. "Keep walking. Not too fast."

The cloaks Favreau had given them were coarse, hooded, heavy. Perfect for vanishing into the sort of place no one wanted to look too closely at. They reached the mouth of a narrow passage and slipped inside just as the vigilants turned their backs. The passage was barely wide enough for a man and his regrets. It twisted like something wounded, lined with damp stones, reeking faintly of mildew and urine. Rats skittered along the walls, quick and nervous.

Michael stepped over a puddle that might once have been water. "Where does this go?"

"Back to the market," Eliza whispered. "Favreau didn't say it, but I know his meaning. If the vigilants are here, the main streets aren't safe. We stay in the cracks."

They moved in shadows until the passage spat them out behind a row of crates stacked against a bakery's back door. Flour dust whitened the ground around them like snow that had forgotten how to be beautiful.

A man dumped ashes from an oven into a bin. Smoke curled around him in pale ribbons. He didn't look up.

Paris was good at pretending not to see.

Eliza tugged Michael's sleeve. "This way."

She led him between two buildings that leaned so close their roofs seemed to whisper conspiracies to each other. The cold air bit harder here. Every sound travelled. Every footstep felt too loud. A group of washerwomen passed at the far end, baskets heavy, their chatter brittle from gossip and cold. One looked their way, frowned, then moved on. Their cloaks worked. For now.

As they reached the wider street, the bells of Saint-Merri tower clanged the quarter hour. The sound rang out like iron striking bone. Michael flinched.

Eliza didn't.

She tipped her chin toward the river. "Jeanne won't wait forever. We need to reach the Pont au Change before word spreads."

Michael felt his pulse tighten. "Favreau said they were already asking questions."

"They'll ask more after they find Durand's body," she said. "And they'll ask hardest in this quarter."

The street ahead opened into a small, busy square where peddlers hoisted their evening lamps. The glow cast long, trembling shadows. Children darted between stalls like minnows. A man roasted strips of meat on a brazier, the scent rising warm and greasy.

Michael's stomach clenched. They tried to blend in—two cloaked figures wandering like people with errands—but he could feel the unease tugging at the edge of the crowd. People looked suspicious tonight. People whispered. And the word spreading was murder.

A shout burst from the far corner. Two men burst from an alley, one pointing wildly down the street.

"Il est là-bas ! Là-bas ! The vigilants found something!"

The square shivered with attention.

Eliza's eyes narrowed. "That's our cue to leave."

They moved quickly, using the swirl of distracted bodies to slip through the south end of the square. The air chilled as they stepped beneath the shadow of an overhanging archway. And the city's voice shifted—deeper, angrier. A whistle sliced through the air.

Michael's blood froze.

"That's a vigilance whistle," Eliza said. "Someone spotted us."

"What? How—?"

Her hand seized his. "Move!"

They bolted. Feet slapped the stones. Michael's cloak tangled around his legs but he kept pace. The alley funnelled them forward, the walls pushing close, the dark swallowing them in one breath.

Behind them, shouts erupted.

"HALTE ! LÀ !"

Boots thundered after them.

Eliza didn't look back. "Left!"

They swung sharply down a cut so narrow Michael's shoulder scraped brick. The darkness thickened, pierced only by the smudge of lantern glow behind them. Paris was a labyrinth drawn by a madman. The vigilants were men who knew every shortcut.

A hand clamped the back of Michael's cloak.

He twisted, panic flaring.

Eliza's knife flashed.

The hand let go.

A grunt. A man fell to the stones, clutching a bleeding forearm.

Eliza grabbed Michael's sleeve again. "Keep going!"

They tore through another alley, boots splashing through filthy water. The river smell thickened: brine, algae, smoke. They were close. Voices echoed behind them, furious now.

THIEVES!"

"MURDERERS!"

"ARRÊTEZ-LES !"

Michael's lungs burned. His chest was fire. He wasn't sure he could keep running.

Then they burst onto the Quai de Gesvres.

The Seine widened before them, black and writhing, lit by trembling lanterns. The Pont au Change arched overhead like a spine.

Eliza scanned the shadows under the bridge.

"Jeanne!" she hissed.

A shape detached itself from the dark, a barge low in the water.

Jeanne stood on the prow, coat whipping in the cold wind.

"Dépêchez-vous! Move!"

Michael and Eliza sprinted toward her.

Shouts flared behind them, five men now, maybe six. One raised a lantern. Another drew a knife. They were closing.

A musket fired. Stone shattered near Michael's foot.

Jeanne vaulted forward, grabbed Eliza's arm. "Allez!"

Eliza leapt onto the deck. Michael's boots pounded the last stretch as another shot cracked the air. Eliza's hand reached back into the dark.

Michael jumped. Her fingers caught his wrist. For one moment, the world held its breath. Then Jeanne shoved off the quay with a long pole, the barge sliding into the river's cold embrace.

The vigilants lunged, but the boat was already drifting out of reach. One threw his lantern in fury. It hit the water with a hiss and vanished.

The Seine swallowed their curses. Eliza pulled Michael fully aboard and he collapsed onto the deck, chest heaving, breath scraping like broken glass.

Jeanne spat into the river. "You weren't followed well," she said. "But you were followed."

Eliza nodded. "That's why we need you."

Jeanne's eyes were flint in the lantern glow. "You'll owe me double."

Michael managed a rasp of a laugh. "Put it on the bill."

The barge drifted under the arch of the Pont au Change, the city's roar dimming behind stone.

Only then did Michael realise his hands were shaking.

Eliza noticed.

She touched his arm, gentle despite everything. "You're alive, Michael."

"For now," he breathed.

"For now is all Paris gives," Jeanne said.

The river carried them deeper into the dark. The barge drifted beneath the Pont au Change, swallowed by shadow. The world above shrank to a muffled thrum of boots, voices, and the hollow clatter of the city shifting its weight.

Beneath the arch the water thickened, slow and sullen, tugging at the hull. Jeanne kept her pole braced, reading the current with the instinct of someone who had learnt early that rivers have moods and moods have consequences.

Michael pulled himself upright, breath still jagged.

Eliza crouched beside him. "Any injuries?"

"Only my pride."

"That'll survive." She dusted mud from his shoulder, her touch brisk but careful.

Jeanne snorted. "Pride's the first thing Paris eats. Consider it a tax."

She nudged the pole deeper, guiding them toward the darker span beneath the bridge.

Michael's breathing began at last to steady. The cold off the river wrapped around him like wet cloth. He shivered, shoved his hands under his arms.

"What now?" he asked quietly.

"Now," Jeanne said, "we slow our hearts."

Eliza glanced at her. "How far will you take us?"

"Far enough." Jeanne jerked her chin toward the southern embankment. "We hug the shadows until Île Saint-Louis. After that, the river widens and the patrols thin."

Michael leaned over the gunwale, watching the river swallow the lantern reflections and break them into shards. The chill of it bit his face.

Behind them, on the bridge above, the vigilants' voices echoed—frustration, not pursuit.

"They'll spread the word," Eliza murmured. "By dawn half the city will have heard there's blood on the Saint-Denis road."

"And the other half will pretend not to care," Jeanne said.

Michael frowned. "Durand had friends?"

"Durand had debts," Eliza corrected. "Friends are optional. Debts are loyal."

Jeanne's lip curled. "His kind always owes someone. And the men he owed will not enjoy being robbed of their coin or their revenge."

"So they'll hunt us?" Michael asked.

Eliza gave him a look that was neither apology nor reassurance. "They'll hunt anything that moves until their pride is satisfied. But they don't know our names yet. Only our cloaks."

"And those cloaks will be ash by morning," Jeanne added.

She wasn't exaggerating. Every alley they passed beneath seemed to breathe in the dark, carrying rumours like spores. Paris wasn't a city; it was a mouth.

And tonight, it had teeth. They slid toward the Île Saint-Louis, the buildings looming like sleeping beasts. The lamps along the quai shimmered in the fog, their light blurred, uncertain. A dog barked somewhere above. A drunken voice sang half a verse and forgot the rest.

The barge bumped lightly against a rotting timber beam. Jeanne adjusted her course, murmuring something under her breath—half a curse, half a prayer to the river.

Michael rubbed his hands together, trying to coax warmth into them. "Feels colder here."

"The river carries every lie in this city," Jeanne said. "Lies are cold."

Eliza's mouth twitched. "You sound like one of those pamphlet poets."

"I sound like someone who's seen men drown because they thought water was kinder than people."

Silence pooled between them.

Then Jeanne pointed. "There. That passage."

They were approaching a narrow cut between two ancient stone walls. Moss clung to the edges; a trickle of water ran down one side and joined the river in a thin ribbon.

"This is our stop?" Michael asked.

"For now," Jeanne said.

She eased the barge against the wall. Eliza took the rope, looped it around a rusted iron ring, and secured it.

Jeanne spoke low. "From here, take the Saint-Louis steps. They spit you onto the Rue Poulletier. Keep to the eastern edge of the island. Less eyes."

Michael peered upward. "Looks steep."

"It is." Jeanne handed him a warning smile. "Paris punishes those who want easy roads."

Eliza lowered herself onto the stone steps slick with moss. The river slapped rhythmically against the wall.

Michael followed, boots skidding slightly. Jeanne caught his arm just long enough to steady him.

"Two nights," she said. "After that, I change routes. The river doesn't stand still—neither do I."

"We'll be there," Eliza said.

Jeanne nodded once, then pushed the barge off with a grunt. It drifted back into the dark like a ghost returning to the water it had escaped.

Michael watched until she disappeared fully from sight.

The river's voice filled the silence.

Eliza straightened her cloak. "Come on. Keep your head down. And whatever happens—don't speak unless I speak first."

He nodded. They climbed the steps and at the top, the world changed again.

Paris breathed differently up here—quieter, but not calmer. The wind lifted fog into thin sheets that drifted through the narrow streets like restless spirits. Lanterns glowed behind shutters. A few silhouettes moved behind thin curtains.

The island felt older, as if the city had bones here. Eliza set off eastward, keeping close to the shadows of the houses. Michael followed, listening to the hollow rhythm of their footsteps. They passed a small chapel with a faded stone façade. A beggar slept in the arched doorway, wrapped in a threadbare coat, breath steaming.

Michael slowed.

Eliza touched his arm lightly. "Don't."

"He's freezing."

"So are we. Keep moving."

Michael hesitated only a moment, then followed her. But the beggar stirred as they passed, lifting a cracked voice.

"Citoyens… a coin… for bread…"

Eliza didn't stop. "We have none."

It wasn't entirely true. Michael felt the weight of his guinea against his ribs, a weight that didn't belong in this century. He shook the thought away and pushed on.

Halfway down the street, the quiet shattered. Voices erupted at the far end—shouts, hurried steps, something crashing into wood.

Eliza grabbed his sleeve. "Back. Now."

They slipped behind the corner of a shuttered shopfront. Michael peered cautiously.

A patrol barrelled into the street—six men in mismatched coats, red armbands stark in the lamplight. Vigilants again. One carried a lantern, its glow skittering crazily off the fog.

They were dragging a man between them, a butcher by the look of his apron. The butcher's face was bloodied; his hands bound.

"Thief!" one of the vigilants barked. "Thief and liar!"

The butcher protested, voice hoarse. "Non! Je vous jure—je n'ai rien volé!"

Michael stiffened. Eliza gripped his wrist— hard enough to warn, not enough to hurt.

"Don't," she whispered.

Michael's jaw clenched. "They're going to beat him."

"They'll beat us too if we step in."

"But he didn't—"

"Michael," she said softly, "we are ghosts in this city. We cannot save every living soul."

The vigilants shoved the butcher against a wall, fists rising. Eliza pulled Michael deeper into the shadows, her breath warm against his ear. "Listen.

Vigilants want a story to tell their captain. A body works fine as a story. We can't be that body."

The butcher cried out as a blow landed. Michael shut his eyes. Eliza tugged him away before the next scream. They disappeared down a side passage, the echo of violence trailing behind them like smoke. When they had put enough distance between themselves and the patrol, Eliza slowed.

Her face in the weak lantern glow was unreadable.

"You can't help every drowning man," she murmured. "Not here."

Michael exhaled unsteadily. "It feels wrong."

"It is wrong," she said. "But being righteous doesn't keep you breathing. Being careful does."

They kept walking.

They crossed the island and reached its eastern edge, where a narrow bridge arched over the water toward the Right Bank. A woman selling boiled chestnuts huddled beneath a shawl near the foot of it. Smoke curled from her brazier, softening the air.

Eliza paused.

"Buy two," she murmured.

"Why?"

"So the watchers think we're ordinary."

Michael stepped forward. "Deux, s'il vous plaît."

The woman handed him two paper cones of steaming chestnuts. She didn't smile. No one smiled in this city unless they wanted something.

Eliza took hers. "Good. Now eat slowly and keep walking."

They crossed the bridge. The fog parted briefly, revealing the vast shadow of Notre-Dame rising above the city, its towers like dark sentinels. Michael slowed unconsciously. Eliza didn't.

"Don't stare," she said.

"It's beautiful."

"It's watched."

They reached the far side, where streets widened and the smell of the river gave way to smoke and horse dung. Lanterns sputtered in the wind. Eliza stopped beneath a sagging signboard that read Chambre à Louer. A narrow stair climbed into darkness.

"This is where we vanish," she said.

"You know the place?"

"I know every place where no one asks questions."

Michael looked up the stair. "And after tonight?"

"We watch. We wait. We learn who wants Durand dead—and who wants us to pay for it."

She put her hand on the latch.

"Paris isn't done with us," she said quietly. "Not yet."

They took the long way back toward the river—down the rue de la Tixeranderie, where cobblers were already hammering soles as if determined to outwork the dawn, then along a crooked stretch of alley where washing sagged like defeated banners from every window. Paris breathed around them: sharp, thin, impatient.

"Keep your head down," Eliza murmured.

Michael did—partly because it was wise, partly because the street was now so narrow that a man couldn't walk upright without knocking someone's laundry into the gutter. They passed a cooper rolling an empty cask, three women arguing in simultaneous, overlapping French, and a priest sweeping filth from his doorstep with the weary zeal of a man who suspected sin had the stronger arm.

When they turned into the Marché des Innocents, noise hit them like a thrown pail. Fishmongers shouted prices; children wove between stalls like pickpockets in training; a woman hurled a cabbage after a man who had insulted her onions. The air stank of river mud, old eel, and woodsmoke. A good place to blend. A terrible place to be noticed.

Which meant, of course, that they were. Michael felt it first—a prickle beneath the skin, the slightest shift in how the crowd moved. Then he saw him. A man stood by the shuttered door of a bakery, wearing the blue coat of the Garde Nationale. Not uniform-fresh; not parade-clean. This was a working man's jacket, patched elbows, worn cuffs. The man inside it had a lieutenant's swagger and a face carved from something that didn't apologise.

Lieutenant Lacombe.

Michael didn't need Eliza's quiet, "Don't look at him," to know it.

Lacombe's eyes swept the crowd with the bored hunger of someone hoping a dangerous face might appear. And then—inevitably, horribly—they paused. Not fully on Michael, but on Eliza. Michael saw the moment Lacombe recognised her. His expression tightened—not surprise exactly, but the satisfaction of a man whose quarry had finally walked into the light.

"Eliza," Michael breathed.

"I see him," she said.

"What do we—?"

"Walk," she said. "Not fast. Not slow. Walk like every other exhausted soul in this city."

She did exactly that—slipping between a bread stall and a cart of turnips, posture loose, hood low, footsteps measured. Michael followed, resisting the instinct to run.

Behind them, Lacombe pushed off from the wall. He didn't shout. He didn't draw his sabre. He simply began to follow, weaving through the noise with a predator's patience.

"Left," Eliza murmured.

She cut into a narrow archway half-hidden behind a stack of crates. It led into a dim passage that smelled of piss and damp stone. The noise of the market faded behind them. Michael's heartbeat hammered in his ears.

"He's still coming," he whispered.

"I know."

They emerged into a small courtyard where washing lines intersected overhead like mismatched rigging. A woman was beating rugs with the flat of a paddle; she barely looked up.

"Through here," Eliza said.

A low doorway led into another alley, this one lined by the backs of taverns, the walls plastered with old theatre bills and political slogans half-torn: VIVE LA NATION, LIBERTÉ, PAIN POUR TOUS. A drunk lay snoring beside a barrel, hat pulled over his face.

Then the sound came—boots entering the passage behind them.

Lacombe. Michael felt sweat break along his spine despite the cold.

"Eliza—"

"Don't speak."

She led him into a tannery that stank so intensely Michael's eyes watered. Hides hung from beams; vats of foul liquid hissed and frothed. No one looked up—the tanners were too busy and too accustomed to people slipping through their domain with questionable motives.

"Up," she said, pointing to a set of wooden steps that climbed to a loft walkway.

He obeyed, boots sinking into slippery sawdust. The walkway creaked dangerously.

At the far end, a shuttered window overlooked a side street. Eliza slammed it open with her forearm, splinters flying.

"We jump," she said.

Michael stared. The drop wasn't far—perhaps eight feet—but the street below held a pile of crates, a stray dog, and a man sharpening knives on a whetstone.

"We can't—"

She had already jumped.

He followed. His boots hit a crate, cracked it, and he tumbled into a heap of straw. The dog barked in outrage. The knife-grinder swore and hopped back. Eliza was already pulling him to his feet.

"Move."

They slipped into a stable-yard, scattering chickens. A groom cursed at them, brandishing a pitchfork, but Eliza tossed him a coin without breaking stride. He caught it instinctively, and they were gone before he decided whether to shout.

Finally, after what felt like an hour but could only have been minutes, they reached the Quai again—broad, cold, watched by the river.

Michael leaned against a bollard, gasping. "Did we lose him?"

"For now," Eliza said, watching the street behind them. "But a man like Lacombe doesn't stop. He watches. And then he steps where you least want him."

"Why after you?" Michael asked, though he already knew.

"Because Durand was his," she said. "Because someone above him wants names. Because men who traffic favours do not like being made fools of."

Michael looked at her in the cold grey light. Hair pulled back, hood low, eyes alert and hard. Paris looked ready to bite, and she looked ready to bite back.

"What do we do now?" he asked.

"We meet Jeanne tonight as planned," she said. "We stay alive until then."

"And tomorrow?"

"Cross the Seine," she said softly. "And vanish before Lacombe rearranges our bones."

The fog lifted slowly through the morning, burned off by a weak sun that had no real commitment to the job. Eliza kept them moving— never in a straight line, never where the crowd parted too easily. She bought a string of onions she didn't need, simply because lingering might have looked suspicious; she paused to talk to a seamstress selling scraps of lace, just long enough to make themselves ordinary.

Paris was beginning to notice them less. Which meant it was the perfect moment for trouble to notice them more. They were crossing the rue Mondétour— a street that stank of stalled drains and bad tempers— when a hand shot out and grabbed Michael's sleeve.

He spun, ready for a knife. It wasn't a knife. It was a boy. No more than ten. Thin, quick-eyed, barefoot despite the cold.

"M'sieur," he hissed. "Message."

Michael glanced at Eliza. She nodded once. The boy shoved a folded scrap of paper into Michael's hand and darted away, swallowed by the crowd. Eliza steered Michael into the shadow of a doorway.

"Open it."

He unfolded the paper. A single line, in a hand that was brisk and unmistakably English:

Lacombe hunts you. Do not return to the inn.

—G

Michael felt something cold settle in his chest.

"Gulliver," he said.

"Of course," Eliza replied. "He is using half a dozen eyes across the city. If Lacombe wants us, Gulliver will know before we do."

"But if we cannot go back…"

"We do not," she said. "We stay in motion."

She took the note, lit it with a tinder spark, and dropped it into the gutter where it smouldered into nothing.

"Come," she said.

The Latin Quarter pulsed with a different kind of noise: students arguing politics with the inflated courage of youth, printers hauling stacks of illegal pamphlets, vendors shouting about roasted chestnuts and ink-worn books. The air smelled of smoke, ambition, and the sour scent of men who slept too close together.

Eliza led him through a warren of back alleys until they reached a coffeehouse so narrow it seemed squeezed between its neighbours. Inside, men argued over Rousseau and language reforms while a boy poured coffee thick enough to stand a spoon in. They took a corner table. Michael's pulse began, slowly, to settle.

Eliza stirred her cup thoughtfully. "Lacombe will expect us to run. He will think we are heading for the bridges."

"Are we?"

"Yes," she said, "but not the way he expects."

"Jeanne?"

"She will be ready. And if she is not, Paris will have one less boatman by the end of the night."

Michael stared into his cup. "Eliza… why does Gulliver trust you so completely? You two barely exchange a civil nod."

Eliza huffed a small laugh. "We don't need to like each other. We need to understand each other. He knows I do the work. And I know he doesn't waste men for sport."

"And me?" Michael asked before he could stop himself. "Why take me to Paris? Why trust me at all?"

Her eyes fixed on him with an honesty that felt like a slap.

"Because you think before you speak," she said. "And because you don't enjoy killing."

"That's a weakness."

"No," she said quietly. "That's what stops you from becoming another Lacombe."

He looked down, throat tight.

She went on, voice lower:

"Do not confuse this work with what you are. Men lose themselves because they think the job must become the man. Don't."

He opened his mouth, then shut it again. The coffeehouse door creaked, and Eliza stiffened. Michael didn't turn right away. He reached for the spoon on the table—not much, but something—and waited for her cue.

"Not him," she murmured. "But someone who might talk to him."

He risked a glance. A guard in the Garde Nationale's blue coat. Not Lacombe, but close enough to make the skin crawl. He was ordering coffee. He hadn't seen them yet.

"We should go," Michael whispered.

"We will," she said, "but not like fugitives."

She stood, left a coin on the table, and walked out with the calm poise of a woman whose world was entirely in order. Michael followed, heart pounding far faster than hers seemed to. Outside, she took his arm briefly—not affection, strategy—and they melted into the street. By the time the guard looked around the room, they were half a street away.

They spent the rest of the afternoon moving like shadows—sometimes safe, sometimes not. Twice they spotted men who might have been watching them. Once they ducked into a dressmaker's shop where the seamstress fussed loudly over Eliza's hem, distracting an officer long enough for them to slip out the back door.

At one point, a pamphleteer shoved a handbill into Michael's chest, shouting:

"La liberté n'attend pas!

Freedom will not wait!"

Michael wondered, not for the first time, what the world would look like when this city finally decided it had waited long enough. By late afternoon, the clouds thickened until the sky sagged under their weight. Lanterns were being lit early along the river.

Somewhere a drum pulsed—not marching, but warning.

Eliza exhaled once, long and steady.

"Night is coming," she said. "And with it Jeanne."

"Are we ready?"

"No," she said. "But we're going anyway."

Twilight dragged itself across Paris, turning the river to dull metal. The city's edges sharpened; shadows lengthened; the bells of Saint-Gervais tolled with impatient urgency. The cold seeped under collars and through seams. Eliza and Michael approached the Pont au Change by a route Gulliver had marked on a piece of leather—scratched lines only, no writing, nothing traceable. They moved against the flow of people returning to cramped rooms, smoke-heavy meals, thin beds. The noise of the day died slowly, reluctantly.

Michael's nerves thrummed like live wire. Jeanne's rendezvous would be the line between escape and disaster. They reached the base of the bridge and slipped into the alcove beneath it—a place where stone sweated and the river muttered about old sins.

Eliza checked the shadows.

"Too quiet," she murmured.

"Too quiet good?"

"Too quiet never good."

The water slapped the arches below.

Then—footsteps. Light. Deliberate.

Michael tensed.

Jeanne emerged from the shadow as if carved from it.

"You're early," she said.

"We like to see trouble before it sees us," Eliza replied.

"Then turn around," Jeanne said. "You'll see it now."

Michael turned. A figure stood at the top of the stair, a blue coat. Sabre. Lieutenant Lacombe. His smile was thin as a razor.

"There you are," he said.

Eliza did not flinch.

"Lieutenant," she said, as if they had an appointment. "You've been walking in circles."

Lacombe descended the steps slowly, one hand on the rail, the other resting near the hilt of his sabre. Two guards followed, boots scraping stone. Above them, the bridge thrummed with wheels and voices, the muffled life of the city carrying on.

"I dislike circles," he said. "I prefer straight lines. From question to answer. From crime to rope."

His gaze shifted briefly to Jeanne. In the half-light she had gone still as a moored boat in frost.

"And you?" he asked. "You are...?"

"Nobody," Jeanne said. Her voice was flat as water. "Just a woman with bad luck in customers."

"Bad luck," Lacombe repeated. "Yes. Paris has plenty of that." His eyes returned to Eliza. "And some people seem to bring more of it with them."

Jeanne's fingers twitched on the boat-hook. Eliza saw it, weighed the odds, and cut across the moment before courage could get anyone killed.

"Lieutenant," she said mildly. "If you mean to question us, may I suggest we do it where someone might think to remember it? I prefer witnesses to rumours. You, I suspect, like to be seen obeying the law."

Lacombe tilted his head. "You are trying to negotiate with the man who can have you arrested."

"I am trying," Eliza said, "to spare you the trouble of explaining lost prisoners to your captain."

For a heartbeat, no one spoke. Then Lacombe laughed once, not kindly.

"Very well," he said. "We'll talk. Up there."

He jerked his chin toward the broad curve of the bridge. The guards shifted, sabres clinking.

Eliza leaned close to Jeanne, voice barely a breath. "Go."

Jeanne was already moving. By the time Lacombe turned to check, the barge was a darker shadow slipping back under the arch, her pole digging into the current with silent power.

Lacombe made a small, irritated sound. "If I'd wanted her," he said, "I would have called for her first. You two will do for now."

He stepped aside, making a courteous little gesture with the hand that wasn't near his sword.

"After you, madame."

Eliza went, head high. Michael followed, feeling the stone steps rise under his feet like a gallows. The top of the bridge was a different world—open air, the smell of the river, the glow of lanterns along the parapet. Evening traffic had thinned but not vanished. A cart stacked with firewood rattled by; a woman with a basket of eels paused to gawk; two students in shabby coats argued furiously about some point of philosophy neither would keep when rent came due.

Witnesses. Just as Eliza had wanted. Lacombe steered them to the centre of the span, where the Seine sprawled on both sides, black and patient. His men fanned out, not quite blocking escape but making any attempt look suicidal.

He faced Eliza, his breath just visible in the chill air.

"Ask," she said, as if inviting him to choose a fish at market.

"Why are you in Paris?" Lacombe said at once.

"Because a man died," Eliza replied.

"Which man?" His smile didn't move, but his eyes sharpened.

"The kind who would be dead if I named him," she said. "Ask something cleverer."

A faint ripple of amusement moved through the small knot of onlookers forming at a cautious distance. Nothing like a woman pricking an officer's pride to pull eyes.

Lacombe's jaw ticked.

"Very well," he said. "Where will your brandy land?"

"In cups," Eliza said. "Or on the ground. That depends on God and men with guns."

He shifted his attention to Michael, as if adjusting a lens.

"And you?" he said. "What are you?"

Michael felt the river at his back, the drop, the cold weight of the coin in his pocket, the tug of two centuries the wrong way. He let Cornwall roughen his vowels.

"A pair of hands," he said.

"Hands hang," Lacombe replied.

"Not if they're busy," Michael said, surprising himself with the steadiness in his voice.

A couple of bystanders smirked. The eel-seller snorted. Lacombe's gaze cooled another degree.

"So," he said. "We have a woman who talks too well and a man who doesn't fear rope enough. Interesting."

He turned back to Eliza.

"Who sent you to Mercier?" he asked.

"Who sends anyone anywhere?" she said lightly. "Coin, need, hunger."

His nostrils flared. "You are not clever enough to dance around this forever, madame. Men talk. Papers talk. Even barrels talk, when one knows how to listen. I know you met Gulliver's people. I know you sniffed around the Quai. I know you spoke to a wine seller, who now pretends not to know his own stock."

"You know a great many things," Eliza said. "None of them useful to you."

"You think not?" He stepped closer, so close Michael could smell cheap cologne failing to hide the tang of metal and sweat. "I know Isaac Gulliver plays his games here now. I know he has friends in Whitehall and fools in Normandy. I know he uses little coastal rats like you to run in the dark where he cannot be seen."

"You know his name," Eliza said. "If you knew how to hold him, Lieutenant, you'd rattle when you walked with all the medals. We are small change. Chasing us is a waste of brass."

A murmur rose. Lacombe heard it. Pride is a thin glass; public scorn cracks it.

"You mock the law," he said quietly.

245

"I mock you," she said even more quietly. "The law is thicker than this bridge. It was here before you, it will be here after you. I just sail round it when it puts its rocks in the wrong place."

Michael saw the moment Lacombe nearly lost his temper. The fingers on his sabre twitched. The guards leaned in, waiting.

Then a drum rattled at the far end of the bridge.

Not the playful tapping they'd heard all day, but the hard, deliberate cadence of the Garde Nationale marching on some other errand. A file of soldiers came into view, shoulders squared, muskets at the ready, faces set in the effort of looking exactly as determined as the law required.

The crowd shifted, hungry for spectacle. Lacombe saw them, saw the other uniforms, saw the watching eyes.

"You will leave Paris," he said. "Today."

"We were going to," Eliza said.

"You will not return."

"We will," she said, smiling—because he could not arrest a prophecy.

For a second, their gazes locked. Then he stepped aside, pride and circumstance compelling it.

"Go," he said. "Before I remember I do not care for witnesses."

Eliza walked past him as if they had concluded a polite business agreement. Michael followed, the guards' shoulders brushing his as he went. Only when they had crossed the bridge and turned into a quieter street did Eliza let her breath out through her teeth.

"Bribes?" Michael asked.

"Later," she said. "He'll want them. I'd rather he ask for them than for our heads."

"Do we actually leave Paris?"

"Not tonight," she said. "Not while we still have use of it."

"You told him—"

"I told him what would make him sleep a little easier." She gave a thin, exhausted smile. "Men like

Lacombe are much easier to step around when they think they've drawn a line."

They didn't risk returning to the inn. By the time the lamps were lit along the rue Saint-Honoré, they had walked enough crooked loops that even Michael's bones had lost track of direction. Eliza paused under the eaves of a bakery, watching the flow of people, weighing.

"We need a roof," Michael said.

"We need a roof that doesn't know our names," Eliza replied.

A small boy appeared at her elbow, as if summoned by thought. It was the same quick-eyed runner who had brought Gulliver's warning.

"Madame," he said, breath puffing in the cold. "From the Englishman."

He held out another scrap of paper. Eliza took it, opening it against the lamplight. Three words, in Gulliver's brisk, ugly hand:

Rue du Renard. Tonight.

No signature. None needed.

Eliza crumpled the paper, slipped it into her glove. "Come," she said.

They followed the boy through streets that grew narrower and meaner—past a boarded-up church with slogans scrawled across its doors, past a line of women queuing at a bakery window for bread that might not last until their turn. One woman had a baby on her hip and another on the way; Michael watched her count her coins three times, still not believing them.

"Here," the boy said at last.

He pointed to a doorway squeezed between a cobbler's and a shop selling cheap tin icons. No sign. No light.

Eliza knocked twice, paused, then once. The door opened a slit, then wider.

Gulliver stood there, hat off, pale hair dampened by the mist. His eyes flicked once to the street before he stepped back.

"Inside."

The room beyond was not quite an inn and not quite a warehouse. It was both and neither: straw pallets along one wall, a rough table, a single shuttered window. A smell of tar, damp cloth, and stew that had been stretched farther than its ingredients. A woman in a plain dress stirred a pot over a brazier; she nodded at Eliza with the wary politeness of someone who had seen too much of other people's business.

"You picked a busy day to annoy the Garde, Trevelyan," Gulliver said.

"Lacombe came to us," Eliza replied. "We simply declined to roll over."

Gulliver gave a short grunt that might have been approval. "He won't leave it there."

"I know," she said. "He told me to leave Paris."

"And you told him—?"

"That I would," she said. "Eventually."

Gulliver's mouth tugged sideways. "He'll hear that as obedience."

"He'll hear what he wants," Eliza said. "Meanwhile we do what we came here for."

250

Gulliver's gaze flicked to Michael, then back to Eliza. "My man at the wine shop says your business there is finished. Mercier is pleased enough, which I take as a bad omen. Jeanne says she'll take you if the river stays honest for one night in a row." He gave a small shrug. "That's all the luck Paris is willing to offer."

"And Durand?" Eliza asked. "You said he had a cousin in customs. I've yet to see a cousin, only a man who smiles too much for an honest Frenchman."

"He asked for a meeting tomorrow," Gulliver said. "Rue aux Ours. He thinks he's snaring you. I think we'll see who's in whose net."

"Tomorrow, then," Eliza said. "We'll hear him. We'll weigh him. And if he's hollow…"

"We throw him in the Seine and see if he floats," Gulliver said calmly. "In the meantime, you sleep."

"I don't sleep in borrowed holes if I can help it," Eliza said.

"You can't," Gulliver replied. "Lacombe's men have your old inn under watch. New faces behind the counter. Old faces gone. Best you leave no footprints of your own tonight."

Eliza looked as though she wanted to argue, then let the fight go.

"An hour, then," she said. "Two. Enough to think with something other than my feet."

Gulliver nodded. "There's stew. Don't ask what's in it."

Michael's stomach answered before he could, loud enough to make the woman at the brazier smile despite herself. The stew was grey and thin, containing more turnip than anything that had once walked on legs, but it was hot, and it filled the hollows. He ate with the dull, ferocious gratitude of a man who'd spent too long thinking about rope and river.

Eliza sat across from him, back to the wall as always, her spoon moving with automatic neatness. Gulliver stood by the shutter, occasionally lifting the edge to glance at the street. Shadows moved beyond:

a man with a sack over his shoulder, a cart with one wheel protesting, a patrol passing in loose formation.

"Why do you do it?" Michael asked when the silence grew thick. "You could have walked away. After Jacques. After Newgate. You could have gone to ground somewhere the sea can't find you."

Eliza's spoon paused, hovering over the bowl.

"Because walking away doesn't un-hang anyone," she said. "Because there are men in London getting fat off taxes on bread that never reaches the plates. Because this trade owes me a life." She looked up, eyes steady. "And I mean to collect interest."

Gulliver made a small approving sound. "Sentiment will drown you," he said. "Arithmetic keeps you afloat. She understands that much."

"And you?" Michael asked.

Gulliver's pale eyes narrowed. "I do it," he said, "because I'm better at it than the men who'd do it without me. And because the law isn't half as good as it thinks at feeding people. The King takes his share before the poor even smell the loaf." He shrugged. "If

I must choose thieves, I prefer the ones who give something back."

Michael thought of Looe. Of Mary's bread. Of Ferris's quiet accounting. Of Jory watching the road with that hollow, wary gaze. Of the tin under the floorboard in the cottage and the coin in his own pocket, warm from his hand and two lifetimes.

"You're still a thief," he said.

Gulliver's smile was brief and without apology. "So are you. You stole yourself out of whatever life you had before you came to that cliff."

Michael swallowed. The stew curdled in his stomach.

Eliza's look cut across the table, sharp but not unkind.

"Enough," she said. "He still owes me another crossing before you break him open like a cask."

Gulliver made no apology. "You'll want to be at Rue aux Ours by mid-morning," he said. "Durand likes to show off on a fat stomach. I'll meet you there.

If I'm late, assume it's because someone is trying to hang me and improvise accordingly."

He straightened his coat, checked the pistol-cane by habit, and nodded once.

"Rest while you can. Paris works best when you're too tired to argue with it."

He left as he had come—without ceremony, stepping into the city like a man stepping into his own shadow.

Eliza watched the door close behind him, the candle's flame shivering in the draft he left.

"He could have at least told us where the damned bed is," she muttered.

But he had—just not kindly.

Michael remembered the vague gesture Gulliver had made toward the stairs, the offhand mention of a room.

"Top of the stairs," Michael said. "He meant the attic."

Eliza snorted. "Of course he did."

She lifted the candle and climbed. The steps creaked under her boots. Michael followed, feeling the air turn colder with each riser. At the landing the low attic door stuck, then gave way with a tired groan.

The candlelight pushed back the dark. Low rafters, a wash-stand with a cracked pitcher, a single narrow bed with blankets that had survived more winters than they should have.

Eliza wrinkled her nose.

"I need to wash. Paris gets into every pore."

She pointed at him. "Turn around. And keep turned."

Michael moved to the small window where frost feathered the glass. Outside, Paris hunched beneath them: chimneys coughing smoke, shadows moving over roofs, distant wheels grumbling across stone.

Behind him came the quiet rustle of cloth. Boots shifted on the floorboards. A faint breath. He fixed his eyes on the glass, but the glass betrayed him.

It held her reflection. Eliza lifting her shirt to wipe under her arms with a damp cloth, brisk and unembarrassed. A pale sweep of skin. The curve of her shoulder. The calm, utilitarian confidence of someone shaped by hard years, not softened by them.

And then the song began in his head.

Without warning.

Without mercy.

Not here.

Not now.

Inside him.

How can you just walk away from me…

Against All Odds. Mara's voice. Mara's song. The one piece of the future that refused to let go.

For a heartbeat, the attic dissolved—replaced by a warm Yorkshire kitchen, flour dust on the counter, the radio humming softly, Mara smiling at him as if she held the rest of his life in her pocket.

His chest tightened. He gripped the windowsill, grounding himself in splintered wood and cold glass.

"You can look now," Eliza said.

By the time he turned, she was tying her hair back, shirt straightened, eyes unreadable in the candlelight flicker. They took turns sleeping. Eliza lay on the pallet nearest the door, cloak wrapped around her, boots still on. Michael sat with his back against the wall, the guinea turning between his fingers in the poor light. The woman at the brazier dozed in her chair, arms folded, head on her chest.

Michael listened to Paris muttering beyond the shutters: wheels, voices, a burst of drunken song, a baby crying somewhere above, someone shouting for a lost dog, a lost child, or lost hope. The city never quite slept; it only changed the subject.

Eventually, Eliza shifted, eyes opening as if she had never truly closed them.

"Your turn," she said.

He hesitated. "Can you rest?"

"Enough," she said. "Tomorrow we listen to a man lie for his life. It's easier when you're not falling over."

He lay down on the pallet she'd vacated. Her warmth lingered in the blanket. For a heartbeat, it felt like home—a word that belonged to another century, another kitchen, another bed.

He closed his eyes, and sleep came quicker than he deserved. The dream was kind at first. Mara in the kitchen, the radio on, some song he knew every word of and could not bring himself to hum. The baby in the pram making soft, questioning noises, not crying yet but weighing the possibility. The smell of toast.

"You're miles away," Mara said, smiling. "Come back."

He reached for her—

—and woke to the rasp of a bolt.

Eliza was upright, hand on the knife at her belt. The door creaked; a shape filled the gap. For a moment, Michael thought Lacombe had come early. Then the woman at the brazier relaxed.

"Jules," she said.

The boy from the street appeared again, hat askew, cheeks flushed from the cold.

"Message," he said, panting. "From Mercier."

Eliza's jaw tightened. "Well?"

The boy held out a grubby slip of paper. She glanced at it, then passed it to Michael. Three words, in a different hand this time—tight, precise, French.

Rue aux Ours. Pas seul.

"Not alone," Michael translated.

"No," Eliza said. "We knew that already. Durand will bring friends. Men who don't ask questions before they hit things."

"Lacombe?" Michael asked.

"Perhaps," she said. "Perhaps just another piece on the board."

She tied her hair back with quick, efficient fingers, retied her cloak, checked the small flat pistol in its holster and the knife at her belt.

"Come on," she said. "Let's go meet the man who thinks he can sell us the Seine."

Michael rose, every hour of the last two days heavy in his bones.

"Paris by day," he said, "no mercy at all."

Eliza's mouth twisted. "That's all right," she said. "Neither have we."

They stepped into the morning together, the city's cold breath rolling over them like surf.

Paris watched. Paris waited. Somewhere near the Rue aux Ours, Isaac Gulliver and a man called Durand were already deciding whether Eliza Trevelyan and Michael—once Graham in another world—would walk away richer, or not at all.

Chapter Eleven

Shadows on the Seine

The fog of smoke and noise that cloaked the streets at night thinned under the winter light, leaving the city exposed, raw as a wound. Market stalls clattered into place along crooked lanes. Hawkers shouted onions, bread, chestnuts, ribbons—voices sharp with need, haggling like knives. Horses stamped in rutted slush that had once been snow. The Seine rolled sluggish and brown, barges pushing through ice floes like tired beasts, their hulls groaning against the current—a low, steady sound that traveled under everything, like a thought too heavy to name.

Eliza walked with her hood low, cloak brushing the slick cobbles. Michael—Graham somewhere inside the skull that remembered radio static and supermarket lights—kept close at her shoulder. His boots hunted for purchase in the muck. His eyes measured the city's appetite. Every turn offered a new stink, a new argument, a laugh with no joy. A woman poured grey water into the gutter; it steamed before vanishing into the city's veins. A boy darted between legs with a tray of hot chestnuts, a grin too old for his face. A veteran with one sleeve pinned empty sold flints from a blanket, staring past his customers into a battlefield that had not released him.

"Keep close," Eliza murmured. "Paris notices who walks alone."

Their carriage left them near the Rue aux Ours, a maze of warehouses, taverns, and men who knew the worth of a barrel before it was tapped. The streets here smelled of wet rope, horse, spilled wine, and the sour trace of river mud dragged up on boots. Isaac Gulliver waited where he had said—broad as a door, pale eyes restless beneath a cocked hat, cane in hand as if it were an extension of his will.

"Late," he said as they approached, Dorset in his mouth cutting through the French chatter like a hawk through pigeons.

"The road was slow," Eliza replied. Not apology—just fact.

"Paris is slower." His gaze skimmed the street, weighing exits, counting witnesses. Then his chin angled toward the shadowed mouth of an alley where a man leaned as if carved into the stone. "That's our would-be partner. Claims he's Durand's kin."

"Durand's dead," Michael said quietly.

"Aye," Gulliver answered. "But the debts aren't."

The man pushed off the wall as they approached. His coat was fine enough, though the cuffs had been turned twice and pressed back with care. His smile revealed more teeth than warmth. His eyes were quick, always moving—counting, measuring, deciding where to put a knife if the afternoon went sideways.

"Eliza Trevelyan," he said in smooth French. "Isaac Gulliver. And a new face."

"Hands," Eliza said. "He lifts things."

The man chuckled. "Then we are all colleagues."

He placed a hand lightly to his chest.

"Étienne Marot. Cousin to the late Durand."

Eliza's eyebrow arched. "Durand has cousins?"

"Had," Marot corrected pleasantly. "Now he has debts. I inherit both."

She glanced at Gulliver. "Truth?"

Gulliver shrugged. "Who cares? As long as we get what we need."

Marot's smile sharpened, pleased by the practicality. "Then we understand each other already."

He gestured for them to follow.

"This way. We speak where walls do not listen so loudly."

Marot led them through the narrowing throat of the alley, boots whispering over damp cobbles, until they reached a modest warehouse squeezed between a cooper's yard and a tannery. Not one of Durand's old showy fronts—this was a working building with scuffed timbers, iron bolts, and the faint, honest smell of stored goods.

A man outside rolled a barrel into place, nodded at Marot, and vanished again without ceremony.

"This is mine," Marot said. "Durand kept his lies in bigger buildings. I keep truths in smaller ones."

He unlocked the padlock with a key hung from a strip of leather at his belt. The door groaned, but not with neglect—just with winter.

Inside, light slanted through high windows, catching dust like drifting ash. The space was low-ceilinged, practical, and full: casks stacked in ordered rows, crates stencilled with ports on the Bay of Biscay, bundles wrapped in hessian. Nothing staged. Nothing showy. Everything real.

Marot watched them take it in.

"Eliza Trevelyan," he said softly, "I cannot resurrect your Durand. But I can replace him."

"Show us," she replied.

He crossed to a workbench and uncovered several items:

— a small wrapped sample of dark leaf for tobacco mixes,

— a narrow cask-head lifted to show clean grain spirit,

— dried fruit sealed with wax,

— a bolt of French cloth, dyed better than anything Cornwall saw honestly.

"These," Marot said, "are the shapes of tomorrow's cargo. What your lanes need. What Paris can still provide—if someone bold enough stands between the law and the river."

Michael lifted a sample. The tobacco leaves were crisp, not brittle. The cloth smooth as water. He didn't know how to judge smuggling goods, but he knew quality when he touched it.

"Good enough?" Marot asked Eliza.

"Good enough to start," she said.

Gulliver sniffed the grain spirit, swirled it, and nodded once. "This will fetch double in Dorset."

Marot smiled. "Triple, if you tell the right story."

Eliza folded her arms. "Durand had a cousin. How convenient for you."

"A misfortune for him," Marot said. "A necessity for me. And an opportunity for you."

Michael watched him. Watched the confidence, the angles, the calculation. This was a man stepping into a dead man's shoes, knowing they still had blood on them.

Eliza's voice sharpened. "Durand had enemies. They won't welcome you stepping into his place. Or us for agreeing to it."

Marot's smile thinned. "Let them be unhappy. They were thieves pretending to be merchants. I am a merchant who knows how to deal with thieves."

"And if they disagree?" Michael asked quietly.

Marot's eyes flicked to him, assessing. "Then we shall all discover who Paris listens to now."

He closed the samples again with the same tidy precision he had shown in opening them. "But first, we sign nothing. We agree nothing. Not until I have proven my worth. And not until I have delivered you safely back across the river."

"Across the Channel," Gulliver corrected.

"One step at a time, monsieur."

Marot tapped the doorframe with a light knuckle. "For now you need shelter and anonymity. Paris is thick with men who believe Durand owed them something. They will not care whether you are here for business or for blood."

He ushered them out and locked the warehouse behind him, careful as a man locking up a church.

"We go to the wine merchant's room," he said. "Neutral ground. And then we discuss prices."

They crossed the Rue aux Ours again, threading through fishmongers, rope-makers, and men shouting odds over crates of oysters. Marot moved like he owned every shadow, every turning; he spoke the language of danger without a word.

He led them through the wine-merchant's back door into a low, narrow room where mould clung stubbornly to one wall and candle grease had colonised the wood. It was neither pleasant nor welcoming, and it did not need to be. Smugglers rarely trusted rooms that tried to impress.

Marot poured wine that smelled of iron and impatience, set out chipped cups, and placed a small ledger at the centre of the table — not Durand's showy tome, but a slim journal, pages inked with real figures and real names.

"My routes," Marot said. "My contacts. My risks. I offer partnership. Nothing more."

Gulliver flipped the ledger open, scanning a few lines with an unreadable expression. Eliza leaned over his shoulder, brow tightening just slightly — not suspicion, but calculation.

Marot's eyes never left them, patient as a gambler waiting for a turn. Michael felt the weight of Paris pressing at the edges of the room, felt eyes where there were none.

Eliza snapped the ledger closed with quiet authority. "All right," she said. "You're not Durand. But you're better than nothing, and Paris is a storm waiting for someone to walk into it."

Marot inclined his head. "Then let us walk carefully."

Before they could move further, a sharp cry split the street — gutter-born, urgent. Marot stiffened.

"Durand's men," he said quietly. "They saw you. They think you come to claim what he owed."

Gulliver's hand tightened on his cane. "Then we leave before they ask questions we don't care to answer."

Marot went to the door, listening, then turned back. "This way. Out the back. Quickly."

They slipped through the wine-merchant's back door into a narrow yard that smelled of vinegar, broken barrels, and cats hardened by winters crueler than most men. Marot moved without flourish or panic — a man used to stepping sideways when danger came head-on.

"Stay close," he murmured. "Durand's men are not disciplined, but they are loud. They will want to make a display."

"A display of what?" Michael asked.

"Ownership," Marot replied. "Of a dead man's shadow."

He guided them through a slit of an alley, washing lines sagging overhead like tired banners. Voices carried — angry, searching, uncertain. Someone shouted Marot's name. Another spat Durand's.

Eliza didn't falter. "They're arguing," she said.

"Seconds," Marot corrected.

The alley spat them into a wider market street dense with baskets and barter. Eliza plucked an apple from a stall and tossed it to Michael without breaking stride.

"Eat," she said. "Look like a man who isn't being hunted."

He bit, sharp and sour, grounding him in the moment.

Behind them came the clang of a crate kicked over, the bark of a man trying to appear important in front of lesser men.

"Move," Gulliver murmured.

They moved.

Eliza's pace was deliberate — not rushed, but purposeful, weaving through the crowd with a smuggler's instinct for cover. Marot cut through a knot of onion sellers, then into a tannery yard where hides hung heavy as grief and the stink punched the back of the throat.

A ladder leaned against a wall. Eliza climbed without hesitation. Michael followed, boots slipping on cold wood. Gulliver came last, cane tucked under an arm until he reached the roof.

Above them, Paris spread under a bruise-coloured sky — roofs clenched together, chimneys coughing smoke like grudges, the river glinting dull as a blade.

"Across," Eliza said.

She didn't run. She flowed, skirts whispering against slate. Michael followed, arms out, breath harsh. A tile broke under his heel, clattering into a courtyard; a pot shattered. Shouts rose below.

Something iron-strong closed on his arm. Gulliver's grip.

"Eyes front," the smuggler growled. "You look where you're going, not where you might die."

Below, soldiers shouldered through canvas stalls, sabres rattling. A musket cracked; dust leapt from the ridge three feet from Michael's boot.

He didn't look back.

They ran until the roofs ended. A stairwell punched down into a crowded market. Eliza dropped through, landing as if she'd been born to fall. Michael tumbled after, nearly toppling a barrel of eels. The vendor cursed, then froze as Eliza flicked a coin into his palm without breaking stride.

"Blend," Gulliver murmured.

Michael did — shoulders slumped, face slack, just another man running late on nothing important.

The soldiers thundered into the square moments later, loud and lost. A goose got free, outrunning three of them; baskets toppled; people shrieked. The captain swore with the full vocabulary of a man who had misplaced both quarry and dignity. He waved his men down another street.

"Good."

They threaded through the chaos and into a wine-shop whose innkeeper knew better than to ask questions. A chin-flick toward the back door was all they needed. They crossed a yard where a boy with a cleft lip watched them, then looked away, having learned early that attention was expensive.

"Riverside," Eliza said. "Closest exit they won't expect."

Marot nodded once. "The river eats tracks."

The lane to the Seine was a seam of damp and muttered business. They emerged under a sky the colour of hammered lead. Barges groaned against the current. Lamps coughed small halos of light into the fog.

This was Paris at its truest, hungry, watchful, waiting to decide who might be worth sparing.

A voice came from the shadow of a mooring bollard.

"Madame Trevelyan."

The woman who stepped into the half-light wore a man's coat cut down and a cap that failed to tame hair too stubborn to stay hidden. Her hands were scarred, which in Paris was as good as a passport. Jeanne.

"You are Trevelyan," she said. "I am Jeanne. And word says you seek water quieter than the roads."

"Dover," Eliza said. "Tonight, if tide allows."

Jeanne spat into the water — blessing and curse both.

"Pont au Change. Moonset. Crates marked for Rouen. Flour on the manifest. Flour on top if anyone lifts the lid. You stay low, stay silent, and stay lucky."

"We'll bring coin," Eliza said.

"Bring faces that don't invite questions."

Jeanne melted back into the fog as if pulled by the river itself.

Michael exhaled slowly. The Seine's black water rolled beneath them like a judgment.

Eliza's sleeve brushed his. "Stay close. Paris eats the unguarded."

Something in him tightened — not fear, not quite. More like recognition. As if he'd stepped into a world that understood the quiet, necessary danger of survival.

They moved upriver.

A patrol shouted certificates and quittances near the fish market. A customs sergeant, cheeks reddened by cold and wine, swaggered toward them.

"Papers," he demanded, already pleased with himself.

Eliza produced a folded packet — forged, but beautifully so — and held it loosely.

The sergeant sniffed near her, insolent with practice.

"Where do you go?"

"Where the river goes," she said.

He didn't like it. But he couldn't argue with it either. His gaze slid to Michael. "Not from here."

"No," Eliza said. "But he knows how to carry things. He knows how to keep quiet."

She let a pouch slip into the sergeant's hand so subtly his fingers closed on it before his pride did.

He stepped aside.

They passed.

Michael felt the soft give of escape under his boots and committed its feel to memory. It surprised him—that almost gentle sensation of slipping free of danger without noise, without blood, without the shriek of something breaking. He wondered if every escape felt like this in Eliza's world: quiet, temporary, the calm before someone noticed the gap where you had been.

Eliza angled her body close enough that her cloak brushed his sleeve. "Don't look back," she murmured. "Paris grows eyes when watched."

Gulliver exhaled once, a thin plume of breath in the cold air. "And noses," he added. "Come on."

They threaded deeper into the streets toward their next errand. Paris shifted around them—the pitch of voices, the churn of boots, the restless movement of a city that hadn't yet decided whether to tolerate them or spit them out. Michael sensed the change first by sound: men shouting over each other a few lanes behind, voices scraping against stone.

Eliza heard it next. "Marot's rivals," she muttered. "They've started hunting shadows."

"Shadows are cheap prey," Gulliver replied, "but noisy. Keep going."

They moved along the edge of the fish market where the river's smell thickened—iron, scale, and old salt. Stalls clattered open, buckets slopped, and a woman yelled prices until her voice cracked. Guards patrolled in loose clusters, too bored to be sharp, too cold to be thorough. Favre's forged papers burned warm against Eliza's ribs.

A cluster of customs officers was demanding papers from everyone who came close to the quay. The sergeant—red-cheeked, wind-chapped, and drunk on his own authority—held out a hand as they approached.

"Your documents," he said, eyeing Eliza first, then Michael, his attention lingering too long on the latter.

Eliza passed him the folded packet with an expression that suggested she had better things to do than tolerate delays. The sergeant pretended to read, lips moving with the effort. She stood still, perfectly patient, which unnerved him more than indignation might have.

"And your business today?" he asked, voice sagging under its own attempt at menace.

"Moving goods along the river," Eliza said. "As permitted, unless your instructions have changed since dawn."

The sergeant hesitated. His fingers played over the paper again. A younger guard behind him shifted impatiently.

"Let them go, sergent," the boy muttered. "We've three carts of salt pork to inspect."

Pork. The magic word. The sergeant's attention snapped back to his real priority—food before frostbite.

"Fine," he grunted, handing back the papers with a theatrical sniff. "Don't dawdle."

"We never do," Eliza said.

They passed through, the city's danger falling away behind them by inches—thin, brittle, temporary inches.

Favre's printshop waited just beyond the river lane, its sign discreet and its windows filmed with dust. Inside, the air was thick with ink and old news.

Lead type clicked together like the bones of a small, industrious skeleton.

Favre slid the last of the forged passes across the counter. "For your crates to Rouen," he said. "And the boy, the tall one—his French is terrible, so this one tells officials he is from Lyon and has a throat ailment. They will make him speak less."

Gulliver grinned. "Worth every coin."

Favre shrugged. "Coin feeds my children. Lies feed yours."

Eliza tucked the documents away. "We'll not forget the favour."

"I hope you remember the price first," Favre answered without heat. "Favour is for priests. I deal ink."

Outside, dusk had begun to smudge the edges of the rooftops. Rain spat softly, the kind that never committed to falling but still found its way into the seams of your coat. Paris again hesitated, unsure whether to let them leave.

They ate in a tavern that steamed with the breath of too many bodies and the reek of stew that relied more on onions than meat. Bread thumped onto the table—hard, grey, honest.

"It'll be tomorrow or the next day before Marot's rivals organise," Eliza said, breaking her slice in half. "Tonight they're still deciding who deserves to be angry."

"Useful," Gulliver said. "Stupidity makes room for business."

Michael warmed his hands around a cup of wine that tasted like a rumour of grapes told through smoke. "Do you trust Marot?" he asked.

Eliza took a slow breath. "No. But he wants the trade alive. That makes him predictable."

"And useful," Gulliver added. "Which is better than trustworthy, in most cities."

Michael let that sit. He thought of Cornwall— the raw cliffs, the cold, the air that tasted of salt instead of coal smoke. A world away. And yet it felt closer now than ever, as if Paris were a tide pulling them out by force.

They slept briefly, badly, in a room that creaked every time Michael thought about closing his eyes.

By the time they reached the riverside again the following evening, the city had packed itself tight with its own expectations. Drums thumped somewhere far off, echoing down streets like a heartbeat shared between thousands. Lanterns bobbed. A riot of smells—bread, coal, horse, piss, perfume—wove together until Michael no longer tried to separate them.

Pont au Change rose ahead like a stone spine bridging two halves of a fraught animal.

Jeanne appeared from the shadow of a mooring post as if she'd been carved there. Her crew moved silently behind her, men and women with river-water steadiness.

"Tonight, not a moment later," she said. "The watch is restless. Someone has been shouting old debts in taverns."

"Marot's rivals," Eliza said.

Jeanne grunted. "Then thank whatever saint you keep for choosing the river."

Gulliver hefted one of the sacks on deck and nodded. "Everything's ready."

Jeanne jerked her chin toward the piled flour sacks. "Under. All of you. Think yourselves cargo."

Michael climbed into the shadowed cradle of bags. Their coarse texture scratched his cheek as he lay still. Eliza slid in beside him, cloak brushing his arm. Gulliver settled near the prow.

The barge pushed free.

The river swallowed sound. The city dimmed.

Under the first arch, torchlight flickered down from the roadway above. A woman shouted at someone. A dog barked at nothing.

Under the second arch, a customs skiff slid out, sudden as a thought. Lantern light swung. Jeanne didn't look up. She let the pole drag and the barge drift with the casual innocence of honest work.

"Papers!" the customs man called, triumph already glinting in his voice.

Jeanne passed up Favre's stamped packet without breaking rhythm.

The officer frowned at the ink as if it offended him personally. "Flour for Rouen? At night?"

"The flour keeps better moving than waiting," Jeanne said, "and so do officials. Your captain would tell you that."

A snort of laughter from the second man wobbled the skiff. Jeanne's boy knocked the head from a top sack. Flour breathed out in a soft white cloud.

The lantern-man sneezed explosively.

"Enough," the officer grumbled, wiping his nose. "Go on."

The skiff fell behind.

Michael exhaled—the quietest breath of his life.

Eliza's hand brushed his sleeve once, a silent praise.

The river widened. The city thinned. The night loosened at the seams.

Paris began—slowly, reluctantly—to let them go.

The barge slid onward, carrying them toward the road that would become the road home.

slid onward, carrying them toward the road that would become the road home.

And as the last smudges of the city blurred behind them, Michael felt something he had not expected: the strange, quiet certainty that they would see Cornwall again.

Chapter Twelve

The Road Home

Two nights after Jeanne's barge had slid under Pont au Change and the guards had sniffed their flour and found nothing else, Paris let them go—reluctantly, like a hand unclenching from a throat.

The road out of the city wound like a thread pulled through dirty cloth. By morning, fog lay low on the stones—a grey veil that smudged roofs and chimneys, muffled bells and trapped the stink of the city close to the ground: fat-soot from cookhouses, the iron tang of the river, cabbage boiled to surrender. Carriages rattled past with wheels splashing through slush, horses steaming in the cold. Hawkers shouted bread, onions, chestnuts; a woman croaked oysters until her voice frayed. Somewhere close, a dog barked itself hoarse at shadows it could not catch. Paris refused to blink, even in daylight.

Eliza walked with her hood low, cloak brushing damp cobbles. Michael—still learning how to fit his bones to this century—kept tight at her shoulder. His boots found the deeper puddles; his ears caught the city's noise—hammering hooves, cart wheels shrieking, laughter sharp as knives. Daylight didn't soften Paris. It showed the cracks.

At the Rue aux Ours, their carriage waited, wheels already crusted with mud from a dozen journeys. The driver hunched on the box, breathing steam into gloved hands, eyes shifting as if he feared a last-minute order to turn back.

Eliza's hand caught Michael's sleeve before he reached the door.

"Not yet," she said. "One stop."

The oyster barrow was a low altar of shells, river-wet and piled high. The vendor, a man shrunk by years but hard in the eye, prised one open with a knife more scar than steel.

"Huîtres! Cancale! Toutes fraîches!" he croaked. "Eat while they still breathe!"

Eliza pressed a coin into his palm, took two shells, and passed one to Michael. "Here. You'll need salt in your blood before the road."

He stared at the creature—grey, glistening, sitting like a dare in its own brine. Eliza tipped hers back and swallowed neat, the motion swift as any command. She licked a drop from her lip, eyes cool.

Michael followed. The taste hit hard—salt, iron, mud, something half-alive sliding down his throat. His stomach lurched. He coughed, hand to his mouth, forcing it down with a swallow that burned worse than whisky.

Eliza's brow arched. "What is wrong with you? You'd think you'd never eaten an oyster before."

He wiped his sleeve across his mouth, trying for a grin. "Just thinking about the sea trip back. Hoping it's not rough seas again. I don't fancy a deck pitching under me while I'm full of these."

Her laugh came bright and sudden, quick as broken glass catching light. Not cruel—alive. She shook her head, braid slipping against her cloak.

"You're hopeless," she said, warmth tucked inside it. "Leave the oysters for men who don't fear the tide."

The vendor cackled, three black teeth flashing. Eliza answered him with a line Michael missed, but her tone left the old man grinning as they moved on.

They should have gone straight to the carriage. Instead, Eliza led him two turns deeper into the warren where vendors' cries gave way to the close clatter of needles and shears. A small shop hunched between a baker and a locksmith, its window crowded with bodices and skirts in faded hues.

Michael stopped. "Why here?"

Eliza glanced back, something unreadable in her eyes. "Because trade isn't all barrels and guns. Paris teaches you to wear masks. Sometimes a dress is sharper than a knife."

Inside, warmth thick with wool and dye swallowed them. Bolts of cloth leaned against every wall, a rainbow bruised by candlelight. The dressmaker was a narrow woman with pins bristling from her sleeve and spectacles at the end of her nose. Her French lilted like a song; her eyes cut like shears.

Eliza spoke low and quick, then turned. "He'll take my measure."

Michael managed to study a bolt of silk while the tape circled her shoulders, waist, and hips. She stood still, calm, as though armour were being fitted. The deep green caught him; he imagined it under Cornish light and could not quite look away.

When the dressmaker bustled off, Eliza's eyes found him. "You disapprove?"

He swallowed. "I was thinking you'd look… different. In colour."

"Different doesn't keep men honest," she said, but a flicker crossed her face—amusement, perhaps something softer. She ordered one gown in plain wool—work—and then touched the green.

"And that. For Cornwall. Not for Paris."

He almost asked why she'd let him see the choice, but the words stuck. When the woman named the price, Eliza reached for her purse; Michael set his hand over hers and laid down coin enough to cover both. Eliza looked at him—not quite frowning, not quite grateful.

"You don't buy armour for the captain," she said, but she let him do it.

The green was wrapped and tied with string. Michael carried the parcel as carefully as a barrel with a fractured stave, feeling foolishly as if every eye in Paris might read the secret in paper and twine.

Only then did they climb into the coach. The driver clicked his tongue, cracked his whip, and Paris began to fall away—markets to workshops to ragged edges of field, smoke trailing thin from cottages. Behind them, somewhere in those streets, men would begin to ask where Durand had gone and who had taken his voice from the city. Michael felt it like weather on his neck.

Soon the roads stretched northwards, the city shrinking behind them like a scab you don't dare scratch.

By mid-morning the coach jolted and limped to a stop. A trace had snapped on the rear team; the driver climbed down, swearing at leather that had forgotten how to be leather. While he fussed, the fog thinned to show a hamlet—crooked well, a Madonna nailed to limewash, a girl of ten barefoot in the frost selling chestnuts from a smoking brazier.

Eliza bought a paper cone and handed it to Michael.

"Eat," she said. "You look the colour of old rope."

The chestnuts burned his fingers and steadied his stomach. The girl's eyes flicked from Eliza's cloak to Michael's boots to the parcel in his hands.

"Pour madame?" she asked, nodding at the bundle.

"For Cornwall," Eliza said.

The girl nodded solemnly, as if that were a place one posted letters to. She watched them climb back into the coach with the measured gaze of a child already counting risks.

They rolled on. Fields ran pale and stubbled; hedgerows wore lace of frost; crows hopped like punctuation. Once, far behind, a rider appeared on the road, then another. They did not gain on the coach, but the sight made Michael's shoulders tighten until a turning and a thicket of beech took them out of view.

"At least one of Lacombe's friends will have our names in his pocket," Eliza said, not looking back. "But he prefers cities. Country makes him itch. We have that, at least."

At noon they reached a toll bridge where soldiers in blue coats lounged with muskets and boredom. The sergeant had a face like an axe head and a taste for coin he pretended to be ashamed of. Papers were examined, purses weighed by eye. Eliza's French softened by a hair; a folded card with wax appeared where Axe-face's fingers could feel it without quite seeing. His thumb tested the thickness; his mouth did the work of disapproval while his hand did the work of acceptance. The muskets stayed where they leaned. The coach creaked on. Michael let out the breath he hadn't admitted holding.

That evening they reached a posting inn whose sign squealed on its chain. The common room roared. Smoke pressed itself to the beams and would not be moved. Michael's stomach had recovered enough courage to consider the stew; it lost some when a man at the next table slammed his fist and snarled about flour cut with plaster, bakers jailed and loosed, soldiers drinking what they could not pay for. Words—liberty, bread—brushed the room in sharp strokes. A pamphlet seller slipped from table to table like a wren among hooves, his bundle clutched tight as a prayer.

Eliza watched everything and ate quickly, her spoon steady as a clock. "Sleep while we can," she said. "Tomorrow they'll be counting the horses on the road and arguing who owns them."

They slept badly. Wind set the shutters gossiping; the floorboards answered back. Once in the night, wheels rattled past at a furious pace, hooves striking sparks; Michael lay awake, picturing Lacombe's neat hat and the men who liked him. Before dawn, the driver hammered on doors and cursed the frost. By first light, they rattled northwards again, hooves thudding a rhythm the cold could not break.

A mile beyond a village whose name Michael lost as he heard it, the coach slowed. Ahead, a tangle of carts blocked the road. A wheel lay snapped, spokes splayed like ribs. Men argued; a woman held a crying child and swore with the disciplined venom that makes air wince.

Eliza leaned out. "We go round," she told the driver.

"Ditch is deep," he said. "Full of last week's water."

"Then we lighten," she answered, already unlatching the door. She stood at the broken cart before Michael had gathered the parcel and followed.

"Where's your jack?" she asked the farmer.

"Jack?" He stared as if she'd asked for the moon.

Eliza sighed, shrugged off her cloak, and set her shoulder under the corner. "Lift," she told Michael, and he did, feeling old muscle memory wake in his back and arms—scaffold boards, steel beams, all the things he'd shifted in another life. The farmer and his boys scrambled to wedge timber under the axle.

"Again," she said. The second heave raised the cart enough to lever the wheel free. A spare was fetched; pin seated; nut coaxed home. The woman spat into the ditch in triumph. The road unclogged.

"Merci, madame," the farmer managed, tipping his hat. His boys stared with the helpless admiration of lads who had just seen the impossible done.

Eliza nodded them off, shrugged back into her cloak, and climbed in with her breath not even quickened.

Michael watched her hands smooth the wool over her knees. "You could lead a war," he said.

"Wars are for men who like crowds," she replied. "I prefer tides."

At Amiens, they changed horses. The ostler's breath smoked while he buckled traces; his hands moved with the speed of a man who had more mouths than coin. Inside, the inn smelled of onion, damp wool, and the sweet-sour of wine nobody loved. A fiddler tried to teach a tune how to behave; the tune refused. Two soldiers at the door watched Eliza with cat eyes; when her gaze met theirs, their eyes slid away with the guilty grace of professional cowards.

They set out before dawn for Calais. The road shouldered into beechwood and narrowed to a seam; branches clicked like bones. Somewhere a fox barked; silence answered. Frost skittered across ruts like a living thing. Michael felt the old ache of leaving in his chest—the sense that eyes were behind every tree trunk, waiting to see if these travellers would be worth remembering.

Calais harbour stank of fish and tar, gull shit, and men who had lived too long on salt. Masts made a forest against a pewter sky. The Channel lay pewter to match it, cold and endless. Michael's stomach tightened.

They boarded a brig bound for Dover—canvas patched, ropes stiff with brine. The deck tilted beneath them as they cast off; memory rose with it: the storm, the hammock, the line burning into his forearms while Eliza shouted, Hold fast.

"Calm today," the master said, as if promising a favour he might withdraw. It was—only a slow heave and a sighing wind. Even so, the world tipped under him, and his belly answered old orders. He set his elbows to the rail and watched grey water slide past, refusing to count the distance down.

Eliza faced the wind, eyes on a horizon he could not see. The green parcel was lashed high in the after-cabin where spray couldn't reach it. Thinking of it there—folded, safe—steadied him more than the rail. It was a small, absurd piece of future in a world that spent itself mostly on the present.

"Why the dress?" he asked at last, not looking.

"For Mary," she said at once, and for a second he thought she meant the woman at the Jolly, then saw her mouth move. "For the men then. For the village. Sometimes they need a sight of what they're fighting for that isn't bread. A colour helps. A feast for the eye costs less than meat."

"And you?"

She considered the horizon. "I'll allow myself a colour if we live to spend it."

They reached Dover with only a gull's insolence to trouble them. Timbers groaned in relief. Men came aboard with accents Michael's bones understood before his ears. Customs poked, sniffed, and made notes to justify their board wages. Eliza's papers were English now, her answers brief and shaped like bars questions couldn't slip through. They were waved into England's winter—hedgerows, flint, and the brown patience of fields.

They took the old road west. Canterbury's spire prised the sky and let it close. At a wayside yard outside Maidstone, a man in a snug brown coat and a hat too tidy for a roadman admired their coach the way a butcher admires a calf.

"Fine team," he said to the driver.

The driver's mouth shaped yes while his eyes said trouble.

Eliza's fingers brushed Michael's knee—a smallest signal. "We change here," she told the driver.

"Still good light," he protested, eager to be paid and done.

"We change," she repeated, dropping two coins into his palm that made agreement the quickest route to dignity.

They swapped to a plainer carriage whose springs had long since ended their quarrel with comfort. Ten miles later, when a tree lay obligingly across the road and three men rose from the ditch with pistols and the wrong smiles, Eliza only shook her head.

"It's always the tidy hat," she said.

The leader began the usual patter—stand, in the King's name, purses—and halfway through noticed Eliza's pistol resting on the window-rail. He forgot his lines.

"No need for—"

"No," she said, cliffs behind the word. "You clear the road and live to wonder whether you should have tried harder. Or you don't, and you learn what gulls eat."

Silence. The men looked at one another and found they weren't heroes. The tree shifted fast; one tried a bow as they climbed back into the hedge. The driver slapped the reins, the coach rolled, and the world exhaled.

"Highwaymen," Michael said, surprised his voice was calm.

"England breeds them like nettles," Eliza answered. "They sting only if you walk into them with your eyes shut."

They ran the miles down like thread. Chalk softened to clay; hedges grew meaner; cottages huddled tight against the wind. They slept a final night in a Dorset hostelry whose beams had heard more lies than sermons and more prayers than either. In the yard at dawn, two men argued over stone and a five-year debt; in the stable, a boy sang to a mare with such patience that the mare closed her eyes. Nettles furred the ditch beyond the gate, dark and wintry—every road's reminder.

By the time a coach dropped them a mile outside Looe, dusk had the village by the throat and shook it. They walked the last stretch. The harbour smelled of kelp and woodsmoke; waves gnawed at the quay as if remembering a grudge. Lamps pricked cottage windows. The air changed—salt sharper, colder, familiar. After Paris's fever, the smallness of the place felt almost like mercy and almost like a trap.

Ferris's bell made the same sound it had last time and would next. Men gathered quick when word ran: Thomas, broad-shouldered, hands scarred; young Will, eyes too bright; old Jago, stooped but sharp. Others too, drawn by the name that pulled them like the tide takes a thrown stick. They looked to Eliza the way a compass needle settles north.

She set her cloak aside and laid the ledger on the table. "François is dead. But Paris isn't closed to us. We have new channels, new names. Gulliver himself has vouched."

Murmurs ran the room—relief, surprise, unease tangled together. Jago spat into the rushes. "Gulliver's word cuts both ways. He'd sell his shadow if the price was right."

Will frowned, voice high with youth. "But if he stands with us—"

Thomas slammed his palm flat. "If he stands with us, we're stronger. If he doesn't, we're meat. Which is it, Eliza?"

Her gaze travelled; calm, steady. "It's risk, as always. Without the trade, we starve. With it, we live."

Still the doubt simmered. Eyes slid. The air thickened with the weight of what-ifs.

Michael felt the moment strain. He wasn't meant to speak—not here, not yet—but silence was worse.

"I was in Paris," he said, rough but firm. "I saw deals struck and men try to bend them crooked. Gulliver called a lie before the man had finished it and made it costly. He's no friend, maybe, but he isn't a fool. Keeping the trade clean pays him same as us."

The room shifted; eyes weighed him—some sharp, some grudging. Thomas's frown eased a notch. Jago's mutter thinned.

Eliza glanced once—flicker of approval, or surprise he'd stepped forward at all. "Two weeks," she said, cutting the moment before it frayed. "Barge east from Paris bound for Dover; from there, Cornwall. Brandy, tobacco, lace—enough to feed the village through spring. It means every hand steady, every voice quiet. No slips. No boasts. You know the cost."

The men thumped the table, not loud but sure. Agreement. Ferris shut his eyes for a breath like a man thanking a god he didn't trust. Mary appeared in the doorway with a basket of mugs, steam rising and something like blessing on her face.

Her eye caught the parcel under Michael's arm. One brow lifted.

"Colour costs less than meat, does it?" she said.

"Sometimes it saves more," Eliza answered.

Mary's mouth twitched. "We'll see if it buys silence." She dealt mugs like absolution.

Later, when the storehouse had emptied into lanes and kitchens, when the square had shrugged them back into themselves, Michael and Eliza took the cliff path without speaking. The sea argued with rock in the old, tired way. Above the gorse, a slice of moon pretended it had new ideas.

At the cottage, he carried the parcel up and set it on the bed. "It will keep," he said, not turning.

"It will," she answered from the doorway, voice looser than it had been in weeks. "If the men run, if the tide obeys, if the French remember our names for coin and forget them for rope."

He looked at her then. The journey had dusted everything with a fine grit—cloak, hair, lashes that made her eyes too sharp to be kind. He wanted to tell her about a kitchen radio in another life, about laughter that sounded like the one she'd let slip at the oyster cart; he wanted to say the word Mara and watch it mean nothing here. He said none of it.

"You're tired," he said.

"So are you."

He thought of the tin beneath the floorboards and the green silk beneath paper—the one a cold promise, the other a warm risk—and felt the weight of both in a world that made weights into destinies. "I'll see Ferris at first light," he said. "Rails for his cellar. Sacks for the kiln."

"Do," she said softly. "And sleep now, while sleep still thinks we deserve it."

She turned away. On the stair she paused. "Michael," she said without looking back. "Thank you. For the dress. For the road." Plain words, unadorned. They settled like another log on the fire— no blaze, more warmth.

When she had gone, he slid the board up out of habit. The tin waited, heavy and patient. He did not lift the lid. He laid his palm flat on the wood and felt the cold creep through. In his pocket, the guinea found its old place and made itself known. He turned it in the firelight—gold making its own small sun— the single thing insisting he was the same man from one day to the next.

He lay back with smoke in his hair, salt under his skin, and the sea doing what it always did. He closed his eyes and saw the green folded in paper; he opened them and saw the beams that held weather off.

Hold fast, he told himself. And now he knew he didn't mean only the cliffs or the tide.

He meant her.

Chapter Thirteen

The Weight of Preparation

The quay smelled of seaweed and woodsmoke. Gulls worried the wind like boys with a new toy. Nets stiffened on walls, sails patched and drying. Dogs nosed the cobbles. An ordinary winter morning—and a calm that felt as if it were waiting to break.

Michael had woken early, the way you do when your body knows work is coming whether the clock agrees or not. The cottage kept its own hours—hearth cough, kettle mutter, a draught that found the same knuckle every dawn. He raked the coals forward, fed them peat and the thin kindling that caught with a sigh, then set the iron kettle near enough to hear it think. Salt pricked the air even indoors; the cliff's breath slipped under the door and made the fire's glow look warmer than it was.

The tin beneath the floorboards had a gravity he could feel through wood and wool. He didn't touch it. He didn't need to. It lived in the place behind his ribs that recorded weights. If he let himself, he could hear it—the softened clink of guineas and pieces of eight, a song that wasn't music but still tuned his blood. He had set the coin—his coin, impossible coin—on the mantel the night before and had to put it away again when it started to become the only thing in the room.

On the settle, wrapped in brown paper and twine, sat the Paris bundle—nothing to look at, everything dangerous. A dressmaker's work folded down to the size of a ledger; the paper smelled faintly of starch and a city that sharpened even kindness to an edge. He did not trust the impulse that had made him buy it, nor the ache that told him he must not give it. Not yet.

He rinsed his hands in the basin; the water took the smell of rope and iron and gave back cold. York slid toward him the way it sometimes did when his fingers went numb: a square of kitchen light, Mara's hair pulled up any old how, a record misbehaving on the stereo. Then the picture shifted, and Eliza stood at a cliff's edge with the wind stitching her cloak to her frame and the word hold fast in her mouth like a blessing delivered as an order.

The cottage felt too small. He stepped outside into wind that fussed at the gorse and walked a short way up the headland, stopping where the path kinked and the sea opened like a door. The horizon wore the grey of old pewter. Below, swell shouldered the rocks and breathed out. Up here the years thinned. It was the strangest thing—how this air could hold both lives at once. He closed his eyes and had a second of the York kitchen and the Minster's bells, and then it was gone, the present shouldering everything else aside. A gull hung, tipping its head as if weighing him. He tipped his head back like a man at confession and said nothing.

A knock at the door broke the quilt of thoughts. Not sharp, not furtive. A neighbour's knock.

Ferris stood there, hat in his hands, scarf damp with sea-mist. His coat carried the smell of iron and oil; you could have found his shop blindfolded by scent alone. He had the look of a man who had spent too long hunched over ledgers and nails, wide across the back but worn at the edges, eyes quick under brows that pretended to be slow.

"Michael." A nod, cautious. "Best I step in."

He did not wait for the invitation, but he would have been welcome even if he had. Ferris moved to the hearth as if the house belonged to him whenever he needed it, which wasn't far from the truth in a place where walls owed each other favours.

"Word is, you're back from France." He held his hands out to the heat, turning them as if roasting his doubts. "And word is, you didn't come empty."

Michael said nothing. He had learnt that a quiet mouth keeps you alive longer than a clever one.

Ferris gave a dry smile that did not bother to reach his eyes. "I don't ask what I don't need to know. But if Eliza's moving barrels, I'll see them shift. Ironmongery doesn't fatten a man through winter. Smuggled brandy does." He rubbed his palms together once, brisk. "And yet."

"And yet?" Michael said.

"The excise men are thick as gulls this month." Ferris shifted to let the kettle have more flame. "Two cutters sit off Fowey. Another near Rame Head, pretending to fish badly. Harker's men took Pentreath's boy on the Rame road last week for a single keg. If we're careless, they'll make a gallows of us."

The kettle sighed. Michael poured willow-bark tea into two chipped mugs; Ferris accepted his with a grimace that meant he would complain and drink it anyway.

"What do you want of me?" Michael asked.

"Tell Eliza. She listens to you." Ferris's eyes measured him, weighing grain for rot. "She may not to me, not as quickly as I'd like. We need new ways. Hide the casks deeper. Move them slower. Keep the carts light—or better yet, don't use carts at all until the moon turns. I can clear the back cellar, but I'd sooner the barrels sat nowhere near the shop floor. The kiln up at Boscawn—" He lowered his voice instinctively, even with only the peat to overhear, "— the old lime pit—may serve again. No revenue man looks for drink where stone used to burn."

Michael pictured it: the scar of the kiln, thistles standing guard, chalk ghosts under the moss. He'd scrambled there in daylight once, hand on gritty brick. In the mouth of it, you could hide a cow and a barrel under her and charge no man for milk.

"She won't slow the tide," he said, because he believed it and because he had learned, too, the shape of her will.

Ferris's mouth made a shape that started as a smile and caught itself. "Then we'd better be sure the tide doesn't drown us."

He set his mug down and hauled his scarf up. "There's buyers waiting. London wants lace, Plymouth wants tobacco, Exeter will drink anything that doesn't taste like rain. If the barrels come, I'll see the coin finds its way. But the King's men have sharper teeth than ever. Remind her."

At the door he paused, hat in his hands, turning the brim. "You've the look of one caught between," he said without heat. "Be sure which side you're on when the night comes, Michael. This trade doesn't forgive hesitation."

When Ferris left, the cottage seemed to lean closer, as if to listen to what he would think next. The fire popped; the kettle hissed at nothing. Michael sat with his mug and let the heat find the cold places in his hands.

Two lives pressed at him from opposite shores. Mara's voice in a warm York kitchen, teasing him about salt he hadn't added. Eliza's voice on a black shore, telling men where to put their feet and where to put their fear. One woman gone beyond reach, one all too near. He had the queer sense that love could belong to two places, and he would be punished by both for daring to believe it.

Outside, a gull screamed like laughter cut by a knife. The tide kept chewing at the shore. Michael, caught between, felt the weight of preparation settle on his shoulders like a yoke.

There is the work you do so the work can be done.

By midmorning he was on the path toward Ferris & Co., where the neat front promised nails and lamps and measuring chains and the back promised nothing to anyone who didn't know how to knock. The sign—& CO., IRONMONGERS — ESTABLISHED 1760—had been freshly gilt, a challenge to the damp. Through the glass, coil upon coil of rope hung like sleeping snakes; drawers of nails had labels in a hand that had been taught to make looped letters by a man who liked order.

Ferris met him at the counter with a ledger that didn't belong to any taxman. "Come on," he said, not looking toward the street. He led Michael through to the clatter and smell—iron, oil, sweat—and then past a stack of hoops and a case of lanterns toward a door that did not promise anything except darkness. The key turned with a small sigh. The air beyond was colder, sweeter, faintly salted from years of wet coats hung to dry.

The back cellar had been the worst-kept secret in the village for longer than anyone would admit. It wasn't a cavern mapped by smugglers with romance in their heads; it was stone and damp and low beams and a practical whiteness of wash on the walls to keep mould from getting the upper hand. Ferris pointed with his chin. "That corner. We can lay three tuns there without them being seen from the stair. If they come searching, we'll have rails over them and sacks of nails. Nails outweigh thirst, even in winter."

A boy—Ferris's nephew, a lad with ink stains on his thumb from trying too hard at his letters— appeared with a broom and a sharp look. He stared at Michael the way boys stare at knives.

"Uncle says you lifted a barrel by yourself," the boy blurted. "Is that true? How do you lift a thing that rolls away when you look at it?"

"With your legs and with a friend," Michael said. "And you look at where it wants to go before it knows."

The boy considered this like scripture. "Do the King's men hate nails?" he added, sweeping at nothing. "Uncle says we'll put nails over the barrels and the King's men will leave them. If they hate nails, why do they have so many in their boots?"

"Because hating a thing never stopped men using it," Ferris said dryly. "Sweep."

The boy swept as if the floor had offended his honour. Ferris lowered his voice. "Not long. We'll not keep them here. It's a mouth. I'd rather the kiln."

"Tonight?" Michael asked.

"Too many eyes," Ferris said. "But watch the road. If Harker's dogs show their snouts, we close early and become men who have always sold hinges and never seen a cask."

They went back up. The bell over the door jangled the way bells do when they are new enough to be proud of being bells. Outside, the day had the colour of pewter; the sea's edge changed its mind between white and grey. Michael crossed the square and cut along a path that led him up over the village into the scrub and gorse toward Boscawn.

The kiln waited where the earth had been taught long ago to harden in a certain shape. It sat like a memory of heat. Bracken had claimed most of the ramp; the pit's lip was greedily green. He climbed down where stones showed a logic of men's hands and stood in a place where countless fires had licked rock to ash. The smell of old lime and damp chalk lived in the stones. A fox had printed a neat story across the dust and left the tail end under a ledge as commentary. A man crouching here could hear the sea without seeing it. The space had the right kind of echo. Two men could roll a barrel in here and lay it behind a stack of broken slates and if they were careful the only witness would be a fox that no one believed.

He mapped it with his feet—entrance, choke point, where to put a man with a reed whistle, where to dump a sack of lime if talk went wrong. Thought like a thief to hide a thief's work. The wind came down the lip and turned his hair into a question.

Back on the path he met Jory and Kit with a handcart that had once belonged to potatoes and now belonged to a dozen lies. Jory's scar looked whiter in the grey light; Kit had a new patch on his coat that did not match anything else he owned.

"Ferris say the word?" Jory asked, breath fogging.

"He said the word and three more," Michael said. "We'll hold before we pour. Kiln's sound. We'll need sacking."

"Got a store of sackcloth in the loft of the capstan house," Kit grunted. "Smells like mice, which will make the brandy smell like mice too if we're not careful, but the excise don't go searching with cats."

They grinned like men who knew a joke about their own deaths and decided to enjoy it while they could. The cart groaned away; Michael followed on foot, choosing ruts that wouldn't tell tales.

On the way down he passed the church where the bell rope hung coiled like a sleeping snake. Old Parson Bray crossed the yard with his cassock caught up out of the mud, face wind-burnt to brick. He nodded at Michael as a man nods to weather— acknowledgment without responsibility. In the porch a woman with a shawl over her hair counted out coppers with winter-swollen fingers for a loaf from Mary's niece. Bread was dear this year; words were cheaper and cut deeper.

Afternoon dropped its shoulder. The light flattened and drained the colour from roofs and hedges; the sea became a ledger you had to squint to read. By three, the storehouse down by the quay had drawn its usual gravity. Men came in twos and threes, some carrying nothing that would upset a parson, others with arms too empty not to be hiding something. Ferris drifted in, having locked his front door for an hour that no sign announced.

Eliza was already there, standing where the light from a high window cut the dust into strokes. She had her ledger open and something of Paris in her face still—the way she had spoken a foreign city into giving her what Cornwall needed. Her braid had dried into the kind of wave women get not from ribbons but from weather. She looked at the men as if they were facts to be laid out, weighed, and then put back into the world with their correct substitutions.

"All right," she said, without bang or scrape. The word found every ear. "Ferris says cutters off Fowey. Harker's boys on the lanes. We change the pattern. Two to a keg. No ponies down the lower track—their prints tell stories. We'll use the gully by the copse and come up behind the kilns. Hide there if the night goes wrong; we can shovel lime over the heads and pretend we've been burning for hours."

"I'll be damned if I—" a man started, but she cut him with a look, not unkind, that said he would be damned if he did not, and sooner.

"We split the load," she continued. "Three in Ferris's back, under rails and nails. Four into Boscawn. Anything left sits in the cliff cave we never talk about. Not the left one; the right, where the water comes up slower. No torches on the headland. No singing like fools. And for the love of your mothers, no boasting in the Jolly. A tongue costs a neck this month."

She started setting watches as if she were setting tables. "Jory at the bend by the ash tree. Kit up above the lime. Tom—you keep the capstan yard until midnight. Stone sober. It's the hinge of the night. No wandering. No sampling."

Thomas Treglown had the decency to pretend to be embarrassed. He saluted with two fingers, as if that could pin his good intentions down. Michael caught it: the unbelief in Thomas's eyes that the order applied to him the way it applied to other men.

"Ferris," she said, "if the revenue walk in, you are selling nails to men with no work and lamps to men with no eyes. Smile like you love their money, and we'll move under it."

Ferris's mouth made a modest theatre of agreement. He had already set the weights on the scale to look like they had always been there.

"And one more thing," Eliza said, voice landing lightly and then holding. "If the night goes to ground, if a man is taken—" she didn't look at Thomas; the room did that for her "—we don't talk him into bravery with our drink. Silence for him is mercy, and silence for us is survival."

There was a murmur that was not argument but the noise men make when asked to be more than they are without being thanked for it. She shut the ledger with a sound that was not a bang and left a small space for questions.

"What if Harker has the lanes from both sides?" Kit asked.

"Then we go to ground and wake with the frost in our hair," she said. "I have no better comfort."

"What of the French?" Jory's voice had a grin in it you couldn't call disrespect. "They still rowing or have they gone to Paris to cut throats with paper?"

"They'll row if we keep our end," she said. "Coin is a boat that will float on any tide."

They started to break—men to their tasks, shoulders finding the shape of weight again. Eliza lifted her head at the same moment Michael did. Some sounds are not sounds; a kind of listening enters a room like weather. She moved and he moved with her without needing to be told, and they found themselves outside where the square took the day into itself, smelling of tar and soap and fish guts.

"Ferris came to you," she said, as if she had sent him and was pleased he had obeyed. "What did you think of the kiln?"

"Good echo. Wrong kind of echo for searchers. It'll do."

Her gaze slid over him and then away, measuring more than geography. "You're quieter," she said.

"I'm thinking," he said.

"Think faster," she said, then softened the line with a breath that wasn't quite a smile. "You did well in Paris."

He felt the heat that lived under embarrassment on its way to something else. "You did," he said. "I followed."

"You held," she said, and for a heartbeat the word held meant something with a shape that was not rope, not barrel, not law.

They took the cliff path for a short stretch to check the sightline from the western bend. The sea rolled as if it had forgotten how to do anything else; the wind had teeth. She walked sure-footed, cloak pulling like a sail, boots reading grit and root. He watched her hands, the way they opened and closed on nothing as if counting seconds, counting men.

"You sleep?" he asked before he decided whether to ask.

"I sleep enough to remember what I must remember," she said. "And you?"

He did not know how to answer a question that asked whether a man could sleep in one century and wake in another without losing his mind between them. "Enough," he said, and the word broke a little.

They stood a while and did not talk; not every silence is debt. When they turned back, the village waited with its doors that claimed to be shut.

The Jolly Sailor had the kind of evening that fills and empties a town. The door wore a bruise of fingerprints. Men who would tell lies about the sea told truths about their wives; men who would boast about their wives told lies about the sea. Mary lifted and lowered tankards with the precision of a surgeon and the mercy of a good priest. Every time she told a man he'd had enough, she was right.

The fire had a strong voice. The dominoes had a weaker one but kept trying. The fiddler tried to teach his bow a tune that had been taught to him by a man who swore he knew how to keep time and turned out to be wrong. A boy by the hearth practised a whistle too near a signal and earned a flick of Mary's cloth on the back of his head. Snatches of talk floated—press gangs in Plymouth, a cow dropped a calf backwards up at Trenant, Parson Bray preached short because his feet were cold.

Michael found the wall he preferred, near enough to see and far enough not to be seen. Mary set a pint in front of him with a look that said don't get clever. "One," she told him. "And keep your ears open and your mouth closed. Ears make money; mouths make widows."

"Preaching pays?" he asked.

"Not in coin," she said. "In necks." She was gone before he could answer.

Eliza arrived without announcing herself, a trick only possible if a room already expects you. She shook rain from her cloak and nodded the fiddle into a key that did not belong in any book. Men shifted subtly to make space and then pretended they hadn't. She took nothing to drink and was fed anyway; this is what power looks like in places where law is not a friend.

Ferris came in with the smell of his own work on him. He did not look toward the back, and thus everyone knew he would be going there eventually. Jory slid into a seat near the wall, hat low, the brim now part of his face. Kit took his usual place with his back to the window because he trusted what came through doors more than what came through glass.

Mary passed again, tray steady. Her eye dropped to the brown-paper parcel tucked under Michael's chair. "If that's what I think it is," she murmured, "best your timing be good and your reason better."

"It's nothing," he said too quickly.

"Nothing weighs lighter," she replied, and was gone.

Thomas Treglown—God help him—had started early and would not stop. He had the shine-eyed look of a man who mistakes feeling large for being safe. He slapped the back of a man who wasn't his friend and told a story about a wave that had never happened. He threw a laugh wide enough to step into and invited everyone to fall over the threshold. When a miner from inland failed to be charmed, Tom puffed and squared and would have made a foolish point with his fists if Mary hadn't slid her ladle between them like a magistrate's baton.

"Soup," she said.

"I'm not ill," he protested.

"You will be," she said, and put the bowl down as if it were a parcel that had been paid for.

He ate the way a boy eats when told the food is free. For three minutes he was quiet. Then he filled the quiet with himself again.

"Tell ye," he boomed to no one who needed telling, "no cutter afloat can match us. Not when Eliza's at the helm."

Half the room smiled because the drink made them feel the size of their own stories. The others shifted in their seats because the word helm said too much in a place where men were good at not saying.

"Quiet," a voice muttered. "Walls."

Thomas was not in the mood to have architecture explained to him. "Walls have ears," he agreed happily, "and I'll tell the ears too: she's sharper than the lot of us. And Michael" - his arm swung out, a friendly blow that would have broken a smaller man's ear - "our quiet friend here carried a barrel up the cliff like it was a basket of eggs."

Michael lifted his pint and put it down again. Heat ran up his neck. You cannot teach a man what danger is when he is drunk on his own cheer.

Eliza's eyes found Thomas and then moved away; her mouth did nothing and said everything. She crossed to Ferris with a ledger already open and said nothing that any man could repeat without sounding like an idiot. Michael watched the way her hand steadied the page when a drunk bumped the table. He watched her not be bothered by the bump and be bothered by the shadow that lingered too long under the door.

A stranger stood there. He held his hat in both hands the way men do when they want to be mistaken for polite. His coat was good cloth poorly worn; his boots had mud that belonged to a road that didn't lead to Looe. He took in the room as if he were counting bolts in a shipyard and sat at a corner table with the look of a man who expects to be served without needing to ask. When Mary brought coffee, he sipped it like a man unused to bitterness.

"Mary," Michael said when she passed, keeping his eyes on the rim of his tankard. "Friend of yours?"

"Friend of no one," she said. "Says he's a salt-pork dealer who forgot where his wagon is. I've never known a pork man drink coffee at this hour. Watch your back."

"Always," he said.

"Especially," she said, and took a mug to a table that never had enough mugs and made it look like she'd done nothing at all.

The stranger's gaze slid. He watched Eliza too long without pretending he wasn't. He watched Thomas with the faint interest people reserve for a candle set too near a curtain. He lifted his cup at the wrong time. He laughed without hearing the joke. There is a way men look when they have been sent to see and another way when they have come to tell. He looked like a man who would do both badly and still be paid.

As the evening folded into itself, a small meeting happened in the room without closing a door. Eliza had a corner, and into it drifted Ferris and Jory and Kit and two others who were good at being seen when they wanted to be seen. Michael stood half outside it and felt more inside than he deserved.

"The kiln," Eliza said, not looking up from her page, "will keep us if we keep it."

Ferris nodded. "I'll lay rails at dawn. Nails over rails. If Harker's man asks me what business keeps me open before light, I'll tell him his own."

"Signs," Jory said. "We need them clean. Three knocks on the capstan post means go. Two and a whistle means scatter. If a man sings anything, I'll knock his teeth out to save his life."

"Eliza," Kit asked softly, "and if they take one of us?"

"Then we do not take him back with talk," she said. "We take him back with silence. If you are seized, say nothing and we will grieve you. If you talk, we will grieve everyone."

No one said aye to that. It was beyond assent. It was a law older than the ones on paper.

From the hearth, Mary cleared her throat the way a bell clears a sky. "And if any man cannot keep silence," she said to the room at large, "he can keep away from my door. I bury men enough without pouring them ale first."

The stranger stood, left coins too large for his drink, and went out. Michael was already moving; Eliza's hand lifted the smallest fraction. "No," she said without breath. "Let him tell his nothing. We'll answer with something."

Thomas had drifted toward the door like a man drawn by a tide he couldn't name. Outside, rain stitched the square together into one piece. A boy slipped, recovered, swore in a voice he would not have used in daylight. The fiddler put his bow down and let the noise be music for a while.

"You'll walk him?" Mary said to Michael, meaning Thomas without measuring his name.

"If he'll be walked," Michael said.

"If he won't," Mary replied, "walk beside him anyway until he turns left at the Marcia. After that, men's choices belong to them."

Eliza heard and didn't say yes and didn't say don't. She had a way of leaving a piece on the board in a position where it could take two directions and somehow both seemed to be her idea.

Michael found Thomas at the door, arguing with the latch as if it were a stubborn mule. "Home," he told him. "That's the cleverest place to stand tonight."

Thomas grinned, loose and wide. "I'll go when I like."

"Like now," Michael said, and the thing about a man like Michael is he could sound kind and still leave no room for argument.

They stepped out together beneath the dripping eaves. Rain stitched the square into one cloth; the lamps breathed their halos on puddles and cobbles. A cart rattled somewhere on the far lane, and a dog barked once, then thought better of it. From a cottage on the slope a woman's voice rose and fell, scolding and fond in the same breath, and a baby answered as babies do, with the whole of itself.

"Do you know," Thomas said, taking Michael's arm for balance and then releasing it, "I could have been a fisherman. Or a farmer. But I chose the right crime."

"You chose bread," Michael said.

"That too." Thomas hiccupped, laughed, and wiped his sleeve across his mouth. "Eliza'll make us rich. You'll see."

Michael saw the rope before he saw the gold. "Turn here," he said, steering him toward the bend by the Marcia.

At the ash tree where the lane narrowed, a shadow moved where a wall jutted. Michael stopped because men like him live longer when they stop. A cat slid out, tail up, and crossed their path without offering an omen. "Go on," he said, letting the breath he hadn't noticed go. "I'm for the quay."

Thomas clapped him hard on the back. "You're a good dog," he said, as if loyalty were the highest title a man could bestow. "Tell Eliza I... no, tell her nothing. She knows already."

He tipped an imaginary hat, swayed, then declared with theatrical clarity:

"I'm leaving!"

And so he did, shoulders swinging to a tune only he could hear, vanishing into the dark beyond the lantern's reach, the lane swallowing him as if it had been waiting.

Michael stood a moment longer, the rain cold at his collar, listening to the fiddler's tune drift out from the Jolly Sailor and into the night. Far off, something metallic knocked twice and then did not knock a third time. He could not name the sound, and so he did not say it. He turned for the quay, leaving Thomas to the shadows. The sea kept its counsel. The village pretended to be a village. And the calm, patient as rope, waited to find a neck.

Chapter Fourteen

The Noose's Shadow

Rain stitched the square into one cloth. Michael left Thomas at the ash tree, watched the big man tip an imaginary hat and lurch toward the dock, the lane-bend by the inn with its iron bracket, and then turned for the quay. Behind him the fiddler's tune leaked from the Jolly and thinned in the wind. Somewhere metal knocked twice and did not knock a third time.

He slept badly and woke worse. By first light the lanes had the colour of pewter; gulls scraped the sky raw. Mary, Mary at the Jolly, was sweeping her step, bristles whispering like someone telling a child to hush. She jerked her chin toward the corner.

"Did he reach home?" she asked.

"He said he would," Michael answered, and knew how little that weighed.

They found the mark of it before they found the story: scuffed prints where the lane narrowed, a poor circle of struggle, a neat skid against the inn wall, a single dark thread snagged high on the bracket as if a rope had brushed it. No one had seen anything, which meant everyone had. The morning made men tidy in their answers.

By noon the tale chose a mouth. A net-mender with more honesty than sense told Ferris he'd heard a cart at the wrong hour, wheels muffled in sacking, a horse shod for quiet. Two blue coats had stepped from the dark and put a hand over Thomas's laugh. No shouting, no wildness. Practised courtesy. The cart took the north lane, toward a farm Harker had been paying by the month.

"Not the watch," Ferris said, jaw tight. "Excise. Harker's own."

Eliza took the news without blinking, but her thumb worried the ledger's page-edge smooth once, the way a person rubs a stone in a pocket. "We don't go blundering after them," she said, and someone's breath left the room as if she had kicked it out. "He chose drink. They chose him. We don't feed the rope with half the village."

Michael's throat worked. "He's one of ours."

"He was," she said. The past tense landed light and hard at once. "If he holds fast, he may be again."

He did not say what sat in him like a fishbone: most men don't hold when you lay their children's names out like knives.

The night before, Thomas's world had narrowed to straw and fear. The barn smelled of damp oak and old hay; the roof beat back the rain in a soft drum. They roped his wrists, not tightly, just enough to teach his skin to obey. A lantern hung too high, making shadows thin and long; the light insisted on his shame.

Harker moved like tide, patient, inevitable. He did not swagger. He did not strike unless it counted. His hands were clean; his boots were mudless. He sat as if the stool had his name on it.

"Thomas," he said, warm enough to peel the cold from the name. "You're a decent lad. These are not decent men you run with. They'll let you swing and drink to your memory. I can do better."

Paper laid the table bare: a crudely sketched coast, marks that might have been guesses or might have been aimed shots, a list of cottages that looked like a prayer written down. Harker fixed the papers with a brass weight such men use to weigh coin. Its ordinary shine was obscene here.

One blue-coat, rope-callused hands, worked the coil as if reminding it how a neck should look. The other, pale and careful, brought gruel and set it down with the competence of a good wife. Thomas did not know which he feared more.

"We've no quarrel with your Mary," Harker went on. "Mary Treglown, is it? Baby, Maryanne? You wouldn't leave them to winter alone."

He said the names without cruelty, and the lack of it was worse.

Thomas tried a laugh; it cracked. "I'm no use to you. I lift what I'm told. I don't count..."

"Exactly," Harker said softly. "You won't be missed for an afternoon. Not by the clever ones. You tell me the night and the place. I give you this." He slid a folded paper across the table. "A pass for the watch. Your good name on loan. Your debts in town, settled by a friend. Bread on the table. The rope, Thomas, is for bigger fish."

They set him under the beam. The noose looked innocent until it kissed his throat. Leather creaked. His knees learned to shake. They didn't hoist him high, just enough that his heels scraped straw and the body's ancient panic rose like a tide and drowned sense.

"Date," Harker said. "And we all sleep."

They lowered him, raised him, let him cough, raised him again, not to bruise but to measure. The rope taught his breath the shape of obedience. The pale man dabbed his mouth with a rag as if kindness were a spice to be added in the right proportion.

"Think," Harker murmured, and from a pocket produced a small square of folded paper darkened by hands. Inside, a smudged list: Mary, Maryanne; rent; bread; midwife. The ledger of a poor household. "It is a pity when a man loves his mates more than his child eats. Whitehall finds that sort of romance poetic. I do not."

Thomas lasted longer than most would have guessed and far less than he had once promised himself. He thought of Mary's cracked hands. He thought of his baby's pink mouth learning hunger early. He thought, filthy, of ale. He gave more than he meant and less than he wanted, and somehow it was exactly enough: the cove with slower water, the path under gorse, the pony yard, the kind of moon that thumbprints the tide, a whistle and two knocks. He tried to swallow the words back after he had said them. They did not return.

Harker's approval was nearly fatherly. "There now," he said. "A good man after all."

They set Thomas on the straw and left him to learn breathing again. The noose's shadow lay along his shoulder like a touch that would not be shaken off. He discovered relief has a twin called disgust, and both wore his face.

At first light they cut him loose and handed him a crust as if mercy needed proof. The cart took him as far as the ash tree. He stood and blinked in the grey like a player shoved onto the wrong stage.

He walked.

No one stopped him because no one knew what to call him. The village reassembled around him as he went: Ferris at his door testing a hinge by sound, old Jago tugging his cap, the milk boy slopping the lane with his pails and pride. A dog came forward and then thought better of it. Smoke went up straight as a sermon. He turned from his own door when he saw Mary Treglown's shawl in the window and washed his face at the trough instead, teeth chattering, the water biting as if it were allowed to judge. When he did go in, the baby reached with both hands and he flinched at the softness. He told Mary he had fallen asleep at the Jolly. He said it with a steadiness he had not earned. She looked once at the raw line on his neck and said nothing. They both understood the price list.

Eliza saw him later, just once, crossing the square with a coil of rope that did not belong to him. He lifted his eyes and met hers. He found no contempt there, only the soft, merciless grief reserved for men who will cost other men their lives.

Word travels in coves like smoke, thin at first, then everywhere. By afternoon, Ferris had the shape of it. He said nothing in the square; he said everything in the storehouse.

"We move," he told them, voice kept low so the walls would have to work at it if they wanted the tale. "We hide deeper. We split the load. We change the song."

Eliza arrived with rain in her braid and Paris still in the set of her jaw. She listened without interrupting, then opened her ledger and made the village into columns.

"Black Copse, then the kilns. Two to a cask. No ponies, prints talk. Three under Ferris's rails and nails; four to Boscawn; the rest to the right-hand cave we never discuss. Signals stand: three knocks go; two and a long whistle scatter. If anyone sings, hit him. He'll thank you alive."

"What of Tom?" someone asked without wanting to.

Eliza did not look at Thomas. "He does as he's told until the tide turns," she said. "After that, we see what the sea gives back."

Thomas stood at the edge of the ring, hands loose, mouth open as if to breathe and then deciding against it. Shame had made him small; fear had made him obedient. He nodded when told, lifted when told, rolled when told. Once his eyes found Michael's and held for a count. There was apology there, and something worse, the knowledge that apologies do not shift a rope.

They set about the plain work of not dying. Jory took the ash bend; Kit the rise above the kiln mouth. Ferris found extra sacking that smelled of mouse and winter and promised to conquer both with spice and patience.

Out by the church, Parson Bray had just finished reading the clouds a lesson when a blue-coat swung down and asked, with practiced politeness, whether the vicarage kept late fires.

"For sinners," Bray said, dry as last year's hay. "And for the dead."

"Do you see much of either?" the man asked, trying a grin that had never been popular.

"I keep my eyes on my Bible," Bray replied, and shut the porch door on the question. He stood a moment in the stone hush, fingers on the bell rope, then went out the side way and found Michael by the stile. "Storm coming of another kind," he said, voice low. "If your work keeps men from starving, do it clean, for pity's sake."

"I'll try," Michael said.

"Try harder," Bray returned, and went away with mud on his hem and guilt on his face.

Mary at the Jolly made her own preparations. She cleared the pig-salting bench in the back, laid down two clean boards that were not quite the same colour as the rest, and fitted the false tongue so it would catch for a stranger's hand and yield for hers. She dragged a salt sack over the seam and set, very carefully, a slab of pork on top with her initials pressed into the rind. She rehearsed two answers in her head, one for Harker (I keep ale and I keep order; brandy's for gentry who can spell it) and one for Eliza (it will hold a nine-gallon if you're not proud). She told her niece to polish the pewter hard enough to see lies in it and to serve any man who asked for coffee with water so weak it remembered beans as a rumour. She set three mugs on the shelf in a row, left, middle, right, and moved the middle a thumb's breadth out. The boy carrying milk glanced, blinked, nodded, the sign to keep to the higher path. No one saw any of it because Mary was a woman who had never done anything but clean.

Near dusk, a ragged boy burst into the storehouse, breath sawed to pieces. "Blue coats," he gasped. "Two by the marsh lane. One at Parson Bray's asking if he keeps late fires."

Eliza's mouth made a shape that started as a smile and wasn't. "We keep earlier ones," she said. "Home. Lamps out. If asked, nobody has a mother and everybody loves the King."

She turned to Michael. "We'll walk the kiln."

They took the higher path. The sea worked at the rocks with its old patience. Wind combed the gorse into whispering. Boscawn sat where it always had, black mouth, green lip, a pit trained to hold heat and forget it. Michael climbed in first and counted footfalls, murmuring numbers like a charm, then called her down. Inside, the world was held and half-silence.

"It'll do," he said.

"It must," she answered.

For once she allowed herself to look tired, leaning on broken slate. The parcel from Paris pressed on Michael's mind as if silk could anchor a night. He nearly told her, nearly said he wanted to see her in colour, if only for an hour, but she turned toward the sea's voice and the moment went by like a gull shadow.

"Do you think he spoke from malice?" she asked, not looking at him.

"No," he said. "From hunger. From the rope. From wanting to keep the small world that knows his name."

She nodded once. "That's the worst kind. You can't hate it clean."

"Before we commit the whole," Eliza said later, "we test the lanes."

A decoy run. Two empty kegs, weighted with stones, wrapped in sacking that smelled convincingly of brandy; a cart without a cart—shoulders, not wheels—men walking as if the load bit. Michael and Kit took the weight first, backs bowed. They went by the long hedge, past Parson Bray's gate where

Christian forgiveness had to share space with state suspicion. A dog barked and then thought better of it.

At the marsh lane the world held its breath. A cough came from the ditch, the same two coughs a man makes when he wishes to seem like a farmer. A boot slipped—lime dust, just a pinch, betrayed the leather. A muttered curse followed, strangled too late. Michael did not turn his head. He counted a slow twelve and let the number carry his feet. The cough did not follow.

They made the ash bend, left the decoys in the copse, and returned by the higher stile one by one with hands in their pockets like men who had only been out to look at weather. From a field a single owl called them fools and wished them luck.

"Lanes are watched," Michael reported. "But not well."

"Good," Eliza said. "I prefer stupid danger. It's less inventive."

Harker re-folded his neat plan and found the night did not care for it. The coughers in the hedge had missed their place. A cutter off the point read the tide badly and had to wear off, making an ugly scrape of canvas that even a sleeping man could have heard if sleep had been granted. He sent a rider inland to fetch two more men and received back a farmer with a lantern who wanted paying first. Harker smiled once, thin and unpleasant, and rearranged his ideas. If not tonight, then the next. The noose works on patience, not punctuality.

The Jolly was quieter than it had any right to be. Mary drew ale with a stricter hand. The stranger from the night before did not show his face. When the door opened to the square's dark, Eliza looked up each time and then returned her gaze to the men she meant to keep alive.

"Midnight," she said at last, voice pitched to carry and not be caught. "Kiln first. Then Ferris. No lanterns, no courage in cups. Hold fast."

She closed the ledger as if closing a mouth.

Michael lay awake for an hour that might have been ten, listening to the sea dismantle the shore grain by grain. He saw again the barn's high lantern, the rope's ugly logic, Thomas's body learning to fear on purpose. He understood something he would not say aloud: a net forgives more than a rope, but a net can strangle if you're not careful.

He rose before his name was called. The parcel from Paris sat under the bed, brown as soap; he left it, because silk had no work to do in this night. Outside, rain had quit; the dark was a hard thing, not a wet one. The village pretended to sleep. The sea did not bother.

At the kiln mouth, Jory stood like a post. "Two knocks," he breathed, and Michael gave them: wood on stone, soft. From below the pit came a single answering scrape. Kit. All as planned.

They lowered the first real weight, a barrel that felt like a choice. Sacking rasped; rope burned; breath ghosted. Michael's palms remembered scaffolds and found old strength. Eliza moved in the dark like someone who had been born here and only borrowed daylight at need.

Halfway through the second lift, a noise stitched the hedgerow—a misstep, a pebble kicked the wrong way. Every body in the kiln went stone. The sound repeated: too careful to be a fox, too clumsy to be a man who belonged. Michael touched Eliza's sleeve with two fingers. She did not pull away.

From the hedge a rabbit burst, panicked by something behind it. Then a whisper: two men arguing through their throats, not their mouths. "—told you the left path—" "—said the ash—" "—shut up—"

Eliza's breath did not change speed. She put her mouth to Michael's ear. "Two and a long whistle," she said, meaning not now, but if the next noise came closer.

It didn't. The men in the hedge, whoever they were, repositioned themselves with the grace of farmers' sons wearing soldiers' boots and, like all men disguised badly, convinced themselves they had not been heard. The rabbit found another hedge to trust.

Work resumed. The third cask settled into lime's old memory. Ferris's rails waited for their share.

By the time they broke the load and started the thin trickle toward the ironmonger's back, the kiln had swallowed seven barrels and wanted more. The right-hand cave would get the rest. Jory ghosted ahead to taste the lane's weather. Kit took Thomas into the shadow with a barrel between them, and Thomas—blessedly—said nothing.

Near Ferris's yard the darkest dark lifted to a colour like iron. Light leaks differently before dawn. Somewhere inland a cockerel tried a note and gave it up. From the marsh side—two soft coughs again, the farmer who was not—then silence.

Inside the ironmonger's back room, the world became nails and rails and the good honest lie of iron. Ferris had cleared a mouth no excise man would think to reach into without getting his suit filthy. Three tuns went under the rails. Sacks of nails—thick, ugly, undeniable—went over. Ferris dusted his hands and made himself smell properly of lamp-oil and metal and nothing else.

"Twice more," Eliza said. "Then the cave."

Thomas lifted his eyes, found hers. "Eliza—" he began, voice cracked.

She turned her face as if a draught had brushed it. "Do the work," she said.

He did. Obedience can feel like penance if you want it to.

Harker, up on the point, watched the cutter pretending competence and felt his tidiness itch. He imagined the kiln as a dark mouth swallowing coin and decided he would make it vomit before the week was out. "Tomorrow," he told Rope-Hands. "Positions shifted. Lanterns hooded. And for God's sake, cough the right number."

Rope-Hands nodded, chastened. The pale one—careful, careful—wrote it down in a neat hand as if the night cared for handwriting.

They reached the right-hand cave when dawn was stropping a thin edge on the horizon. The cave accepted four barrels and muttered about a fifth. Eliza made a small subtracting motion with her fingers—enough—and the night, as nights do, decided it had done all it could.

They scattered the way birds do when someone claps. Michael ghosted the long hedge; Eliza took the high path with Jory; Kit folded himself into the copse and became a bush for a while. Thomas stood at the ash and looked like a man who had been given back one breath and did not trust the next. When the two coughs sounded again, they were further off and annoyed at themselves.

The village woke the way villages do: dogs arguing with their collars, a woman scolding a child for the shoes he had not thought to dry, smoke finding its way into morning, gulls writing their same rude note across the same rude sky. Ferris opened his respectable door and sold a man two hinges he did not need. Mary threw wash water into the lane with the righteous splash of a woman who had never done anything but wash; the pig-salting bench looked like a pig-salting bench.

Eliza met Michael in the lip of shadow by the capstan house. For a moment neither spoke. Their breath smoked like a promise that could not be kept long.

"You see?" she said at last, voice low. "A net holds. If one knot slips, the rest take the load."

"And the knot?" he asked, because he could not help himself.

"We mend it," she said. "Or we cut it out."

She turned to go, then paused. "Tonight bought us a day," she added. "Maybe two. Harker will not forgive being made to wait. We move again tomorrow—with better luck or better lies." She glanced toward the cliff where the kiln sat like a taught-to-behave mouth. "Keep your hands ready. Keep your head low."

"Hold fast," he said.

Her mouth tilted the smallest fraction. "Hold fast," she answered, and was gone into the morning as if she had been drawn there by the tide and not by her feet.

Michael watched the square collect its daylight. The rope's shadow reached further than the barn; it lay across the cove, the lane, the Jolly's door—thin, patient, ready. He felt it graze his own neck (Graham's neck, Michael's neck; some days the difference hurt) and knew the next chapter of the village's life would be written in the dark again, with fewer mistakes and sharper quills.

For now the kiln held. The rails lied. The right-hand cave kept its mouth shut. And somewhere up on the headland, a cutter with a captain who had misread the tide pretended it had meant to do that all along.

Chapter Fifteen

The Breaking Tide

The word went out like a tide, quiet at first, then in every mouth that mattered. Clouds had banked low all afternoon, a grey lid pressing the sea flat. By dusk the wind died, leaving the cove held in a brittle hush. Men came by sheep paths in ones and twos, cloaks dark, hats low, lanterns hooded to a thread. From the headland the beach looked empty; from the beach the world felt watched.

Barrels arrived as shadows—blunter shadows heaved from the French boats, humped over gunwales with the soft grunt of men who had carried weight their whole lives. Hulls hissed on wet shingle. Rope thumped. Orders came in clicks and single syllables. Eliza moved through it without fuss: a touch to a shoulder, a chin to steer a barrel's roll, the knife's weight familiar under her cloak and out of sight.

Michael stayed on her quarter, hands to casks, working before thought could make trouble. Isaac Gulliver stood near the run of rocks, a dark block against darker cliff, cane in hand, eyes everywhere at once.

"Faster," Eliza murmured, not raising her voice. "The tide turns on its own clock, not ours."

The French captain—bearded, scar at the jaw—nodded once. "Deux de plus, madame." Two more boats nosed in, their oars a whisper. Men bent, lifted, rolled. The beach breathed with them.

For a span there were only practical things: grit under boots, the slosh of brine in a cask's belly, the scrape of plank, that wet thunk when a barrel took its first bite of turn. Work as shelter. From the notch above, two soft coughs—the wrong farmer again—then boot leather scuffed where no furrow lay. Michael's neck prickled.

A smell rode the next gust—horse and leather, powder and damp wool. Footfalls skidded.

"Lanterns!" someone hissed.

"Douse 'em!" another snapped, though none showed.

Too late. From the notch two lights bobbed, then three, then a scatter flared up the beach like foxfire. The shout cracked like a musket: "Stand there!"

Revenue.

Everything held—men, breath, sea. Then the night shattered.

"Split!" Eliza's voice cut clean. "Barrels to the west path! Leave what you must! Michael—Isaac—up the headland!"

"Caves!" Gulliver's bellow carried like a signal horn. "You lads, into the teeth! Lose 'em in the rock!"

The beach broke into two minds—one bolting downshore for the black mouths in the cliff, the other surging up the goat track where gorse snagged and the path turned mean. The Frenchmen heaved two last casks into the surf; the barrels bobbed and swung back toward their boats like reluctant dogs. Oars bit water; hulls scraped; hard Breton swears struck stone.

Soldiers spilled onto shingle, red coats ghosted to umber, bayonets a scatter of cold moons.

Michael took the slope with Eliza and Isaac, boots clawing at grit. The revenue shouted behind, voices falling into that rhythm men find when they think the rope is already on the other fellow's neck. A shot cracked; chips sliced off a boulder near Michael's ear. He tasted grit and copper. Eliza didn't look back.

"Keep going," she said. Not bravado. Instruction.

The path kinked at a thorned outcrop. Isaac dipped the cane and fired; the pistol hidden in its head coughed, and a lantern below shattered, throwing wild light and wilder shadows. "Up," he barked, smoke curling around his teeth.

Down shore, the cave-chasers vanished as if the cliff had eaten them. The scream that came back out wasn't death—more the sound a man makes when he's chased his own courage into a place where it cannot turn. Another shot. Echoes cracked rock.

Barrels thumped. One soldier slipped, went under, came up cursing, musket ruined.

On the rise, the headland narrowed to a spine. Gorse crouched, ready to tear. Three revenue men had chosen this chase—quick and sure, boots made for this land. "Stop in the King's name!" the biggest roared, as if names meant anything to wind.

"Down," Eliza snapped, dragging Michael and dropping behind a tumble of stone. Three shots answered at once—three bright mouths. Stone spat fragments. A gorse bush caught, hissed, guttered. Resin and threat stung the air.

Isaac eased the cane to one side and drew a second pistol from his coat. He peered past the rock, eyes cold. "Three," he said.

"Three's a fair number," Eliza answered. To Michael: "Can you fire straight?"

He swallowed. "Aye."

"When I rise, take the left. Isaac has the middle."

"And you?"

"The right." That look: don't argue.

A breath. Two. Wind whining through thorn. Below, the sea worked at its endless job.

"Now," she said, and stood.

The world compressed: three shapes, three muzzle flashes, three answers. Michael pressed the butt to his shoulder, stock slick under a hand gone wet. He didn't think of York or Mara or the coin in his pocket or the tin under the floor. He saw the left-most flash and a hat's tilt, and squeezed.

His pistol cracked. The man on the left jerked, stumbled, went down hard and stayed, legs twitching out the last of their orders.

Isaac's shot was a surgeon's stroke. The middle man's hat spun; his body followed, string cut.

Eliza's ball landed true—but as she rose to take it, the right-hand revenuer's shot found her under the ribs, where cloth meets bone. The sound that tore from her was not a cry so much as a breath cut in two. She folded, slid against stone, leaving a smear of black that gleamed even in bad light.

"Eliza!"

Michael had her before the name finished, hands already finding the press, but warmth flooded his fingers and refused to answer pressure. The last man—hit but not ended—lifted his pistol again with a shaking hand.

Isaac didn't hesitate. His second piece coughed; the man went backward as if laid out by a careful mother.

Only wind then, and the click of cooling metal, and Eliza's breath—fast and wrong.

"Up," Isaac grunted, hauling her. "No more noise. Others'll climb."

Michael shoved his shoulder under her. The shock was the weight itself; she'd always been weightless in rooms—an angle, a fact. In his arms she was terribly light and terribly heavy. They stumbled over the crest, down the lee where wind cut less, across heather hiding holes.

Behind them, calls tangled and thinned. On the beach the soldiers had lost their prey; on the water the

French were halfway to the black. The only sound that kept pace was Eliza's breathing and Isaac's effort, the old smuggler taking more than his share without cursing it.

They made the cottage by a route Michael could not later draw: a seam of path, a gate black in the dark, a wall he'd leaned on last week for air. He shouldered the door; warmth flared like a friend who didn't know the news.

"On the bed," Isaac ordered, cane clattering aside. "Fetch the doctor."

Ferris seemed to have been waiting for feet; he was gone like a bolt toward the village. Men spilled in and out, one with a lamp, one with peat for the hearth, one standing useless, trying to find a thing to make his hands helpful.

"Hold this," Isaac said, pressing linen into Michael's palm.

Michael held. He pressed until his wrists shook, until his palms slid, until his mind whispered stop that's her blood—and his hands answered, press harder.

The door banged and then behaved. Mary pushed in sideways with a basin and a stack of linen that had seen more christenings than deaths. She didn't ask permission; she set the basin by the hearth, rolled her sleeves, and met the doctor's eye like one professional to another. "Tell me what you need and don't waste words," she said. To Michael: "You— hold. Don't count. Just hold." Her hands moved without fret, the way women's hands learn to when men insist on bleeding in their kitchens.

Eliza's eyes found him through it—dazed, then focused, then soft. Her mouth was white at the edges.

"Michael," she said, the word a thread.

"I'm here." His voice broke on the second word. "I'm here."

"Do you remember the cave… the keg… how angry I was? You only said 'Aye.' I thought—God help me—I thought you were a fool." A flicker touched her mouth, there and gone. "You weren't."

"Don't talk. Save it. Save it for later."

"Later," she echoed, as if trying the shape of the word.

The doctor arrived in a flood of cold air, hair wild, coat over nightshirt. "No laudanum—there's no time," he snapped, already at the bed. Knife flashed; cloth parted. The wound showed itself, obscene in lamplight. "More light." He pressed, packed, swore softly when the packing soaked red between one heartbeat and the next. "Arterial," under his breath, not for them. "Hold that," he told Michael, and Michael did, because the world had arranged itself around the command.

Eliza didn't look away. Pain was there, and something that wasn't pain.

"Listen," she said. "If I don't—"

"You will."

"If I don't," she insisted, with a shred of her old steel, "you take the run. Ferris knows which buyers keep quiet. Gulliver—" A breath broke.

"Gulliver will try to hold it alone. Make them share the risk."

"Don't ask me to plan without you."

Her fingers found his wrist, leaving a wet print. "You can. You will." She searched his face, and for a moment something unguarded moved there, softer than command. "Michael... I—"

"Don't," he said, because the word he knew she meant would tear him, and he still had to keep his hands steady.

The doctor pressed harder, then slower. He looked older by a decade for each minute the bleeding didn't stop. "I can't reach it," he said at last, low with defeat. "It's taken too much."

Michael shook his head, a child refusing an empty plate. "No. Try again."

Eliza drew breath as if the air had grown heavy. Still, she held him. "I love you," she said, the rest a whisper that carried all its weight.

The words slammed through him and opened what he'd boarded since York. He bent until his forehead met hers. "I love you," he said back, reckless because nothing but truth belonged here. "God help me, Eliza, I love you."

Her hand fluttered, steadied on his wrist. He felt her grip weaken and clenched his own as if he could hold her by will.

Something small slipped free of her cloak— tired gold. It bounced once on the board, rang high and hard, then spun for a breath that seemed a lifetime. It rolled—slow, inexorable—toward the crack between two planks.

"Don't," he said—to a coin, to fate, to the night.

It tipped, paused at the lip, and dropped with a sound that made men flinch. Gone into the dark under the cottage where he had hidden so much and now could not keep this, could not keep her.

The doctor's hands stilled. He closed his eyes for a beat, then opened them not to argue but to witness. "I'm sorry," he said, and in his voice lived the truth of all men who have failed at the border between flesh and whatever comes next.

Eliza's breath eased by degrees. Her eyes stayed on Michael's until the last. Something unknotted in her face—a slackening that was not pain. Her hand lightened. The weight of her in the world changed in the way you always know, even if no one tells you, even if you refuse it.

"No," Michael said, a word too small to carry it. He bowed over her hand, over blood and linen and his own useless strength, and made a sound that had no language.

Mary laid Eliza's hair flat with a palm as sure as a lid. "We'll have her washed and laid proper," she said, not asking, not inviting dispute. She looked up, found each man in turn, and did the hard mercy. "You can cry later. Tonight you do as she told you. I'll keep the door." She turned to the latch, set the bar, and in that small sound the house learned a new law.

The room remembered itself by inches. Someone fed the fire and then looked ashamed for having done a practical thing. Ferris set a hand to Michael's shoulder and left it there, pressure steady and human. Isaac stood back by the hearth, jaw clenched, eyes on some far point men look at when they won't let the room see them break.

No one moved the fallen cloak. No one spoke her name. The cottage spoke it for them.

Michael stayed until time loosened its grip. When at last he lifted his head, the rushlight guttered, recovered, guttered again. Blood had dried on his fingers in stiff maps. He rested her hand on the sheet, stood because men will stand even when the ground has done them no favours.

He crossed to the table. The lamp threw a small island of light and ignored everything beyond it. He stared at the gap where the coin had gone. His mind offered the absurd hope of levering the plank and reaching in, as if retrieving gold could undo the last ten minutes; as if coins and time obeyed the same laws.

The door pushed open and night breathed in. Cold salted the room. The sea kept doing what it had always done—chew, breathe, pull—indifferent and eternal. Once its sound had steadied him; now it sounded like a thing that would go on without her, which felt like blasphemy.

Isaac picked up his cane and set it down again. He found only gravel in his throat. "We'll give her the night," he managed. "Then we do what men must. The run—"

Michael turned. Whatever Isaac saw in his face made the older man stop, then nod once, as if the answer he'd been ready to insist on had already been spoken.

"We'll do it your way," Isaac said, low. "For her."

Ferris wiped at his eyes with the heel of his hand, angry at tears. "I'll send word to those who should know—and no one else. The village'll hear soon enough." He looked at Eliza then—really looked—for the first time, like a man memorising a sun that won't rise again. "God keep you, girl," he said, and the word girl held father, ally, debtor.

Men left as men do, backwards a step, then another, then gone, the room lighter and heavier by turns. The doctor packed what skill could pack and left what no man can.

Michael sat again. He set one palm on the board where the coin had fallen, felt only old timber. He laid the other on the sheet near her shoulder. Between wood and cloth, between the living and the place that had no right to claim her, he found the only ground left to hold.

"Hold fast," he whispered—the words he'd clung to in storms when rope burned his forearms. He didn't know to whom he said it—himself, the men, the world—but he said it until the edges rounded and the phrase turned to prayer.

Outside, in the caves and under headland shadow, men hid, breathed, counted their pulses, waited for dawn to judge them. Inside, the cottage remembered whale oil on the wick, lavender folded into linen, the old smell of tallow and salt. The night stretched. The fire settled to a red patience.

When sleep came it did not negotiate. It took him like a wave taking sand from under your feet and left him standing on bone.

He dreamed nothing. He woke to everything.

Dawn scraped a thin line along the sill and showed the room without mercy. Eliza lay where he had left her, still as the coin under the floor. The doctor's bandages were a map of a country no one should have to learn. Michael stood because standing was what he had.

He fed the fire like a penitent. He washed his hands and found the creases still red. He set the kettle near the coals and heard it begin to fuss, ordinary as any morning.

On the table, next to the lamp, sat the other guinea—the one that had crossed time and sea with him. He set it on his palm; its weight was insult and comfort both. Without knowing why, he laid it on the board above the crack and watched light slide along its tired edge.

A knock—soft, deliberate.

Michael closed his hand around the gold and turned. "Come," he said, and the word was not what it had been the night before.

Ferris stood there, hat in hand, eyes red. Behind him, two village women, shawls tight, faces set to work that must be done. Isaac followed a pace back, carrying a different weight than any barrel. Mary slipped in last with her basin, already in charge of the kindnesses no man can manage.

No one spoke her name. The room spoke it.

"Tell me what to do," Michael said, and his voice was steady. That steadiness scared him more than the shaking had.

Isaac met his gaze. "We bury our dead," he said. "Then we make the tide pay."

Michael nodded once. It wasn't vengeance he agreed to. It was duty—and, under it, the ache of a love that had arrived too late and would not leave.

He slipped the guinea back into his pocket, where its circle burned. Somewhere under his feet, in the dark between boards, another coin lay lost, bright in dust.

Two suns, two weights. Two lives. One gone where he couldn't follow. Not yet.

He set his hands to the work of grief, because there was nothing else he could set them to that would not shame him.

Outside, the sea said the only thing it has ever said.

Inside, the cottage listened.

Chapter Sixteen

Against All Odds

Morning bled slow across the horizon, layering the sky rather than lighting it. Frost held to the grass as if it had reasons. Michael walked the cliff path with the careful tread of a man who didn't trust the ground. Each breath smoked and broke apart; each exhale left him emptier.

The cottage had not been still when Eliza died. It had been a storm in a box.

She'd coughed—no, fought—for each fragment of breath. Michael had held her upright while Mary shouted for Rowe, and the little room had filled with bodies and panic and the thick, sour smell of fear. Eliza's fingers had clawed at his sleeve, not to hold on—she wasn't that sort of woman—but to warn him, to insist she wasn't done. The doctor's bag had hit the floor. Rowe's voice had risen, then broken. Someone knocked a lantern against the wall so hard the flame guttered sideways. A cup smashed. A woman cried out.

And then—just like that—the sound left the world.

Her body slackened as though someone had cut a rope.

Michael had made a noise he didn't recognise as human. Mary had caught his shoulders before he could follow Eliza to the floor. The hush afterward was the cruellest thing he'd ever heard: a silence that had teeth.

By first light, the cottage was busy with the small, stubborn work of love that happens after death. Mary and two women came with a tin basin and quiet competence, braided Eliza's hair smooth, pinned it with the same plain pins she'd worn on storm nights, folded lavender into the linen until the room remembered summer and not the choking dark of the night before.

Michael stood useless, hands open, until Mary put a cloth in them and said, "Hold this," the way you'd speak to a child or a man underwater.

By the time the bed had become a board and the board had become a box, his fingers smelled of soap and salt and nothing like blood. He slipped the old guinea into his pocket because he could not carry her—not really—and the weight steadied him like a stone in a sling.

By the lychgate the church hunched against the weather as it always had, its tower the back of an old man watching the sea. Villagers lined the path— shawls pulled tight, coats darned to their last thread, faces set to the work of grief. The coffin was pine and honest. No carving. No gilt. Not a thing in or on it that you could sell or steal.

The parson tried for strength and found duty. "Friends, we are gathered…" His words thinned in the wind and fell between boots and frost. People leaned in and caught what they could: dust to dust, mercy, rest.

Michael didn't hear much. He heard rope creak and gulls circle and, somewhere inside his chest, something old give way. He kept his hand in his coat because the guinea wanted to jump. He pressed its tired edge into his palm until it hurt—a circle of the life that still claimed him sitting over the other coin he could not reach beneath the cottage floor. Two suns, he thought, one burning, one buried.

Boots crunched the path.

Three blue coats came through the gate as if it owed them. Harker didn't remove his hat. He looked at people the way a clerk looks at numbers.

"This burial pauses here," he said, hard as an iron hinge slamming shut. "We open the box. If she hid the King's goods, the King will see them."

The crowd tightened like a fist.

Michael felt his body turn to iron.

No one moved.

Doctor Rowe did.

He had the coat he'd put on in the dark and the calm of men who learned long ago that hands matter more than titles.

"Open it," he said mildly, "and you'll breathe what killed her."

Harker's mouth twitched. "What killed her?"

"Consumption." Rowe didn't look at Harker. He looked at the younger two soldiers—boys, really—at the place on a man's jaw where fear shows first. "You'll take it home. To your wives. Your babies. They won't last the winter."

A ripple moved through the villagers—a subtle, low, dangerous sound.

Someone spat. Someone else shifted closer to the coffin.

One soldier lifted his musket, not in threat but in miserable instinct—like a child raising a hand against thunder.

Mary said, almost kindly, "Go on then. Be brave for once."

Harker weighed the weather, the rows of grieving faces, the priest's stillness, the tinder-dry hush of a yard full of people with empty hands and too many reasons to stop being afraid. For one long second, the world held its breath. Michael had the wild thought that a spark—one word, one wrong gesture—would send the whole churchyard into riot.

Finally Harker spat into the frost.

"Let the ground have her," he said, saving his temper for later, and turned his back.

Only when the soldiers left did the crowd breathe again.

The service finished like a boat run on muscle after the wind has failed—rope, grunt, the lowered box taking its first dull knocks of earth. Michael waited to the last. He let a fist of soil fall and flinched at the sound it made. It felt obscene that dirt could speak and she could not.

They drifted away in pairs and clumps, the way people do when there's stew and talk and nothing useful left to hold. He stayed. The sea worked at the rocks without shame. He said her name once, and it hung white in the air and fell.

"Michael."

Mary again. She hadn't needed the apron to be formidable, but she wore it anyway.

"You'll freeze your bones," she said.

"I'm fine."

"You're not."

She hooked his elbow. "The living need you more than the dead."

"I can't—"

"You can." She tugged. "If you won't do it for yourself, do it because I'm asking nicely, and you won't enjoy what comes after nicely."

He let himself be taken. The guinea pressed his palm until it left a welt.

The Jolly Sailor glowed against the grey, a lantern pretending to be a sun. Inside, the usual music had been dismissed. No dominoes, no fiddle, no dice. Just stories, which is what people play when the tune has gone out of them.

"She told Harker the barrels could take the King by the hand and walk up the cliff themselves," someone said, and there were small, grateful laughs.

"She carried two casks in a blow," another put in. "Called them 'babes' and swore they were lighter than men's opinions."

"She fed us," a woman said simply. "All winter that year."

Each tale raised her and laid her down again. Michael sat at the edge of it with a mug he didn't drink. To them she was legend; to him she was weight and breath and the way a hand can find your sleeve in a room full of knives.

In the back, smoke had opinions. Ferris had eyes rimmed red. Isaac Gulliver stood like a door that wouldn't yield to weather.

"She's gone," Isaac said. He didn't lower his voice for the dead. "The tide won't mourn with us."

Ferris's jaw worked. "Men will follow who she trusted. That's you."

"I'm not—" Michael began.

"You are," Ferris said, as if finishing a sum. "Or someone softer takes it and we all hang."

The room did that thing rooms do when they agree: nothing moved. No breath wasted. No dissent dared.

Michael felt the mantle come for him and tried to step aside; it moved with him. He thought of the ledger on Eliza's table, columns waiting. He thought of Thomas with a rope-shaped shadow across his neck. He thought of the kiln swallowing barrels the way the ground swallows anything you give it.

"I'll try," he said, and it wasn't enough and it was all there was.

That night, the cottage remembered her— whether he asked it to or not. The fire sank into itself, the way grief does when no one feeds it. He found the brandy because not finding it would have required sense. The first swallow burned and didn't help. The second did less. By the third he was on the bed, face buried in the hollow her head had left, and whatever sound came out of him wasn't language.

The bottle rolled, tapped the wall with a dull, forgiving clunk. He slept like a man dragged under by a wave he hadn't seen coming.

And then—before thought, before time—Mara.

"Graham," she said softly. "It's me."

He turned toward the voice, though there was no direction to turn to. "Mara," he managed, the word half-breath, half-break.

"Graham, you have to go back," she said, her voice clearer than air, warmer than any fire. "You have to live. For the three of us."

You need to stop being afraid to start again. We're all right—truly. We're happy. We're surrounded by love. But you—" she paused, and he could hear the smile she always wore when she wanted him to listen—"you made me a promise, remember? You said if anything ever happened, you'd keep going. I need you to do that, love. For me. For us."

He tried to reach her, but his hands found only light and the faint scent of her hair, and it broke him all over again.

"I love you," she whispered. "I will always love you. But you have to go now. Go, and live for us all."

"I don't want to go," he choked. "I want to stay here with you both."

"Graham," she said gently, with the kind of firmness only the dead can manage, "you must go back. We will be here waiting."

The world trembled. The light rippled like cloth. For a heartbeat he thought he could follow her, step into that warmth—but then—

At first he only heard the sea.

Then another rhythm bled through it, thin and tinny, like a gull learning to sing and failing. A beat from another century. A voice he knew too well from kitchens and broken radios.

Not the words—not all of them—but the hook you don't need the words for.

Phil Collins. Against All Odds.

The ache of it punched straight through the dream, harsh and bright.

The room narrowed to white.

A cold sheet.

A vice around his throat—plastic, rubber.

Hands on his wrists.

A machine shouting in beeps too fast, too sharp.

"He's awake!" someone barked, too close, too loud, too real.

Graham—ripped from dream, from sea, from her—came back gasping, thrashing, choking on the tube. Panic tore through him like fire through dry brush. The lights were knives. The voices were storms. His pulse hammered until his vision pixelated at the edges.

"Hold him—he's disoriented—"

Someone pinned his right arm. Another clamped his shoulders.

He fought anyway.

He fought because he'd lost her twice now.

Cold climbed his vein—clean, merciless, medical.

"Easy," a voice said, like Mary when she wasn't. "Easy now. You're safe."

Safe.

The word insulted him.

Safe meant nothing in a world where she wasn't.

His body betrayed him—limbs heavy, lungs burning, the darkness rushing in like a tide that didn't listen to prayer.

"Welcome back, Graham."

The dark took him—clean, efficient, merciful.

When he surfaced again, the machines had settled into smug little confirmations of life. The tube was gone; his throat felt flayed. A curtain guarded a small square of sky that didn't belong to any coast he knew. One hand wore a clip; the other panicked, searching, until a nurse found what it was looking for.

"Here," she said softly, placing the coin in his palm with a smile that felt practised and kind in equal measure. "Been through it, haven't you?"

She tucked the blanket around him the way you might secure a child on a boat or a man who'd fallen between centuries.

He nodded—or thought he did—and stared past her at a wall that had never seen salt or rope or the mark of a net. A sheet was pinned there in neat black capitals:

DO NOT REMOVE — VENT SETTINGS

The world had rules about air now.

And then it came—everything, all at once.

Gulliver's cane. Ferris's ledger. Mary's "nicely."

The green dress folded under paper.

The kiln mouth.

The right-hand cave.

The rope.

The barn's high lantern.

Eliza's breath catching against his ear.

Eliza dying.

Eliza gone.

They came and went in a single pulse, leaving behind only wreckage: the man he'd been, and the man he was, both marooned.

He closed his fingers around the coin until it bit deep enough to make meaning. Somewhere else—under another floor, another life—another coin lay bright in dust. Two suns. Two weights. One pulled him forward. One would never let him go.

The monitor counted his heart in numbers.

Outside the curtain a trolley squeaked over un-oiled floor.

Farther down, a television laughed on cue for no one.

"Hold fast," he whispered.

His voice wasn't the same, but the words worked anyway. They always had. They built a wall inside him, something to lean his forehead against.

He slept without dreams, but he was back.

Chapter Seventeen

Coming Up For Air

The machines were the first voices he understood. Soft beeps counting seconds he couldn't feel. Air moving through plastic with a low, tidal sigh. Somewhere close, a pump clicked on, clicked off, steady as a metronome.

When he tried to swallow, something gripped his throat and wouldn't let him. Panic hit hard and stupid—he clawed at the tube until hands closed over his wrists and pinned them gently but firmly to the mattress.

"Easy, love. Easy," a voice said above him. Not the sea. Not Eliza. Flat vowels from the here and now. "You're in hospital. You've been asleep a while. Let us do the work."

He tried to nod but the tube held him hostage. He blinked instead, and the lights bled into stars.

A day or a week later—time had lost all teeth—the tube was gone. His throat felt flayed. Water came in tiny sips off a spoon. The first burned, the second blessed. He cried without meaning to, a ridiculous leak he couldn't stop.

"Welcome back," the nurse said, actually smiling now. "Knew you'd come up for air sooner or later."

His voice arrived in scraps. "How… long?" It came out like sand.

"Six months," she said gently. "You gave everyone a fright."

Six months. The number didn't fit anywhere inside him. He licked dry lips and tasted hospital air—bleach and boiled linen and old toast. The smell of peat smoke and salt—the smell that had been his entire world—was gone.

He slept. He woke to murmur and metal. He slept again. He dreamed in sea-colours and gunshot. In one dream Eliza's hand wouldn't warm in his no matter how he begged it. In another, Mara moved through a kitchen's pale light, tying her hair back, smiling like none of it had happened. He woke gagging on an empty grief that had no century to live in.

When the world settled long enough to hold still, a woman in a navy cardigan took the chair by his bed. Rosy from the cold outside, hair pinned up with more hope than success, scarf round her neck like armour. She twisted the paper lid off a coffee and looked him over with eyes that didn't allow much nonsense.

"About time," she said, and only then did her mouth tremble. "Bloody stubborn man."

He tried the name on his tongue. "Mary?"

"That's me." She scooted the chair closer, set the coffee where he could smell it. "Barmaid, dog walker, part-time rescuer of idiots. Mary Trelease, for forms and funerals. I'm the one who found you. In your hall. Door off the latch. Radio on. Milk still on the step. I knocked till my knuckles hurt. When you didn't shout back, I pushed in."

For a fractured moment his heart lurched—
Eliza, he thought, seeing a woman at his bedside.
Eliza in her apron, braids pinned back. The mistake
hit him so hard his vision whitened at the edges.

Mary kept going. "You were cold as stone. Blue
lips. Eyes rolled back. Sick on your shirt." She shook
her head once, sharp. "Ambulance was fast. They said
hypothermia, alcohol, maybe a bang to the head from
the fall. You'd taken yourself off good and proper."

Shame rose in his throat like bile—shame that
she had found him like that, that he'd left his own
body as a warning for the first kind person to knock.

Mary's hand found his and gave it a quick,
practical squeeze. "Anyway. They hauled you out and
kept you. I brought your post to the nurses, told them
not to let the electricity lot cut you off. Ferris sorted
the stopcock for the mains. We kept the cottage from
going mouldy as best we could. You're welcome."

He tried to laugh. It scraped his throat raw.
"Thank you," he managed, and meant it more than
any two words he'd ever said.

"Don't go making a fuss," she said, brushing at her scarf like it had offended her. "You'd do the same for anyone." She lifted the coffee, took a sip that steamed her lashes. "And before you ask—no, I didn't go poking under your boards. Your secrets are your own."

Eliza's coin flickered in his mind: tired gold, the sound of it dropping between two planks that didn't belong to this century. The nurse's hand was steady on his wrist long before panic could root.

"Slow," Mary said, like a referee between body and mind. "One thing at a time. Today you breathe. Tomorrow you stand up. After that, we'll see."

He nodded. This time it worked.

Recovery was humiliating and holy by turns. The physiotherapist—a woman with calves like a fell runner and the patience of a saint—coached him through sitting, then standing, then shuffling the length of the ward. His legs were matches. His hands shook when he lifted a mug. He slept after each effort as if he'd run miles.

The next morning she wheeled a chrome frame to the foot of the bed and looked at him the way a cliff looks at a climber: not unkind, not indulgent either.

"Feet over," she said.

It took an age to persuade his legs they were legs. The floor was cold, a shock he was grateful for. She belted him in and set her hand at his scapula the way you steady a door in a gale.

"On three." A breath. "One—two—"

He stood a quarter of the way, the room tilting, the machines putting their twopence in—beep, breathe, beep. His heart knocked too loudly for the work he was doing. He thought of lifting barrels, of scaffold boards, of the weight of a body that had lain too long.

"Good," she said, meaning barely adequate and miracle both. "Again."

On the fourth try he was upright enough to see the ward from a different height—the window square and grey; the nurse at the station scratching dates onto a chart; a man in the next bay asleep with his mouth open like a child. His legs shook. Sweat prickled his lip. The physio didn't let go.

"Tell me three things you can see," she said.

"The rain," he managed. "Your… shoes." A pair built for purpose. "And—"

"And?"

"The world," he said, because it was there, inconvenient and huge, waiting.

She grinned. "We'll count that as four."

By the time she eased him back down he was crying in a way that had nothing to do with sadness. He didn't apologise. She didn't ask him to.

On good days, he ate scrambled eggs and toast that tasted faintly of cardboard and triumph. On bad ones, everything smelled of disinfectant and old copper, and nothing stayed down.

Mary came when she wasn't pulling pints. She brought village gossip packaged as medicine: Mrs Trelease's cat had finally had the kittens, Ferris had nearly taken the top off his thumb on a new tin-opener, the bus from Plymouth had lost a wheel but no one was on it who'd paid a fare anyway. He let her talk him into the present because it was easier to sit in her sentences than in his head.

The consultant—tired eyes, good hands—talked of "prolonged coma," "aspiration," "deconditioning," "remarkable neurological recovery." None of it. What stuck was the leaflet the speech therapist slid across the tray: After ICU: Finding Your Way Back. A list of simple things with impossible weight. Eat. Drink. Wash. Walk. Call someone. He circled walk twice.

Six weeks after waking, he put on his own clothes. The jeans hung loose; the jumper smelled faintly of the cupboard where Mary had rescued it. He walked to the window and stood. Outside, a bus leaned at the stop and steamed in the rain. A man in a red anorak shook a newspaper like it had insulted him. Life, relentless, ordinary. He pressed his palm to the glass and felt the cold.

"Ready?" Mary asked, appearing at his side in the reflection.

"No," he said honestly.

"Good," she said, just as honest. "Come on."

The cottage took his breath with both hands. It always had. Even on nights he'd stumbled into it half-drunk, it had been there, stubborn as a stone in a river. Now, thin and mended and raw-eyed, he stood on the threshold and let the sea blow through him.

For a split, delusional moment, he expected movement inside—the rustle of a skirt, the scrape of a chair, Eliza turning from the hearth with an impatient look that meant Come in, then, don't hover. Or Mara humming over a pan. For a heartbeat, he let the impossible exist.

Then Mary barged past (her way) and the illusion fell apart.

She made the fire as though she'd been doing it for years. Peat and driftwood and a fistful of sticks that cracked and argued their way alight. She put the kettle on like a flag. "Tea first. Then plans."

"What plans?"

"The kind that stop you drowning in your own head." She pointed at the drafting table, still under its dust, shoved against the wall like a guilt. "That thing hasn't earned its keep since you dragged it down here. It moves to the window today."

"Mary…"

"Do not Mary me. The view's the only free therapy you've got."

He gave in because he was tired and because she was right. Together they shunted the table across the floor, legs biting at the boards, breath steaming. They set it under the window where the world was all cliff and sky and muscle-thick sea. He wiped dust with his sleeve. It left stripes like war paint.

Mary stood back, hands on hips. "Right. That chair by the fire is for sitting and not thinking too hard. The table's for drawing and not thinking too hard. The bed is for sleeping and not thinking too hard. Any questions?"

"Where do I think too hard?"

"Outside," she said. "On the path. Where the wind can bully it out of you."

He smiled, small and sore. "I'll try."

"Good man." She fussed with the kettle. "You hungry?"

He wasn't, but he ate because she looked like she'd make him anyway. Bread and cheese, an apple that tasted of something alive.

Mary pulled on her coat and headed for the door. "I'll leave you to settle," she said, already halfway onto the path. He nodded out of politeness.

She walked a few steps into the wind, then paused — a hesitation sharp enough that even the sea seemed to wait. Something tugged at her.

She turned back toward the cottage.

He washed up because it felt like an apology to the house.

He opened the cupboard above the bread bin without thinking and found what he'd left himself months ago: two miniature bottles from the off-licence, the sort that pretend smallness equals mercy.

406

He stood there with one in his hand, the cold weight digging into the palm he'd once pressed around Eliza's coin. A tiny bottle, a tiny door back toward forgetting—toward silence.

For a moment he imagined disappearing into it, leaving the world as quietly as he had six months before. The cottage felt watchful, waiting to see what kind of man had come back.

He turned the cap. The sweet sting licked his throat before he'd even lifted it.

Someone knocked—three quick taps. Mary's way of opening a conversation with a building.

He left the cap on the counter and went to the door.

"You forget your halo?" he said, because jokes were cheaper than confessions.

"Always." She stepped inside and glanced past him, her eyes landing on the bottle without judgement or surprise. "You pour, or shall I?"

He carried it to the sink. The liquid hit porcelain with a soft hiss. The smell vanished under the tap. The second bottle went easier.

Mary handed him the tea towel. "Good. I'll tell the priest you're making progress."

He tried to laugh, but it came out thin. "I don't need that stuff anymore," he said quietly. "After... after everything."

"I know." Her voice softened. "Kettle's going on. Coffee—not the cheap granules, either." She nudged him toward the table. "Sit before you fall over."

He sat. His body still felt foreign—like someone else's limbs stitched loosely to him. Mary moved around the kitchen with the easy authority of someone who refused to let him vanish back into himself.

"You're mending," she said as she set down two mugs. "Slow as winter, but you're mending. The trick now is deciding what to do with the days you've got back."

"I don't know where to start."

"That's fine. No one does. Start anyway."

He looked out at the sea, calm for once. "Everything feels… unfinished. Like I walked away from something halfway through."

"You did." She sipped her coffee. "But that was then. This is now. You get to choose who you are from here on."

He let the warmth of the mug settle into his hands. "Feels easier said than done."

"Most worthwhile things are."

She stood, tugged open the curtains. Light pooled onto the table—thin, winter gold. "You've got a cottage that needs you. A life that needs rebuilding. And…" She hesitated, surprising them both. "People who'd rather see you alive than drunk."

He swallowed, the truth sharp and real. "I'll try."

"That's all anyone can ask."

Later, when she'd gone and the house had settled into its own breathing again, he drifted into sleep on the chair by the fire.

Dreams came, soft-edged.

Mara first—standing in the doorway of their old kitchen, sunlight on her hair, the baby weightless in her arms. She smiled the way she had before pain ever touched them.

Then Eliza—wind in her braids, one brow raised in impatience, as though she'd been waiting far too long for him to find his feet.

Neither spoke, but both looked at him with the same quiet insistence:

Go on.

He woke with tears drying on his face and a steadiness in his chest he hadn't felt since before the storm.

The cottage creaked in the cold, a gentle, living thing. A board under his heel gave a single, familiar click.

"Soon," he told it. "I know."

For now, there was coffee cooling on the table, a winter sun lifting over the sea, and a life that—miraculously—hadn't let go of him.

Chapter Eighteen

The Knock

Morning came slow over the sea, a thin wash of light that took its time pulling colour out of the cliffs. Frost crusted the grass to sugar. The kettle muttered. The cottage stretched itself and remembered how to be a house again.

Trex had been Mary's idea, of course.

"You sit too much, Graham," she'd said across the Jolly Sailor's bar, polishing a tankard to a shine that would last exactly five minutes. "Doctor says walking mends better than brandy. And a man shouldn't come home to silence."

He'd muttered something about liking silence, but Mary had ignored it in the way only Mary could.

A week later she turned up at the cottage with an Alsatian pup whose paws were too big for the earth

412

and whose ears looked borrowed from a larger animal. She barged past him as if she owned the place, a bundle of fur wriggling under her arm.

"Didn't have the heart to say no at the rescue," she said, already letting the creature down on the rug. "He needs miles and you need miles. Sorted."

The pup sniffed once, twice, then collapsed flat on the hearth rug as if it had always been his. Graham stood there, jaw slack.

"I don't—" he began.

"You do," Mary said firmly. "And if you don't, I'll have your hide before the RSPCA has mine."

Graham named him Trex (he couldn't say why) and the name stuck as surely as the dog did.

The first nights were awkward. Trex whined in the dark, unsettled by new walls, and Graham sat on the edge of the bed listening to the sound pierce through him. He considered shutting the dog out, but in the end he lay down on the rug beside the pup until exhaustion knocked them both under.

By the third night, Trex had learned that the cottage was safe, and Graham had learned that silence broken by a steady canine snore was a kinder silence than the one he'd been keeping.

Trex soon understood the geography of the days better than Graham did: when the kettle clicked, when the fire needed banking, when the light at the window went that particular pewter that meant the cliff path would be slick. He shadowed Graham from table to hearth to door, a quiet metronome of breath and patience.

On a dry, hard-skied morning, a month after Graham returned from the hospital, Trex butted his knee and padded to the door, eyebrows commanding an answer.

"All right, you tyrant," Graham muttered, pulling on his coat.

They set off along the lane. The sea was a bruised blue, white seams showing where it met the rocks. The cold had that clean, metallic smell that makes your teeth ache. Far out, a trawler moved like a fingernail across slate. Gulls wrote their restless hooks in the air.

Trex trotted ahead, tail flagging, stopping at every gate as if to ask permission. Graham followed, surprised by how natural it felt.

They took the long way into town, past the sheds where nets were mended and the place the crab pots went to rust, past cottages with their neat little walls and winter-hungry geraniums.

The Jolly Sailor was already warm as a loaf; light ran down its windows and turned the road to shallow gold. Trex's tail thumped twice against Graham's thigh as if to say, Here, here is where the world still works.

Inside: peat smoke, wet wool steaming, that yeasty beer smell that lives in old wood. The same half-dozen voices you could locate with your eyes shut. Someone had dragged the settle close to the fire; two old boys had staked it as theirs and were already arguing about a reef no one had seen since '63.

Mary looked up, clocked him, and poured without asking.

"One," she warned, sliding the pint over with the look she used when fishermen tried to argue with common sense. "And bring that beast nearer the hearth—he's dripping on my floor."

Trex accepted the compliment with a thump of approval and stretched in exactly the one spot that would make leaving later an act of betrayal. Graham took the chair with the good back and let the heat find his spine.

For a moment the room doubled. The same hearth, different evening, different century: men with rope burns across their palms and salt drying in their hair; maps spread on the back table, elbows over them like weathered brackets. And Eliza (no one else folded a room around themselves as if it were a chart to be read) standing just inside the door, cloak damp, braid pulled tight, gaze moving so quick you felt seen, measured, and stored.

He blinked and the present swam back into place: dominoes clacked; Jimmy laughed that laugh that always cracked in the middle; Trex sighed and put his muzzle on Graham's boot.

He nursed the pint, not rushing it. The fire made a conversation of its own, the pop of resin, the soft fall of ash. He watched the door open and shut, the same stripe of light lay itself across the floor and slide away. He watched the way Mary listened to a blow-by-blow of a haul that hadn't gone to plan and said exactly the thing that let the teller keep his pride.

"Mind's quieter today," she said when she came down the bar, topping him up with a splash of soda unasked. "You look like you're starting to belong to your days."

"Some days," he said. "Some, I belong to the days I've already had."

She followed his eyes to the back corner, to the table the smugglers had once taken without asking. "A lot of history in one room," she said lightly, but her hand touched his for a second, the quick, practical comfort of a woman who knows when to offer it and when to pretend nothing's wrong.

That night, back at the cottage, he lit one lamp, then another, and the little rooms became themselves again. The drafting table took the window, as it had since Mary bullied him into dragging it there. He sharpened a pencil and ruled off a margin. Trex, satisfied with his part in the enterprise, made a neat circle of himself on the rug.

He worked until the lines started to float. No arches tonight, no gorgeously unnecessary cornices; just a lintel detail he couldn't get to look honest and a note to himself about a staircase that wouldn't foul a window. He wrote numbers, rubbed them out, wrote them again.

He set the guinea (the old gold coin that should not have been in this century and yet was) on the paper and let it sit there like a borrowed sun.

The coin always grounded and unsettled him at once. Heavy, warm-ish, the worn king's profile softened by fingers long dead. It didn't belong on squared paper in 1987, but there it glowed, refusing to deny itself.

His eyelids grew heavy. He was in the flat in York. The good kettle (the one that didn't wheeze) shook just before it clicked. Mara stood in the kitchen's square of light, hair tucked messily up, one curl refusing to obey. She wore that grey jumper he had claimed and she had stolen back, sleeves shoved to her elbows.

"Taste," she ordered, lifting a spoonful of sauce to his lips. "And don't say 'needs salt' like a man in a cartoon."

He tasted. Tomato, garlic, a hint of the wine she swore made everything better.

"Perfect," he said, and she narrowed her eyes because he always said it.

"Liar," she murmured, affectionate, bumping his hip with hers.

A record played in the other room; a Phil Collins ballad held the air like breath. She mouthed a line at him and made the sad thing light. Flour dusted her fingers; she wiped them on his T-shirt and left ghostly palms he pretended to mind.

The fragile miracle of an ordinary evening caught his heart hard.

Light shifted. Wind pushed in. Eliza stood on the cliff path, the sea climbing and falling behind her, a lantern cupped in her hand.

"Hold fast," she said. Only that. As if it were instruction for knots, for life, for grief.

The night smelt of kelp and peat and brandy in unmarked casks. She was close enough that he could see the tiny white scar at the corner of her mouth, the one that only showed when her face was relaxed, which was almost never.

"Are we safe?" he asked.

"We are never safe," she said, eyes on the bay. "We are only careful—and sometimes lucky."

He reached out and the kitchen came back— the pram by the table, the tiny fist of a baby punching the air just to prove the air was there. Mara bent and lifted him.

"James," she said softly, laughing under the word as if it tickled her to say it. She looked up at Graham. "You need to wake up now, Graham."

Hearing that name in her mouth should have jarred; it didn't. It felt like someone straightening a picture.

"Don't keep living halfway," she said, rocking James, who blinked solemnly at the world. "Not for me. Not for him. Be alive."

Eliza's lantern flared as if it heard and agreed. She tilted it, light painting her cheekbone.

"We made our choices. We lived them. You must live yours. We're happy," she added, and for once her mouth softened. "So you must be, too."

The wind carried their voices together, Mara's and Eliza's, like a tide pulling from two directions. He reached for them (towards both, towards neither) and at the moment his fingers would have found a hand, the lamplight on his table (or the lantern by her boot) flared and guttered.

421

Knocking came up through the floor of his sleep like a sound from the bottom of the sea.

Trex got there first, chest low, a rumble in him that said he approved of caution. Graham pushed the chair back and felt his neck inform him drafting-table naps were the choice of fools.

The knock came again. Morning had sketched itself over the water; the window was the colour of iron.

He opened the door. She was twenty-something, maybe thirty. Dark hair in soft waves brushing her collar (not pinned, not deliberate, just lived-in). Her coat was the kind people buy optimistically and wear for a decade. Her face (Mara, if Mara hadn't known the things Mara had known). Not the same, and yet near enough it ached. The likeness hit him cleanly, not cruelly this time, simply as fact: here is a face you have loved.

"Sorry," she said, cheeks pink from the cold. "My car's given up at the bend. I saw your path. Do you—could you—?" She gestured toward the lane, embarrassment and hope sharing the work.

He opened his mouth and nothing came out.

Trex solved the moment by shoving his head into the space between them and demanding acknowledgement.

The woman laughed (relief catching on the sound). "Hello, you," she said, offering her hand palm-down like someone who knows dogs.

Graham found his voice. "Of course. Let me get my coat."

They walked up the track together, Trex scouting and reporting back, tail a metronome. She kept pace easily; she didn't fill the silence with apologies, which he liked her for.

"You look like you've seen a ghost," she said eventually, not unkindly.

"I had an accident last year," he said. "Still making friends with the world again. You just—"

How does a man say *you have the face that holds half my life?*

"—you remind me of someone."

"Good, I hope," she said, quick sideways glance.

"The best," he managed.

She let it sit. Didn't prod the sore place.

"I'm new here," she said. "Teaching at the primary. Started last week. The roads have opinions about my timing."

They reached the bend. A red convertible sat there with its hazards blinking a statement of the obvious. He lifted the bonnet. Condenser lead (loose). He fixed it with the satisfaction you get from a job that doesn't involve ghosts.

"Try it," he said, stepping back. The engine coughed, considered, then caught.

She grinned (sudden, unwary). The way her face lit made the ground tilt under him.

"Thank you. I don't know anyone yet. I'd have been here until spring."

"What brought you?" he asked, half to hear her voice, half to steady himself.

"Honestly?" She looked to where the sea flashed between hedges. "A map and a finger. And a job advert. Sometimes that's enough."

He nodded. He knew about maps and fingers and starting again.

She watched him watching the water and seemed to decide something.

"You really are far away," she said gently. "Penny for your thoughts?"

He stopped as if the lane had hiccupped. The words were nothing (and everything). A well-worn phrase, a thousand English mothers' favourite. But they rang down a corridor in him and rattled a coin at the far end.

"What did you say?" he asked softly.

She laughed, flustered. "Just... a penny for your thoughts? Sorry. Silly thing to say."

He shook his head, pulled air back into his chest. "It's all right. Let's get you moving."

Trex, who had no patience for metaphors, leaned hard into Graham's thigh until the moment folded away.

"Thank you, Mr...?"

"Graham," he said. "Graham Jones."

"Anna," she said. "Anna Cooper."

He turned the name over. It sat comfortably against the day.

"Do you—" He cleared his throat. "How about a coffee? In town? There's a place by the harbour that remembers how to heat milk."

"I'd like that," she said. And it didn't sound like politeness.

Trex launched himself into the back seat with the entitlement of a lord. Anna laughed. "You're coming too, are you?"

"He doesn't believe in missing out."

They drove slowly down the lane. The village laid itself out gently, as if trying not to spook him: the butcher's with its chalkboard; the window where someone always displayed three pairs of socks and a

tin of boiled sweets; the harbour with its neat chaos
of lines and buckets.

The Jolly Sailor's sign creaked; the same gull
voiced the same disgust from the same chimney.

As they passed, the room in his head flickered:
Eliza at the back, head bent over a ledger; Isaac's pale,
measuring eyes; the scrape of a quill; the smell of tar
and danger. Then, as quick, it was Mary levering open
the sash to let out steam, and a lad in an apron
carrying empties. The present made its case.

They parked where you always have to reverse
twice and still end up an inch too far from the wall.
Inside, the café was steam and scratched tables and
the cheerful chime of a till that thought it was in Paris.
The woman behind the counter knew how to warm
cups. The coffee came with the right weight in the
hand.

They took the table by the window.

The sea did its endless arithmetic beyond the
glass.

Anna cupped her mug with both hands, as if admiring the engineering.

"So," she said. "Tell me what this place is really like when the postcards go away."

He told her about the wind that learns your name; about rain that arrives sideways and ruins washing with artistry; about the morning the bay lies like poured pewter and every man suddenly remembers a job he can do alone. He told her how you can tell the time by which boat noses out first, how the cliff path gives you endings when you need them, beginnings when you don't.

She told him about classrooms: five-year-olds who hand you their secrets like receipts and then forget; the difference between children who've been read to and children who've been shushed; the smell of pencil shavings and poster paint like a second childhood for free.

"When I was little, I wanted to be a lawyer," she laughed. "Can you imagine? Me. A courtroom."

She shook her head. "Teaching suits me better. I like the bang and crash of days."

Mara's voice flickered in the corner of his mind—talking about briefs and cases with the same brightness, the same certainty that careful work could dent the world. He let it ring. Let it fade.

They talked easily. No urgency to impress; no need to guard anything.

When the mugs sat empty and the steamy glass gave them back their faces, blurred at the edges, he said, "I should get back. Work to pretend to do."

"Me too," she said. "Children to civilise."

They stepped outside. Pearly light sat on the water. Trex pretended not needing a wee, then immediately needed one, which made Anna laugh and—unexpectedly—made Graham laugh too.

At the car door she hesitated, then tore a corner off a receipt and wrote a number with a stubby pencil.

"In case the road has more opinions," she said. "And in case Trex needs an emergency walk if you're late home."

He took it. The scrap felt like something larger.

"I'll ring," he said, and knew he would.

They climbed the lane. Passing the Jolly Sailor, Mary shouldered the sash up to let out steam and spotted them. She gave a brisk little wave that managed to be both dare and blessing. Graham lifted two fingers back.

At the bend where the car had sulked earlier, Anna glanced at him.

"You look better than when you opened the door."

"I am," he said—and for the first time, it was true.

"For now's big enough," she said, setting the indicator with a small, certain click.

They drove into the now. Trex's breath fogged the rear window. The road unwound. The sea kept pace. The village waited with the same old buildings that quietly held new lives.

In his pocket the guinea rested against his palm, warm from the café, the car, and the decision he hadn't yet named. He didn't press it. He didn't need to.

At the harbour, Anna checked the time and grimaced. "If I don't go, thirty small people will mutiny."

"Then go," he smiled. "Tomorrow? Same café. Trex insists."

"Tomorrow," she said—simple as weather.

She scratched Trex between the ears. "Don't let him talk you out of cake."

She drove off. Graham stood a moment, watching the car climb the lane.

No tug in his chest.

Something steadier sat there now—ballast.

On the way home he cut across the square. Mary met him at the door of the pub with a dish towel over her shoulder and a look that softened into approval.

"Well?" she asked.

"Well," he answered.

"That'll do," she said, and let him go with a pat that could've been to him or Trex or the day.

Back at the cottage he lit the fire, put the kettle on, moved to the drafting table. Trex curled on the rug, already dreaming.

He set a fresh sheet in place. This time he drew the cottage as it might be—a table that could carry laughter. Shelves expecting books. A hook by the door where someone else's coat could hang without asking permission.

A board underfoot clicked—the hidden coin calling to him. Not today, he thought. Some truths steady the floor. He left it be.

Next morning the sky opened blue in a way it hardly ever does in winter. Sun already had a warmth to it, soft against his face when he stepped outside.

Graham and Trex met Anna at the harbour without saying they would. She had a scarf the colour of new leaves; he had a pocket full of dog treats and more time than he'd had in years. They took the cliff path. Trex scouted ahead, checked back, delighted with his leadership. Anna laughed at the wind, and the sound landed in him like good bread.

They walked until the village looked small and kind behind them. On the headland, three shadows kept pace—man, woman, dog—and for once the horizon felt like an invitation, not a dare. When they turned back, the road laid itself out obligingly, the cottage waiting with its hearth and its drafts and its space for more.

He didn't know what came next. He only knew he wanted to find out, and that—finally—he wasn't walking toward it alone.

Trex bumped his knee. Anna's sleeve brushed his. The three of them went down the path together, the day opening ahead like a door someone had left on the latch.

The following morning, sunlight glazed the path like honey. The air was already soft with the promise of heat; the sea below flashed bright, cheerful blue instead of pewter. Trex nudged his leg insistently, eager for the world to begin. Graham shrugged on his light jacket, and the two of them stepped out into the warm, clear day.

They followed the lane down past the hawthorn hedge—and Graham stopped. The bright red convertible waited at the end of the path, roof down to meet the sun, exhaust sending up lazy curls that wavered in the warmth. Sunlight clung to its paint in a way that felt like possibility.

Anna sat behind the wheel, hair tugged by the breeze, cheeks touched gold. When she saw him, she lifted a hand, a smile blooming warm as a hearth.

Trex made the first move—a delighted sprint, a leap, and he was in the back seat as if born to it.

Anna laughed. "Well, someone's ready."

Graham reached the car and opened the passenger door.

434

The radio crackled—static, then a DJ's voice, warm and easy:

"…and now, for your morning—Starship, 'Nothing's Gonna Stop Us Now'."

The drums cracked; the intro rose like light breaking open.

Graham leaned across and kissed Anna's cheek—gentle, sure.

She smiled at him, bright as the day.

He slid into the seat beside her, drew his Ray-Ban Wayfarers from his pocket, unfolded them, set them on.

Anna grinned. "Ready?"

He breathed in sun and salt and petrol, the whole bright spill of the morning. "Are we ready, Trex?"

The dog gave an agreeable bark from the back seat.

"Ready," Graham said.

The engine rumbled. The tyres hummed on warm tarmac. Trex steadied himself in the back, proud captain of adventures.

They took the cliff road with the roof down, the music blaring, the heat shimmering off the sea, water flashing silver and blue beside them—

and Graham, at last, drove toward his life, not away from it.

THE END

www.ingramcontent.com/pod-product-compliance
Lightning Source LLC
Chambersburg PA
CBHW050106120726
47904CB00004B/1237